# HIGHLAND Hero

CHILDREN OF THE MIST SERIES

# HIGHLAND Hero

CHILDREN OF THE MIST SERIES

# CYNTHIA BREEDING

This book is a work of fiction. Names, characters, places, and incidents are the product of the author's imagination or are used fictitiously. Any resemblance to actual events, locales, or persons, living or dead, is coincidental.

Copyright © 2021 by Cynthia Breeding. All rights reserved, including the right to reproduce, distribute, or transmit in any form or by any means. For information regarding subsidiary rights, please contact the Publisher.

Entangled Publishing, LLC
10940 S Parker Rd
Suite 327
Parker, CO 80134
rights@entangledpublishing.com

Amara is an imprint of Entangled Publishing, LLC.

Edited by Erin Molta
Cover design by LJ Anderson/Mayhem Cover Creations
Cover photography by Period Images and olliemt1980/Deposit Photos

Manufactured in the United States of America

First Edition June 2021

**AMARA**
an imprint of Entangled Publishing LLC

# Content Warning

*Highland Hero* is a historical romance between enemies from rival clans, full of witty quarrels and sexy romps. However the story includes discussion of a rape from a character's backstory and scenes depicting graphic violence, so readers who may be sensitive to these elements, please take note.

# Prologue

STRAE CASTLE, SCOTTISH HIGHLANDS, DECEMBER 1774

Juliana Caldwell wandered down the path to the burn behind Strae Castle. In just a few hours, her sister Emily—an English countess and clearly an outlander—was going to marry the laird of Clan MacGregor. Who would have thought, just months ago, when they'd come up from London to claim the title to these lands, that it would have inspired a marriage? While she was happy for her sister, it meant her own life would be changed monumentally.

So, before the event took place and the raucous festivities of a Scottish *ceilidh* began, she needed some solitude.

She walked along the grassy bank of the burn, rounded a set of boulders, and stopped so abruptly she nearly fell over her toes. There was a man standing knee-deep in the water, half turned toward her.

He was naked.

She shut her eyes quickly, but not before the image of Rory MacGregor, the laird's brother, had planted itself in her mind. Long black hair, slicked back and wet, gave him the look of the devil himself, which was a pretty accurate description since he seemed to delight in tormenting her for being a Sassenach. Still…it was hard not to look at his broad shoulders and sinewy ridges of muscles everywhere… At least she'd only seen his posterior.

"Ye can open your eyes, lass."

Slowly, she pried one eye open, then closed it quickly. "You are not dressed."

"Nae yet."

He didn't sound at all perturbed, which he probably wasn't, drat him. From the first day she and her sisters had arrived, he'd enjoyed vexing her. If she said the sky was blue, he'd insist it was grey. If she offered her opinion, he always managed to argue the point. Plus, he was arrogant and obviously used to having women flatter him—which, of course, she would never do.

"I am clothed now."

Carefully, she opened both eyes, then widened them. He'd stepped onto the bank but only wrapped a plaid around his waist. "Your chest is bare."

He grinned. "Ye noticed?"

She frowned. "How could I not? You are still practically naked."

The grin widened. "Ye want me to remove the plaid?"

"*No!* I did *not* say that." She crossed her arms. "It is most improper of you to engage in conversation half-dressed." Muscles flexed in his chest, although she could have sworn he hadn't moved his arms at all.

"I doona want to get my shirt wet. I havena finished my bath." He placed a hand on the plaid and started to loosen it. "Will ye be joining me?"

"I certainly will not!" Her face grew hot. "I only came here for some peace and quiet before the wedding."

He quirked a brow. "Ye've heard of our Scottish weddings then?"

She frowned. "What about them?"

"'Tis nae anything like a staid, proper English one, I would wager. When there's a gathering of clans, ye never ken what might come of it." He grinned. "Some man who doesna ken your temper might be wont to make off with ye."

She glared at him. "I can take care of myself."

His grin widened. "I doona doubt it. Mayhap I should issue a warning to our guests—"

"Do not be daft. I promised Emily I would mind my manners." She sighed. "All I wanted was some peace and quiet before the crowds arrive."

He reached for his plaid. "Well, then, I will leave ye to it while I finish—"

"You are not going to take that off, are you?"

An eyebrow rose. "'Tis nae practical to keep it on."

"In front of me? You should apologize!"

His brow went slightly higher. "For what? Ye are the one who invaded my space."

She ignored that. "For…for…insulting me. I am not a doxy!"

He grinned again. "If ye were a doxy, lass, ye would be joining me."

"You are incorrigible."

"Aye. I'll nae argue that." He gave her a slight bow that was probably a mockery. "But I canna finish my bath without removing my plaid. So, if ye intend to stay—"

"I will not!"

She could have sworn she heard him laugh as she hurried away. For a moment, she was tempted to turn back just so she could have the last word, but he'd probably be naked again. And she'd already seen far too much of Rory MacGregor than she ever wanted to. Really. The man was infuriating.

# Chapter One

"Ye expect me to do *what*?" Rory looked at his brother Ian over a pewter mug filled with steaming black coffee as they sat in the morning room where he and his brothers normally broke their fast. The inside of his head was pounding like a whole contingent of fife and drum players were marching through it, with perhaps a piper thrown in. The result, no doubt, of too much whisky and ale at Ian and Emily's wedding feast last night.

Ian frowned at him. "I want ye to find Juliana, as I said when I summoned ye down here."

Rory shook his head, although that just made his situation worse. "She's missing?" He almost added *good riddance*, since the blasted female felt it her duty to disagree with him on every point made—including yesterday at the burn—but a look at her sisters' faces, as well as his own sister, Fiona's, made him hold his thoughts. "I thought ye were jesting." Rory rubbed his throbbing temples. "Probably some man caught her eye and she succumbed—"

"Juliana? Succumb to a man?" her younger sister, Lorelei,

asked incredulously.

It sounded absurd even as he said it. Juliana Caldwell, with her fiery temper, could put a fishwife to shame with her viperous tongue. A man would be a fool to lure that one to bed for fear he might wake up a eunuch.

"You know very well that is not a possibility," her older sister, Rory's new sister-by-marriage, Emily, said.

"Och, aye." Rory frowned. "There are wedding guests all over the castle as well as tents inside and outside the walls. She's probably tending to them."

"Carr and Devon are searching the grounds," Ian said and then hesitated. "It seems the Camerons are gone, too."

Rory's head snapped up. "What? Why…" He let his voice trail off. Not three months ago at the Campbells' autumn harvest ball, Neal Cameron, son of the laird, had been quite taken with Juliana, and he'd boasted he'd tame her as a wife. Rory had nearly laughed out loud at that, and Neal had been drunk at the time, so he hadn't given it more thought. "Ye think Cameron stole her?"

Lorelei widened her eyes. "Highlanders do not *really* steal brides, do they?"

"Your sister is gone, isn't she?" Rory relented at the fallen look on her face. "Auld ways die hard here, lass. Neal—the damn arse—camped outside the walls at the far end of the field. Made it easy to leave from there."

Emily gave him a startled look. "You think he planned this ahead of time?"

"I wouldna put anything past a Cameron."

"He tried to talk to Juliana yesterday at the wedding feast," Fiona said. "Actually, he was a bit insistent and she looked like she wanted to pour her drink on him, but Lorelei and I were close to her the whole time."

"That doesna prove he intended to hie her away, though."

"But she is *gone*," Fiona said.

Ian nodded. "I've sent men to ride after the Camerons, although I doubt they—or at least Neal—will take the direct road to Fort William, if they have Juliana. They would be too easy to catch."

"Ian says you are the best tracker the MacGregors have," Lorelei added.

He didn't bother to acknowledge the flattery. It was a well-known fact. Years ago he'd managed to rescue Devon when his brother had been captured by dragoons, and he usually managed to find MacGregor sheep or cows that had been reived, along with a bit of interest in the form of additional animals to add to their stock.

"Most likely they'll head through Glen Coe," Ian said.

Rory groaned. Not only was the glen surrounded by rugged, mountainous terrain with dozens of deer paths that led in different directions, but Ben Nevis, the highest munro in Scotland, stood just to the north of the glen and squarely in the way to Cameron lands. They, no doubt, knew the mountain's trails well.

"'Twill be like looking for a lost sheep in the Great Glen," he said.

"Why?" Emily asked. "Surely they will return to their castle."

Ian grimaced. "Well, they doona have a castle…exactly."

"What?"

"The castle at their clan seat was burned after the defeat at Culloden," Ian replied. "They move about now, with nae permanent home."

Emily looked confused, and Rory could only guess she was thinking how ironic it was that the MacGregors—who'd been proscribed by the Crown for nearly two hundred years and forced to hide in the mountain mists—had managed to return to Strae Castle while the Camerons still roamed from place to place. But Ian would explain all that later.

The stomping of boots heralded Carr and Devon's arrival. The two came through the doorway looking glum.

"Still nothing?" Emily asked.

Carr shook his head. "We questioned everyone encamped in the bailey and outside the walls."

"We even looked into each tent," Devon said, "which dinna set well with some of the men who had wenches inside."

"Ye did make sure none of them was Juliana?" Rory asked, ignoring Ian's glare.

"Aye, she would have been hard to miss with that red hair," Carr replied.

Lorelei frowned at Rory. "Did I not already tell you Juliana would not—"

"You did," Emily interrupted her sister, "but it is best to be sure Juliana is not somewhere on the premises before sending Rory out."

"I think 'tis affirmed," Carr said. "She is nae here."

"Nobody saw anything last night?" Ian looked from one brother to the other. "Or heard anything?"

"Nothing unusual," Carr answered, "but the revelry dinna die down until late. 'Twould have been fairly easy for a man to carry a wench off and nae be questioned."

"Juliana would have screamed her head off," Lorelei said. "Would that not have been heard?"

Devon smirked. "Half the lasses were screaming last night."

Lorelei stared at him, and Rory almost felt sorry for her as a blush stole over her cheeks when she understood the implication. He diverted the conversation. "No one saw riders moving out, either?"

Carr shook his head again. "They were camped close to the burn, away from the crowd. 'Tis nae hard to slip into the woods from there."

Emily made a distressed sound, and Ian put his arm

around her shoulders. "Rory will find her."

"But...in time?"

Rory was almost tempted to suggest that Neal might have come to his senses and already abandoned the harpy—who would want to put up with the screeching banshee?—but one look at Ian made him keep his mouth shut. He didn't particularly want to engage in fisticuffs this morning.

"She should be safe until they get to wherever the laird is staying."

Emily's eyes widened suddenly. "Laird Cameron did not come with Neal, did he?"

"Nae." Ian looked at her. "Neal said he was ailing."

Her expression turned hopeful. "Surely once his father hears about this, he will see how insane it is and make Neal release Juliana."

A moment of silence greeted that remark before Devon spoke.

"Laird Cameron follows the auld ways."

Alarm grew on her face again. "Which means he will think it is all right to steal a bride? Against her will?"

"He might," Carr said, his own face grave.

Emily looked wildly around, then her gaze settled on Rory. "You have to stop him. Please. I know you do not get along with my sister, but... Please. *Please* bring her home. I will make sure she never says an unkind word to you again."

He doubted that were possible, but the look of anguish on Emily's face was nearly unbearable. Not to mention Ian's threatening glare. While it was true there was no affection lost—or even tolerance—between him and Juliana, she still didn't deserve the fate of being Neal Cameron's wife. The man was a total arse. Not only could he not hold his liquor—or his temper when drunk—he mistreated his horse, and his hounds ran from him. At a gathering three years ago, he'd raped a girl—a MacFarlane lass that Rory had an eye for—

and she'd come to Rory the next day, battered and bruised. Neal had denied the rape. Worse, the lass had quickened, and Neal had refused to acknowledge the child.

As shrewish as Juliana was—at least with him—she didn't deserve that fate. Rory set his coffee mug down and sighed.

"I will go after her."

...

Fool. Fool, *fool*, FOOL. She had to be the biggest fool in all of Britain. Juliana yanked against the ropes that bound her hands, but they didn't give. Instead, her efforts only seemed to tighten them. Frustrated, she let her hands drop onto the pommel of the saddle and tried to avoid making contact with the man seated behind her—an impossible feat given that the horse's cantering rocked her against the damn bastard. And against that male part of him that felt very hard.

"Da…mm…phh," she muttered, the words ineffective against the gag that had been stuffed into her mouth early on when she wouldn't be quiet. "Da…mm…phh."

"I told ye to shut your yap." A rough voice spoke into her ear, followed by a sharp bite to the side of her neck. "Next time I will draw blood."

Juliana seethed silently, forcing herself to still. That was the second bite Neal Cameron had given her. The next one might indeed draw blood and, if it hit the big vein in her neck, she'd bleed to death. She needed to survive.

But, dear Lord, she'd been stupid. Neal had hounded her at the festivities yesterday, although with Fiona and Lorelei beside her, she'd been able to thwart his advances. When he'd finally seemed to give up and had left with his clansmen, it was late, and she'd wanted nothing more than to get a bit of fresh air, away from the still-reveling crowd in the bailey. She'd told Lorelei not to wait up as she'd gathered her cloak.

She'd only intended to sit in the quiet garden for a moment behind the castle.

She hadn't gone very far when she'd heard a rustling and then, before she could turn around, she'd been grabbed, something foul-smelling held against her nose, and the world had gone black.

She'd awakened hanging upside down over a man's shoulder and immediately started pounding her fists on his back and screaming, which only got her a heavy fist to her thigh and someone sticking that foul-smelling cloth under her nose again. When she'd regained consciousness the second time, she was astride a horse, bound and gagged, and they were galloping madly down the road.

And her head hurt. It was pounding in rhythm to the horse's hooves, and she felt nauseous. Dear God! What if she needed to cast up her accounts? She'd choke to death. And she didn't dare try to talk again.

Her situation modified slightly from hell to purgatory when the horse finally slowed and veered off the road. But soon her gown was catching on bramble and gorse, ripping the silken skirt to shreds. Not that it mattered, she supposed, since the skirt had already torn when she'd been thrown over the saddle to ride astride.

But she still felt sick. Frantically, she began twisting in the saddle to try and make eye contact. She brought her bound hands to her mouth in a gesture she hoped would communicate she needed the gag out. It must have registered, because Neal signaled the other riders to stop, and he yanked the cloth out.

"If ye start screeching again…"

He hadn't finished the sentence when she leaned over the animal's withers and emptied the contents of her stomach on the ground. He cursed, one of the men said something in Gaelic, and the rest of them laughed. She didn't see anything that was one damn bit funny.

"Are ye sure ye want that one?" one of the men finally asked. "A blethering crabbit who blaws like a bairn?"

*"Dùin do bheul!"*

She had no idea what he said, but it effectively silenced the man. But…he had given her an idea.

"I…have been ill the last few days. You should let me go. It might be ague or the grippe."

While his men gave her startled looks and a couple of them edged their horses away, Neal just laughed.

"Ye were just fine at the weddin'." He smirked. "And I'm nae givin' up me prize."

"I am not your prize!"

He raised a brow. "I would say ye are."

Well, she wasn't going to win that argument out here in the woods. Wiping her mouth indelicately on her sleeve—Lorelei would have swooned at such a thing, but she wanted to make a point—she asked, "Where are you taking me?"

"Home."

That wasn't much of an answer, but Juliana remembered the MacGregors saying something about Cameron holdings north of Fort William. She wasn't quite sure how far that was, since she'd only come to Scotland when her widowed sister, Emily, had been granted her English husband's claim to land here. But anywhere was too far. She had to get away before… before… She quelled the thought. *Focus on the present. Survive.*

"Why did you leave the road, then?"

He looked at her as though she might be slow-witted. Daft, the Scots called it. She raised her chin defiantly. "I would think it easier for a horse to travel on a road rather than through a forest."

"It also makes it easier for the MacGregors to follow us."

A bit of hope sprang up. Surely Ian would send some

of his men out to look for her. She was Emily's sister, after all. But when would they discover her missing? She'd been abducted shortly past midnight. Dawn was just breaking, and they'd been riding hard. And now that they'd left the road...

She cursed under her breath. "Damn fool."

Neal's eyes narrowed. "I'll nae put up with ye calling me names I doona like."

Juliana glanced up at him, startled that he'd heard. "I was not calling you a fool. I was calling myself one for allowing you to capture me."

He snorted. "Ye dinna have a choice in that."

"I did." She hated to admit it, but it was true. "I should have suspected you were not content to leave things be. I should not have gone into the garden."

He shrugged. "I would have taken ye anyway. Ye just made it easier for me."

She frowned. "What do you mean?"

"I bribed one of the servants to tell me which was your bedchamber, and then I offered more coin for the door to be left unbarred." Neal gestured to his men. "We were waiting for the right moment to enter."

"You would have been caught."

His eyebrow rose again. "Would we? MacGregor was nae about to leave his bed, and his brothers were still in the bailey drinking."

Juliana closed her eyes briefly, not wanting to admit defeat. Would Neal have been successful? It was quite possible. There were still servants who resented Englishwomen—*Sassenachs*—invading their castle. Whoever had been bribed proved the point. She shuddered to think what would have happened to her younger sister, Lorelei, if these oafs had actually gotten to the bedchamber. Perhaps it was better that she'd been abducted from the garden, but it was essential she go no farther with this man. She could find her way back to the road if she could just escape. She opened her eyes and clutched her stomach.

"I needs must relieve myself."

He gave her a suspicious look, but she gave him her best imitation of Lorelei acting totally naive. "Please. I would hate…to soil myself."

Neal grunted, then swung off his horse and none too gently hauled her down. He pointed. "Ye can go as far as the trees over there."

That wasn't much distance, and she'd probably have only a few minutes' head start, but she had to try. At least the trees were thick and the sky hadn't quite lightened. She nodded with what she hoped was a demure expression. "Thank you."

As soon as she was out of sight, she picked up her skirts and began to run, ignoring the sharp twigs and hard stones beneath her ill-shod feet. At least the satin slippers didn't make any noise.

She dared not pause to determine if she were being followed, just ran blindly into the hilly woods. She heard the sound of water and switched direction, hoping and praying there would be boulders along the bank that she could crouch behind or even a rocky ledge jutting out from an overhang that she could crawl under.

Instead, she suddenly burst into a small clearing by the burn. And then she heard the crashing sound of boots behind her. Wildly she looked around for somewhere to hide. She raced toward the stream, determined to leap across when her arms were caught in a hard, cruel grip.

"I'll nae hit ye this time," Neal snarled, "but doona try it again." He jerked her around and pushed her back the way she had come. "And ye best remember this. What I want, I get."

Sheer terror struck her heart. The memory of another man forcing himself on her—taking her virginity with it—rose from the depths of her mind where it had been long buried. She had vowed she'd never let another man have his way with her. And then a coldness settled over her and she realized: she would kill this man if she must.

# Chapter Two

Rory cursed silently, although why he didn't just speak aloud since he was alone in the woods in the misty dawn, he didn't know. He led his horse along a narrow deer trail, trying to pick up prints. This was the third he'd followed that appeared to lead nowhere other than the burn, which wove its way through a rocky wash. He huffed a sigh of frustration, and his gelding snorted his accord.

He stroked the sleek sorrel neck. "I ken, Baron. 'Tis nae easy to get through these brambles. Ye'll get a good brushing when this is done."

He peered through the trees as he proceeded, seeing no sign of broken branches or trampled lichen along the path that inevitably led to the winding burn once again. He dropped the horse's reins so he could drink and pondered which way to go.

When he'd set out yesterday morning, it had been easy to follow the Camerons on the road toward Fort William, but then half of them had turned off a few miles later. He'd contemplated which group would have Juliana. Logic would dictate the ones who'd taken to the woods. Why else would they do so? But then, they could simply be a decoy, since Neal was smart enough to know they'd be followed. Getting Juliana to whatever fortress his father was residing at would be much faster taking the road. However, a party on the road would be easier for the MacGregors to catch up to. He'd decided to follow the trail in the forest and leave the road to the men Ian had sent out.

He thought he'd hit the right path when he'd found churned-up grass and hoofprints a short distance in. He'd followed a trail of broken branches and trampled leaves, as though someone had run through them, but the track had abruptly ended on the banks of the burn. Rory had walked along the banks looking for any clue that Juliana might have escaped, plunged into the shallow water, and come out on the other side, but he could find no telltale signs. Whatever had occurred on this side had stopped here.

The second trail had not offered a lot of clues, either. The men seemed to be walking their horses single file, and fewer branches were broken. He'd found some horse dung early this morning, but as dry as it was, it had probably been left yesterday. There were no signs of a camp or fire, which meant they must have traveled throughout the night.

While that must have been exhausting for Juliana—she was an Englishwoman, after all—it was a better alternative than spending the night in a tent with Neal. He must have decided it best to get her home before he bedded her.

But it also meant Rory's chance of catching up to them before they reached their destination was slimming down. If they'd not stopped except to rest the horses, they'd easily get to Cameron lands by this afternoon. And therein lay Rory's other problem. He wasn't even exactly sure where they would've gone, since the Cameron laird moved around. Rory had an inkling where he might be residing at the moment, based on what someone had said at the wedding feast, but if he were wrong, then Juliana might very well disappear into the mists—just as the MacGregors had done for so many decades.

He cursed again, aloud this time. The woman had been a thorn in his side since she'd come with her sisters to Strae Castle this past summer. She was prickly as a thistle and never failed to put him in his place—or, at least, *try* to. She'd challenged nearly everything he said. Yet he enjoyed sparring with her...only to prove *he* was right, of course. But he had to admit—he also liked provoking her temper. Her hair seemed to bristle and flame as though it was on fire. There was something about seeing her riled—her ginger-colored eyes blazing with indignation—that oddly appealed to him. Aroused him, even, if he were totally honest with himself. Which was just another thing about her that was irritating. He preferred biddable lasses who succumbed to his charm and were happy to have his attention. Juliana had none of those traits, and he certainly didn't want to be *aroused* by her. Good God almighty.

He looked across the burn once more, looking for any sign that they'd crossed, but didn't see any. The Camerons had come this far, but the trail ended here. He frowned. Perhaps they'd been clever enough to take the horses into the water and follow the stream a ways to avoid detection. If they did, it meant they suspected they were being followed.

Gathering his reins, he patted his horse once more, then mounted. "Looks like ye will be getting wet feet for a bit."

He couldn't just lose Juliana to the hills and mists. He couldn't go back empty-handed. It wasn't Ian's wrath he feared, but the looks on the faces of her sisters when he had to explain that he'd failed. He set his mouth in a tight line. Not if he could help it. He *would* find her.

• • •

Juliana was tired, sore, dirty, and disheveled the next afternoon when Neal signaled for his group to stop atop a ridge that overlooked a small glen. Except for several stops to rest the horses, they had continued on for a day and a half. Neal had kept well away from roads, staying hidden in the forests, not approaching a village or anything that came close to a coaching inn. Which meant there'd been no opportunity to escape. Unfortunately, her last attempt had resulted in being watched constantly, so she'd not had the chance to relieve herself, either. She really was out of sorts.

"Is that it?" she asked, pointing to a two-story stone building in the distance, surrounded by a number of buildings and a wooden fence. "Where we are going?"

"Aye. 'Tis home for now," Neal answered.

*"Finally."*

He gave a raucous laugh. "Are ye so anxious to get married, then?"

She rolled her eyes, although he couldn't see it since she was still sitting in front of him in the saddle. "I am *anxious* to get off this horse. I am *anxious* to speak to your father about the stupidity of abducting me. I am *anxious* to return to Strae Castle, where my sisters are worried out of their minds."

"I will send word to your sisters…once we are married."

Juliana clasped her hands—at least they were no longer tied—to keep them from trembling. She needed to find a weapon if her wits would not serve, but it would not do to show fear. She just hoped her voice didn't shake. "I have not agreed to marry you, and I never will."

He made a sneering sound. "Ye doona have to agree."

She turned slightly so she could look at him. "That is ridiculous. You cannot just…just…*steal* someone and force a marriage."

"Aye, I can."

"That is *illegal*."

"Mayhap in London. Ye are in the Highlands now. Clans have been stealing brides for centuries."

She glared at him. "You still have to obey English law. Or have you not heard of the Act of Union? Scotland agreed to it in 1707."

He snorted. "Ye will find Scots are nae afraid to defy the English Crown."

"I do not care about that. You cannot force me to marry you."

"Did ye nae hear me before?" Neal asked. "I can. Ye are nae spoken for, ye doona have a father who will demand your return—"

"Ian MacGregor will!"

Neal shrugged. "MacGregor is married to your sister. He canna claim ye, too."

"The MacGregor clan has had its rights restored. My sister is now married to their laird. Do you want a clan war?"

He laughed again. "Ye need to study your history better. While we consider our lairds rulers, your English king does nae. He willna take kindly to MacGregor starting a war, especially so soon after granting the clan recognition."

"My sister is a favorite of the king." Actually, it had been their father whom the king had been patron to, but that was a detail better not mentioned just now. "King George personally granted my sister special dispensation for the deed to Strae Castle." She lifted her chin. "His Majesty will not be pleased to hear of this abduction."

Neal studied her for a moment. "By the time your English king finds out, we will be long wedded"—he smirked—"and bedded."

A chill ran down her spine. The accursed man might well be right. By the time she sent word—*if* she could send word—

to anyone, it would be far too late. Even English law would uphold a marriage that had been consummated. Women were considered chattel.

Juliana clenched her jaw. She would not fall victim to a man again. Even if she must commit murder.

...

He'd just missed them, damn it. Rory lay on his belly, his head poking over the ridge as he watched Neal and Juliana, accompanied by a half dozen men, ride into the glen below. If he tried to rescue Juliana now, he'd be exposed in open land, and Cameron's men would see him coming. Seven-to-one odds weren't good any time, but not having an element of surprise was pure stupidity. Besides, it would be foolish to attack this close to their destination.

He cursed again. Not only had Cameron had a good several hours' head start on him, but he'd lost valuable time on the first two attempts to pick up the trail. On the third try, he'd had to travel a good half mile in the burn itself before he finally found a muddy patch on the bank where Cameron's group had exited the stream. Baron had shown his displeasure at keeping his hooves wet by kicking up his back ones as he climbed out of the water and had nearly unseated Rory.

His first plan had been to follow them, wait for nightfall, overtake whatever guard had duty, snatch Juliana, and ride for home like the hounds of hell were chasing him. Which they would be, no doubt. He'd even thought, if he were lucky, the Camerons would all be drunk and no one would be standing a watch. He should have known such wishful thinking was tempting the fae. While he might outwardly claim that faeries were the stuff of myth, no Scot with half a brain would ignore the possibility that the stories had truth to them. In any event, the Camerons hadn't even stopped for the night.

At least he knew where Juliana was and wouldn't have to spend more time searching. Rory watched as the group approached the gate and said something to the man standing guard atop the barbican. A moment later the gate swung open, and Cameron and his men—with Juliana—disappeared inside.

He studied the property. The main building was stone, but it wasn't a castle. There were no merlons or embrasures along the roof, nor towers at either end. Although there were no other men posted along the top of the wooden fence, it likely had a battlement walk, since there was a watch house by the gate. The number of outbuildings, including what looked like a large stable, indicated that a sizable group of people lived there.

Rory narrowed his eyes. The place was a fortress of sorts, but not one blatant enough to draw the attention of English soldiers. Whoever the owner was, it was a perfect place for the Cameron laird to seek refuge. As it was seemingly not guarded, King George wouldn't consider it a threat, but Rory would wager that, if need be, well-armed men could be summoned to assume positions at a moment's notice.

He sat back on his haunches and thought. He could wait until it was dark, then ride down and circle the barricade, looking for a back entrance. But because no visible guards were posted during the day to draw attention, there was still a good possibility that men would be standing watch at night. The holding was situated in the middle of an open glen, and he'd be spotted since the moon was full.

The other problem with that idea was that he didn't know where the hell Juliana would be once he was inside. He couldn't very well stroll through the halls, looking about. He had no idea of the layout of the place, either, although bedchambers were usually on the second floor.

And *that* thought made his blood chill. *Bedchambers.* So

far, Juliana's virtue was intact since Cameron hadn't stopped, but how long would that last? How long before Neal accosted her in one of those bedchambers? Would he give her time to rest? Or even have a meal? Rory knew the bastard had a reputation for taking what he wanted.

He glanced up at the sky. The sun was still fairly high. Nightfall was several hours away. By that time, he might be too late. He thought about what his brother Alasdair—who had been to London—had told him of English society. If a woman were found in a compromising position, the man was obligated to marry her. And, if he didn't, she would be considered ruined. Rory didn't give a tin farthing about any of that, but Neal had said he wanted to marry Juliana. And, in any event, he would certainly bed her, even if he had to tie her down.

Rory grimaced as he stood up and walked toward Baron. He really only had one option left, something time-honored by Scots. Something he'd never thought he would do. And certainly not with *Juliana*, who hated his guts.

Marriage had not been something he'd contemplated, at least not for several more years. Now that the MacGregor name had been reinstated by King George, there were lands to be reclaimed, battles to be fought to get them, and honor to be restored. He didn't have time—and he didn't need the diversion—while he sought to make their clan great and worthy once more. And, when the time for marriage came, he always thought he'd choose a Scottish lass, willing to raise bairns and tend his house. *Not* one to cause him any trouble. Juliana was nothing *but* trouble. He just hoped the blasted woman had the sense to keep her mouth shut when he claimed her for his own.

# Chapter Three

Juliana looked around the bedchamber as the door closed behind her, and she felt like she'd swallowed hot coals. Neal's cloak had been thrown over one chair, and his muddy boots stood next to it. The breeches and tunic he'd worn lay crumpled on the floor. There was no doubt whose room she was in.

There was no adjoining door to the next room, only the one she'd been pushed through. Since she could hear boots scuff on the floor outside, she didn't need to open it to know she was being guarded. She went quickly to the small window to see if there was an escape route there. Unfortunately, the room was on the second floor. There was no portico below with a welcoming roof for her to jump to. No trees offered a branch to crawl out on, and there wasn't even a vine trellis to climb down.

She was stuck, and Neal would return soon.

Juliana reached into her pocket and fingered the knife she'd managed to purloin by dropping several utensils at the quickly arranged meal they'd had once they'd arrived. The blade wasn't that sharp, but it would have to do.

Hearing a feminine voice outside, she wondered if a maid had been sent to help her undress. Not that she had any intention of taking off one stitch of clothing. Perhaps, though, she could convince the maid to help her escape? It was a far-fetched notion, but worth a try. The house was not the Cameron seat, so the servants might not feel any sense of loyalty to Neal. A bit of hope sprang within her.

That hope was dashed when the door opened and Neal's sister Margaret appeared.

She was probably only a few years older than Juliana and had been quiet at the table earlier.

"I've come to help ye get ready for the night," she said as she carried a pitcher to the dresser. She wrinkled her nose at the dirty water in the basin. "I figured Neal would forget to order fresh water for ye." She emptied the contents into a brass chamber pot standing in the corner, then filled the basin with hot water. "I brought ye some soap, too."

"Thank you." Even though Juliana wasn't about to remove any clothing—not even her cloak—just washing her face and neck would feel wonderful. She eyed the girl as she performed a hasty ablution. "Do you know why I am here?"

"Aye, of course. Neal means to marry ye." She smiled. "'Tis what he's speaking to our father about now."

The coals in her stomach burned hotter. "This is insane. I do not want to marry your brother."

Margaret's brow rose. "Why nae?"

Dear Lord. She didn't want to insult the other woman. "It is not Neal specifically. But I do not want to get married."

The brow rose fractionally higher. "Never?"

Juliana shook her head. "I do not want to be controlled—owned—by any man."

Margaret grinned at that. "I've nae intention of allowing that, either."

A glimmer of hope rose. "Then you will help me escape?"

The grin faded. "I canna do that. Neal has a fierce temper when he is crossed."

Juliana took her hands. "All the more reason that I get away. Please."

Margaret withdrew her hands. "I canna."

"Why not? Surely, you do not want to have me in your family when you know I will always resent you?"

"Ye will change your mind eventually." She shrugged. "Besides, your sister is married to the MacGregor. That makes ye a sister-by-marriage to him. And when ye marry Neal, ye become *my* sister-by-marriage."

"What difference does that make?" Juliana asked.

She smirked. "'Twill give me a chance to see Devon at clan gatherings."

"Ian's brother?" For a moment she was confused, then she widened her eyes. "You fancy Devon?"

"Aye."

"He is half-mad. I could tell you things..." Juliana paused. "Now is not the time, but think of how your children may turn out."

"Och, I doona want to *marry* him or have his bairns." Margaret gave her a sly look. "Devon kens how to please a woman, if ye get my meaning."

Juliana stared at her. "You cannot be serious."

"Oh, I am. Why should men be the only ones to enjoy a tumble? Ye have to admit, the MacGregor men are verra braw and strong." She sighed. "And all of them have that inky-black hair that makes them look a wee bit dangerous."

That might be true, Juliana supposed, remembering the first day she'd seen them. All five had been standing on the front steps of Strae Castle when Emily's carriage had rolled to a stop. Although they all had different-colored eyes, they had looked rather fierce and barbaric with that long, dark hair flowing around their shoulders.

"Actually, I found them to be more annoying than dangerous." Especially Rory. That very same day they'd arrived—she'd barely been out of the carriage—one of the large wolfhounds had nearly knocked her over. Rory had stopped her fall by catching her, but he'd also held on to her well after she'd regained her feet. She was sure it had been a gesture to let her know who was in control. And the irritating man seemed to enjoy making her temper rise at every occasion...although, she had to admit, she didn't mind sparring with him. As long as she won, of course. *And* when he was wearing clothes. The image of him standing in the burn still lingered in her mind, as much as she tried to ignore it.

"Annoying?" Margaret asked. "But—" Her sentence was cut off by loud voices from below. "What in the world?"

She rushed to the door with Juliana on her heels. The guard that had been outside was nowhere to be seen, although he might have gone downstairs to see what the commotion was about.

The rectangular house had a rather odd design. There was a foyer with a central staircase that led to the second floor. Instead of hallways leading to the right and left, chamber doors opened onto walkways with railings, allowing someone standing on the second floor to look down into the open area below. Juliana wasn't sure if the design had been influenced by London town houses or if the builder had thought the occupants might fend off intruders by firing arrows or muskets from this position.

Either way, her mouth dropped open when she saw Rory MacGregor standing below, one hand on his sword hilt and his eyes flashing blue fire.

...

Rory supposed he should consider himself lucky that the fae hadn't decided to intervene again. The holding in which the Cameron laird had taken refuge was owned by a MacLean—they had enough trouble with the MacDonalds not to want to clash with the newly un-proscribed MacGregors—and he'd been granted safe entry.

And the fact that the MacLean owner was standing in the entryway was keeping the very angry Cameron laird and his son at bay. Not that Rory would have minded drawing his sword on Neal. His fingers itched on the hilt.

"I suggest we take this conversation into my library," MacLean said.

Cameron nodded curtly while Neal scowled at Rory. "I ken ye are lying."

"Not *here*," his father said.

Rory managed not to grin at the chastisement, but his humor faded quickly when MacLean suggested that Juliana be present. He had hoped he could convince the Camerons that he was handfasted to Juliana and therefore had the right to claim her *without* her being present. Without her actually being a part of his ploy. It would make his task much simpler if he could simply tell her afterward that he'd been able to persuade them to see reason and that he was taking her back to Strae Castle. She might even consider him a bit of a hero, although that was most likely stretching the truth.

"She is well aware of the situation," he said, not specifying what kind of situation. "There is nae need to subject her to this discussion."

"I would think she would want to hear it," MacLean said mildly.

"Aye." Neal glared at Rory. "Are ye afraid she might deny it?"

That was *exactly* what he was afraid of. Juliana had a tendency to say what was on her mind without giving it thought. A denial would make it difficult to proceed, although he supposed he could say they'd had a bit of an argument before she was abducted. *That* wouldn't be stretching the truth at all. They argued over everything.

"Verra well. Summon her, then." He glared back at Neal. "It will give me a chance to make sure she has nae been injured by ye."

Neal narrowed his eyes. "Are ye accusing me—"

"*Enough,*" his father said.

MacLean nodded to one of his men and then led the way to the library, Neal scowling while Rory held his gaze.

Juliana must have been nearby, because she appeared a moment later, although why she was wearing a cloak he didn't know.

"Please close the door," MacLean said. "It seems we have a small problem."

Juliana looked around. "I would say we have a rather *big* problem, my lord."

He nodded his assent. "Is it true that ye are handfasted to MacGregor?"

She frowned. "Handfasted?"

"Aha!" Neal all but shouted. "She kens nae of this."

"Aye, she does. She is simply nae familiar with the Scottish wording." Rory moved quickly to stand beside Juliana. "She prefers the term 'betrothed.'"

For a moment she stared at him, and he prayed she would not deny it, or worse, try to slap him. He grabbed both her hands to make sure she didn't. For good measure, he squeezed them now, hoping she'd understand and not argue, for once.

She took a deep breath, her eyes sparking, promising a fiery tirade, which he could only hope she'd wait to unleash. He managed to give her a beseeching smile. "Tell them we are betrothed, love, so we may leave and return to Strae Castle."

Her mouth opened, then closed. She took another deep

breath. Her expression changed as understanding dawned, and she smiled sweetly. Something she'd never done before. At least not to him. An odd little jolt shot through his belly. And she wasn't pulling her hands away, either.

She turned to Neal. "I told you I could not marry you. Now you know why."

Clever lass. Rory breathed a sigh of relief. "'Tis settled then. We will leave immediately."

"Yes, of course. I am sure my sisters are quite worried."

"Nae quite so fast," Neal said. "I dinna see ye exchange one word with MacGregor at the wedding feast. *Nae one word.*"

"Well, we'd had a bit of a…disagreement earlier, and I wasn't quite ready to forgive him." She gave Rory another smile. "Besides, we were busy celebrating not only a wedding, but also the lifting of the proscription." Juliana withdrew her hands. "I had duties to attend to."

"Aye, and so did I," Rory added, managing not to remind her *she* was the one who should be apologizing for their… *disagreement.* He'd been at the burn first, after all. But that argument could wait.

Neal glowered. "Ye never made an announcement, either."

"It would not have been appropriate to spoil my sister's wedding day with an announcement of our own," Juliana replied.

Rory was beginning to appreciate the way her mind worked. "We had planned to do that the morning after, but ye abducted my woman."

Juliana shot him a look, and he cringed inwardly at his choice of words. Thankfully, she was keeping in what would be a full-blown tempest later, but the sooner they could leave, the better.

"We will see ourselves out."

Neal moved to block the door. Rory raised a brow and put this hand on the hilt of his sword. "Make way."

"Just one more thing," Neal said, "and then ye can leave."

Juliana frowned. "What?"

"I want ye to kiss MacGregor."

*"What?"*

They both spoke the word together, but Juliana recovered first.

"That would be most improper, especially with my English upbringing."

Neal shrugged. "Ye are in Scotland now."

"True enough," his father said.

MacLean nodded. "A true handfasting is sealed with a kiss."

Juliana's face paled, and for a moment, Rory thought he saw something akin to fear in her eyes, but that would be ridiculous. She might not like him, but she certainly wasn't afraid of him. Was she afraid to be kissed? That didn't make sense, either. The lass was past eight and ten. Surely she'd had suitors who'd at least attempted to steal a kiss? Or made a sloppy job of it? Had some idiot been that inept?

Rory felt his cock stir at the thought of showing Juliana how good a kiss could be. He moved a bit closer, and she stiffened. He sensed her fear again, somewhat like a trapped animal with nowhere to run. He took her hand, which now felt like ice. She *was* afraid. But if they expected to leave here without trouble, the easiest way was to simply do what Neal demanded.

Rory looked into her eyes, imploring her silently to understand as he took another step closer. Her eyes widened briefly, then she closed them tightly and lifted her chin. As he lowered his head and brushed his lips across her closed mouth, he had the strangest feeling she was offering herself up like some sacrifice. And it certainly was not going to look believable if she didn't respond to him.

He brought her hands to his shoulders, then cradled her head in his palms as he pressed his lips gently against hers, angling his position to better claim them with light brushing. He nibbled at the side of her mouth, his tongue barely stroking the crease, and she gasped, her lips parting. His cock hardened at the unintentional invitation, and he wanted nothing more than to plunge deep into her mouth and plunder her sweet taste, but somehow he managed to control his base urge and pulled away.

Juliana looked dazed and, for once, speechless. He felt a little that way himself. He hadn't expected to… Well, kissing Juliana was quite a pleasant surprise.

Rory glanced at Neal. "I hope ye are satisfied, because I will continue the rest of this in private."

He looked like he wanted to argue, but his father nodded. "Go."

Rory didn't wait for any more sentiments. He took Juliana's hand and propelled her toward the door. The movement seemed to revive her. In another moment she was keeping stride with him.

Margaret met them by the door. "Ye are leaving?"

"Yes," Juliana answered, not pausing to stop. "Thank you for everything."

"I've only one horse," he said as they reached the courtyard and he unhitched Baron from a rail.

"As long as he will carry both of us, I do not care," Juliana answered. Pulling her cloak tighter, she hiked up her skirts and clambered onto a mounting block, hoisting herself into the saddle before he could assist. "Just get us out of here."

He sighed and mounted behind her. It seemed the Juliana he knew was back. They had just cleared the gate when a shout came from behind them. Several shouts.

"You might want to go faster," Juliana said.

The hairs at his nape rose. "Why?"

"I think Margaret just told them we are not betrothed."

"How would she know that?" His question was met by silence. "Juliana? How would she know?"

She hesitated. "I might have told her I had no intention of getting married. Ever."

Damnation. The Camerons would no doubt be giving chase as soon as they were mounted, which meant he couldn't head straight home. Riding double on a tired horse, they'd be overtaken. Rory turned in the opposite direction and spurred Baron on.

It seemed the faeries had decided to intervene after all.

# Chapter Four

Perhaps it was just as well that the galloping horse was making Juliana concentrate on staying astride, else she would be thinking about Rory's kiss. She swayed dangerously to one side and felt Rory's arm slip around her waist, tucking her firmly against him. While that did help her secure her balance, it also made her aware of his hard, muscled body, which, of course, led back to recalling the kiss.

She hadn't known how gentle a man's hands could be cradling her head. The man who'd taken her virtue had been anything but. His kisses—if they could be called that—had been foul and brutal, and she'd had a cut lip and bruised mouth for a week. She'd vowed never to let another man touch her that way.

Dear God in heaven, she'd nearly swooned—and she *never* swooned—when Rory had stepped closer to her. It was through sheer will that she'd managed to remain standing. She'd told herself that enduring Rory's kiss in order to escape was better than being raped later by Neal. And certainly better than having to stand trial for murdering the buffoon.

To her own amazement, Rory's kiss had not been harsh nor painful. The opposite, in fact. His lips had been warm and firm, but only brushing against hers. His nipping had been teasing, making her tingle in odd places, and, when he'd lightly swept the tip of his tongue along her mouth, the strangest sensation had washed over her. She'd nearly fainted again. And she did *not* swoon. *Ever.*

The horse veered off the road suddenly, snapping Juliana out of her reverie as he slowed the horse and she swayed dangerously.

"Why are you leaving the road?"

He dropped his arm from around her waist. "Baron canna run all night."

His tone was curt, as though she should have known that, which she should have. Strange, though, how cool the air suddenly was now that she was no longer pressed against Rory. Juliana chided herself inwardly. He certainly didn't need to hold on to her now that the horse was walking. Given the fact that they were barely civil to each other most of the time, he probably didn't even want to hold on to her.

"I need to thank you for coming to my aid."

"I'm the best tracker we have, nae boast intended." His voice sounded gruff. "'Twas nothing."

She remembered Ian saying as much. It was a skill Rory had put to use in finding her. Obviously, *kissing* was another skill he'd put to use, and she was pretty sure he'd had a lot of practice. What he'd done at the MacLean's home was out of necessity. He'd done what he needed to, just like she'd managed to. It didn't mean anything between them had changed. It would be wise to remember his words. *'Twas nothing.*

"Where are we going?"

"For now, we are headed for the protection of the forest. With the moon full, I doona want to take the chance that we will be seen."

"You think Neal will follow us?"

"Eventually." His voice sounded grim behind her. "It will nae take them overlong to realize we dinna take the direct road back to Strae Castle."

"Maybe they will just give up. I did tell Neal I had no intention of marrying him. Surely he would prefer a willing bride."

Rory made a noise that sounded like something between a snort and a groan. "Ah, lass. All ye did was kindle the fire."

"What do you mean?"

"The more ye say 'nae,' the more determined Cameron will be to get ye to say 'aye.' 'Tis the way he is."

"He is a lout and a cad."

"Ye doona have to convince me," Rory answered.

"Perhaps Mr. MacLean will talk some sense into him. Or his father. He seemed reasonable."

"To a point, mayhap. But ye need to understand ye wounded Cameron pride."

"How?" She twisted slightly in the saddle to look at him. "The blackguard *abducted* me. There are laws against such things!"

Rory lifted one shoulder in a shrug. "Ye ken Highlanders doona take kindly to English laws."

"But…but… It's preposterous to think a man can just *steal* a woman…" She let her voice trail off. English law might not force a woman to marry a man she didn't want, but didn't Society often dictate who would marry whom? And, once wed, the woman was chattel. The *property* of her husband. She'd seen what that had done to Emily. She turned back around and lifted her chin. "I will not marry anyone."

"I will nae argue with ye on that." Rory reined in the horse and dismounted, holding out his hands to assist her. "We will walk for a while to give Baron a rest."

Juliana tried to dismount without his help, only to find her legs turned to lead. She half fell, half slid down the horse's side. Rory said something in Gaelic and caught her, which reminded her of how he'd done the same the first day she'd arrived. She looked up, expecting him to laugh like he'd done that time, but she saw only concern. He held her a moment longer while blood flowed back into her limbs, then dropped his hands.

"Are ye able to walk?"

She took a tentative step, then two. Her feet felt like sharp needles were piercing through, but she ignored the pain. Baron did need a break, and she wasn't a hothouse flower. "Yes."

"Good." He turned and led the way into the trees. "We need to keep going."

At this point, all she wanted was some sleep. She'd have gladly curled up on top of fallen leaves for a rest, but she wasn't about to let him think her weak. Still. "Will we be able to stop somewhere for the night?"

He looked at her as though she were daft, which she could very well be.

"We can," he said, "but the Camerons will branch out come morning, if nae before."

"You really think..." She stopped. Rory had already explained all about idiotic male pride. "Then how are we going to get home?"

"We will go north."

"North? But that is in the opposite direction."

"Aye. We will head to MacDonnell lands, then circle around to the MacPhersons' and Murrays'."

"How long will that take?" When he didn't answer, she asked again. "How long? A day or two?"

He shook his head. "More like a fortnight."

"A *fortnight*?"

"If the weather holds."

"If the weather holds." Lord help her, she was sounding like a parrot. "What are we… Where will we… I mean, how can we travel together for two weeks? Or…more?"

He hesitated, then took a deep breath. "To keep ye safe, it would be better if we declare we are handfasted, as I said earlier. Ye will be mine, and nae one will question us then."

Juliana stared at him, and then she began to laugh as hysteria rose in her throat. The irony of saving herself by doing exactly what she didn't want to do was madness.

...

Rory watched her uneasily, wondering what could possibly be laughable about his proposal—a word that made him shudder, considering she was the last woman he was compatible with. He supposed he should be grateful that she hadn't slapped him outright. He frowned. The lass was practically bent over, clearly finding the whole thing hilarious. He didn't think the idea was *that* funny. He had simply suggested that they act like a couple in public, but it was a wee bit of a sore point that she could not stop laughing. The lass didn't have a weakness in her head, not with the sharp retorts she always made to him.

When the sound changed and turned to a high keening, he grabbed her shoulders and gave her a shake. Her eyes widened, and he saw that look of apprehension in them before she jerked away. She started to put her hands up defensively and then suddenly dropped them.

"Are ye all right?"

For a moment, she looked around as though she wanted to bolt, then she slowly nodded. "I…I am fine."

He didn't believe that. She'd never seemed like one to succumb to vapors or any other odd maladies that befell some women. Yet, when he'd kissed her, she'd looked fearful. And now she acted as though she wanted to defend herself. Maybe she thought he was going to take advantage of her? The thought made him grimace. He'd never forced himself on a woman. He didn't *need* to.

Besides, this was *Juliana*, the woman with a viper's tongue…although the image that flashed through his mind of her tongue just now had nothing to do with how sharp her words were. Instead, his wayward mind wondered what would have happened if he hadn't stopped the kiss when he did. His cock twitched, and he pushed the thought firmly aside. He was obviously in need of rest as much as his horse, since he wasn't thinking straight.

"Mayhap we need to find a spot where we can get a bit o' sleep before we move on."

Her eyes widened again. "But you said we should move on so the Camerons do not catch up to us."

"Aye, but neither of us has had any rest in near two days. Ye must be tired."

"I…am…but I do not want to be caught." She fished for something in her cloak and pulled out a knife. "I do not want to have to use this."

Rory glanced at the blade and managed not to laugh. It was one used for cutting meat in a trencher, not very big and not overly sharp. He supposed it could do some damage, but it would hardly kill a man. Then he frowned. Was she sending him a message as well?

"Ye are nae planning to use that on me, are ye?"

She took a step back. "I do not want to—"

"Good." He took a step forward, grasped her wrist, and applied pressure to a spot between her thumb and forefinger. Her grip on the weapon loosened immediately, and he caught it.

"Give that back! You cannot do that!" She scowled at

him. "I have a right to protect myself!"

He grinned. "Ye are sounding like your old self now."

"It is just like a man to want a woman defenseless."

His grin faded. "Ye are more a danger to yourself than anyone else if ye doona ken how to use a knife. Ye saw how easy it was for me to disarm ye."

She furrowed her brows. "You did that just because you could."

"Aye, I suppose I did." He took hold of her hand and pressed the handle of the knife into it, then closed her fingers around the hilt. "Ye keep it for now. I will show ye how to use it properly another time."

She looked as though she wanted to retort, then changed her mind and put the knife away.

"I ken we are both tired," he said, "but I would feel safer if we could put a few more miles between us and the Camerons. I'll lead Baron and ye can ride."

Juliana looked at him and then the horse. She reached up to stroke Baron's neck. "I will not subject this poor animal to carry me. He has done enough. I will walk."

Rory studied her for a moment. She had to be nearly exhausted, but as stubborn as she was, she wouldn't admit it, any more than she'd admit she had no idea how to handle a knife. Still, he liked the fact that she'd considered his horse when most women would have taken him up on the offer.

"How long before we can stop for the night?"

"Only an hour or so more."

She didn't answer but simply nodded as he started to walk. That she was quiet as they stayed within the tree line was an indication of how tired she must be. Rory squelched a twinge of guilt. She probably was thinking they'd be stopping at an inn and she'd have a hot bath and a soft bed, but that wouldn't happen until they were much farther away. He could take no chances on word getting back to the Camerons that they'd been sighted.

But that information could wait for later.

...

"Damn the MacGregors to hell and back." Neal yanked his horse's head back as the animal skittered to a stop in the MacLean courtyard and tried to lessen the tight rein on its bit. He paid it no mind as he dismounted. "We'll need fresh horses," he said to the stable boy who came running out.

"Ye canna think to set out again in the middle of the night?" one of his men asked.

"Why nae? The damn MacGregor is getting away with my intended!"

"We doona ken which way he went."

"Well, we ken for damn sure he dinna ride south," Neal sneered. "We were chasing ghosts for a good ten miles or more."

"Aye, we ken he dinna ride straight for home," another man said, "but the more reason to wait until morning when we can pick up tracks."

"I willna let the bastard get away!" He'd already been made a fool by letting Rory MacGregor bluff his way into making him believe the handfast was true. He should have known better when Juliana didn't know what the word meant. He'd almost—*almost*—accepted that might be the reason she didn't want to marry him. That made him an even bigger fool. And the fact that Margaret announced in front of both the MacLean and Cameron men what she'd been told made it imperative that he right this wrong. His pride demanded it.

"Think on it," the first man said. "We ken he dinna ride south. It wouldna make sense for him to ride west. Loch Linnhe is in the way. If he rides east, there are nae villages and he has the Grampian mountains to cross. More like, he will head for Fort William."

The second man nodded. "We can get to the fort by tomorrow afternoon. The dragoons stationed there are nae fond of MacGregors, even if they have been un-proscribed. A letter from the MacLean stating his *lady guest* was abducted from his home by one of them should get the general to issue orders for a search."

"Aye and we'd have the king's men looking for them," a third man added. "We ken now the Sassenach doesna want to marry him, so she will corroborate the story. MacGregor will be arrested."

"He might even be charged with ravishing her if the lass claims he forced himself on her. The English will take offense at a barbarian taking her against her will."

Neal ground his teeth. The idea of MacGregor plowing that virgin field enraged him. English ladies prized their virtue above all else, and he wanted to be the one to pierce that maidenhead…to show no mercy until she realized that her pleasure—or pain—depended entirely on how submissive she became. She had made him a fool in front of his men. Once he found her, he would show her who was in control.

That damn woman was going to be his, one way or another.

# Chapter Five

Juliana woke to the sound of gurgling water, the smell of pine, and the realization that every bone and muscle in her body ached beyond belief. And she was cold, even though she wore her cloak and was covered with a saddle blanket. She opened one eye to see bare brown branches below a leaden sky. Her groggy mind told her this was not her bedchamber. But where…

Both eyes sprang open as she recalled the events of the past two days. She'd been so exhausted, she didn't even remember stopping somewhere in the forest for the night. No wonder she was cold. It was December. No wonder everything ached, given that her bed was pine needles over hard-packed earth. And where was Rory? Had he left her?

She sat up, pulling her cloak more tightly around her, and looked around. He was nowhere to be seen. But Rory's plaid covered her, so hopefully that meant he hadn't deserted her. She rose, wondering where she should start looking, when she heard rustling nearby. In another moment, Rory emerged from the trees, leading Baron.

"'Tis good ye are awake," he said. "Ye can see to your ablutions at the burn. Then we best move on."

Juliana managed to stifle a groan as she took a stiff step toward the sound of the water. Lord have mercy! She wasn't used to being in a saddle for so long, and she certainly wasn't used to a bed that was nearly hard as stone. She winced as she took another step.

"Riding will take the aches out, lass," Rory called after her.

She frowned. Was she being that obvious? She wasn't delicate. "I will be fine. Just give me a few minutes."

"Doona take too long. Dawn broke near an hour ago. The Camerons will be on the road."

All remnants of sleep left her. "Why did you not wake me sooner?"

"Ye only got a few hours' sleep as it is." He shrugged. "Besides, Baron needed the rest, too. He's going to have to carry the both of us until we get to Fort William."

She glanced at the saddled horse. "Just give me one minute, then." Ignoring the aches of sore muscles and stiff joints, she hobbled toward the bushes near the burn. She'd never been one to take long with her toilet and it wouldn't have really mattered, she supposed, since she didn't even have a comb to do something with her hair, most of which had come down. "I'll be right back."

Five minutes later, after a quick bite of the bread and cheese Rory had brought along, she was back in the saddle, stifling another groan. She didn't know if Rory was jesting—if so, it was a poor attempt—but her inner thighs felt raw from rubbing against the leather of the saddle. A satin ball gown and thin chemise did little to help. How in the world was she going to endure another day of this? She clamped her mouth shut, determined for once to stay quiet and not complain.

She almost laughed at that thought. Emily would be

proud of her restraint. And then reality struck her.

"My sisters are going to be worried."

"They will ken ye are with me."

That sounded a bit smug. Twisting in the saddle, she knitted her brows. "How will they know that, pray tell?"

He lifted a shoulder and let it drop. "Since I have nae returned, Ian will ken I am tracking ye still."

"Your brother may think that, but my sisters might well reason that you have not found me."

Rory looked somewhat affronted. "Then my brothers will set them straight."

"They are that confident in your skills?"

"Aye."

*That* answer was definitely smug. Juliana turned around to face the direction they were going. "I would still feel better if I could let them know that I am safe, but just delayed."

"Well, since we have nae messenger to send, 'tis nae likely to happen." He nudged the horse to a trot as the tree line ended and they were on the road once more.

"Why can we not send a post from Fort William?" Her voice bounced as she was jostled by the trot. "Surely there is a coach that runs from there."

"We are nae stopping at Fort William."

She glanced over her shoulder. "You said we were going there."

"Aye, but nae stopping."

"Why not? I think we should, so I can send a letter."

"Ye will just have to trust me that I ken what is best."

Her temper began to rise. This was exactly why she didn't want to marry any man. A woman's opinion didn't count. A man always thought he knew what was best.

"You have not convinced me. Surely a quick stop at a coaching inn—"

"Nae."

She glared at him as much as she could—since she couldn't twist in the saddle and could only turn her head slightly. "Why *not*?"

"Because..." He urged Baron to a canter, which had her clutching the pommel. "...there are too many dragoons about. Ye would certainly be noticed dressed in your torn finery, with your hair askew. And watchful eyes would note we had the one horse. And a coaching inn will be the first place the Camerons will stop."

That probably made sense, although she didn't want to admit it. "Do you think they will really ride all the way to Fort William?"

"Aye. Neal Cameron is nae going to give up easily."

*Drat that man. Why couldn't he just take no for an answer?* "Then where are we going?"

"We will stop at Spean, near the high bridge that crosses the river. 'Tis less than ten miles past the fort, but far enough that I think we will be safe."

"We will stop for the night? Will there be an inn?"

"The hamlet lies along the path to Fort Augustus, so there should be something."

"And shops?"

"We are nae going to spend time dawdling over clothing."

Her temper flared again. "I am not asking to go *shopping*. I need a simpler garment to wear so I do not stand out like a...a *Sassenach*."

Rory grunted. "I suppose ye are right. 'Twill be better if ye blend in."

"Well, I am glad to hear you think I am smart enough to be right about something." It was hard to keep the sarcasm out of her voice.

He laughed. "Doona let it go to your head, lass."

"Oh! Of all the—" She stopped talking as he urged the horse to a faster pace and she concentrated on keeping her balance. But that didn't mean she wasn't going to have her say later.

*Men.*

...

He probably should not have goaded her, but it was better to have her riled at him, lashing out, than for her to be compliant and…pleasant. Because when she was not hissing and spitting at him like a feral cat, his thoughts turned to how good it felt with his arms around her, steadying her while he managed the reins. Of course, once Baron had started trotting, the motion had her bouncing her rounded little arse against his cock, which happily ignored his attempt to minimize the effect and rapidly grew hard. Cantering lessened the rigorous bumping, but the rocking of the faster pace had his arms jostling the sides of her breasts as they rode.

The fae weren't through with him yet…

He would much have preferred they continue on past Spean—he didn't like being on a road between two military forts—but the lass was right. She did need other clothes…and warmer ones, since they were heading north and the weather was unpredictable in the Highlands.

And he needed to purchase another horse. He was going to be driven as mad as an English hatter if he had to continue riding pillion with her.

They rode in silence until near noon. Juliana was probably fuming over their earlier exchange, but at least she was quiet about it, which was good, since he was battling lustful urges brought on by the constant contact with her. God only knew what direction the conversation would have taken had there been one.

He was jolted back to reality when she finally spoke.

"Are those dragoons over there?"

Rory reined in Baron and followed her pointed finger to a ridge a few hundred feet from the road. Five horses stood abreast, their riders in bright-red coats and black tricorn hats.

*"Mhics an Diabhail! Droch crioch ort!"*

Juliana twisted in the saddle. "What does that mean?"

He blinked, not realizing he'd cursed out loud. From the curious look on her face, he doubted Juliana would take "nothing" as an answer. "May the sons of the devil come to an evil end."

She lifted an eyebrow. "They are dragoons, then?"

"Aye. And they have definitely seen us."

"We are doing nothing wrong."

"They will be suspicious, just the same."

"Do you think they will follow us?"

"They might." He lifted the reins, signaling the horse to walk. "Damnation. We doona need anyone remembering us."

"Bloody hell."

For a moment he was nonplussed, not sure he'd heard correctly. "Did ye just say *bloody* hell?"

"Yes." Juliana shrugged. "It is somewhat the English equivalent to your cursing."

"I...I ken that. I just thought..." He let his voice trail off.

"That ladies did not use such language?" Juliana finished for him. "You are quite right. Emily would be appalled, and Lorelei would probably swoon."

She didn't seem particularly worried about those facts, but why should she? There wasn't anyone around to hear her except himself. He would have laughed, except their situation was too dire for humor. "Let's just hope the Camerons doona run into the dragoons or there will be *bloody hell* to pay." He found he rather liked the word "bloody." It was easy to say and summed up the situation quite nicely.

"I have an idea," she said after a moment's silence.

He looked at the back of her head warily, wishing he could see her face. He remembered all too well when her sister Emily had had an idea. It had involved using herself as bait to catch their madman uncle as he'd attempted to murder her.

"What is it?" he asked cautiously.

She turned in the saddle again. "Since we have obviously been seen, it will not hurt to stop at Fort William."

"What? I am nae about to become a sitting target for dragoons to question us." He frowned at her. "Or Camerons to find us."

"Precisely," she said as if he would understand.

He muttered another Gaelic curse, making sure to do it silently this time. "Ye are making nae sense."

She gave him a look as though *he* were the daft one.

"Well, ye aren't."

Juliana sighed, as if willing herself to have patience with a halfwit. He started to open his mouth to defend himself, then snapped it closed and waited.

"As I said, we have already been seen. *If* the Camerons come to Fort William and *if* they happened to see these dragoons, the soldiers need to tell them it was not us whom they saw."

He felt the beginning of a headache. "Has all this jostling in the saddle rattled your brain? Ye are making nae sense. *At all*," he added just to make sure she understood.

She simply looked heavenward as if for guidance. "Let me explain then. We stop at a merchant's to purchase a new dress for me—"

"Ye want to shop? *Now?* Ye can do so when we get to Spean—"

"Yes," she said in the same tone one would use with a small bairn. "But if we stop here, we can introduce ourselves to the merchant by some other name and come up with a story that we were returning from a feast from somewhere and our carriage was waylaid by highwaymen and we only managed to escape by untying the horse we had behind the carriage and that we are heading home to wherever we are not going. That way, if the Camerons do start asking questions, they will not be getting the right answers." She smiled at Rory as if all that were perfectly clear.

He stared at her, sure his head would start pounding any minute. How she'd manage to put all that together in one sentence without stopping for breath was a truly amazing feat. He was still processing the whole of it when she spoke again.

"It is a good idea."

"It doesna make sense."

"You would think so if it were *your* idea." She gave him a reproachful look. "Go on, admit it. You just do not like it because I thought of it."

"That isna true."

"No? Then can you come up with something better?"

"Well…nae…but—"

"Then let us do it." She gave an exasperated sigh. "At least it gives us a fighting chance to mislead the Camerons."

"Well…aye…but—"

"We have nothing to lose by trying it."

The idea was flimsy at best, but Juliana was right that they didn't have anything to lose. It wouldn't take much time to purchase a serviceable gown—he hoped—and if the dragoons or the Camerons questioned the merchant, it might buy them some lead time, at least.

Rory sighed, too. "All right, lass. We will do it."

She smiled at him before turning forward. "You will see that I am right."

He muted a groan. He had a suspicion he'd be hearing that a lot in the coming days. But she was right about one thing for sure.

Stopping in Fort William would give him the opportunity to purchase another horse. In her mind, it would add to their alibi. But for him, it would be a means to finally stop tormenting himself with crazed lust.

*Hopefully.*

• • •

To her relief, there was a general merchant's shop on the main street that led to the garrison. She pointed. "We can stop there. They should have something I can wear."

Reining in the horse, Rory dismounted and helped her down. "Doona take long to decide, aye? We are nae safe here."

"No one seems overly interested in us."

Rory grunted. "We are in the midst of Cameron country. These people are related to the laird. They'll remember seeing us."

She pursed her mouth. "All the more reason to make our story believable, then. Are you sure we should be Grants?"

"Aye. There's a clan of them north of here, so 'tis reasonable we are headed to Castle Grant."

She frowned. "But you also said some MacGregors took the surname Grant while proscribed. If Neal and his father come here and ask questions, will they not be suspicious of that name, especially if their clansmen give a description that fits us?"

"We have already been over this." Rory sighed heavily, as if she was asking too much of him. "Aye, they probably will think that. Your red hair stands out. My black does, too, since 'tis nae a common color. If Cameron comes to the conclusion that we are traveling under a false name, Grant would be the logical one. And," he added emphatically, "that logic will make them head northwest overland, while we will stick to the east side of Loch Lochy to Invergarry Castle."

"And you think we will be safe there?" She knew she'd asked this question before, but she was still a bit put out with Rory for questioning *her* idea of using this alibi. She'd had to explain it several times, so turnaround was fair play.

He gave her a look that told her he knew what she was doing. "As I have mentioned, the castle is well fortified. The Camerons would be foolish to try and breach it. They would lose and it would stir the clans to war, something the king's dragoons doona want happening."

"However"—she probably shouldn't prod further, but for some inexplicable reason, she wanted to make Rory realize she had a brain in her head—"what if that clan simply invites the Camerons in?"

He took a deep breath. "The MacDonnells have allied with the Grants for nigh on two centuries since a MacDonnell lass wedded the son of the Grant laird. They'll nae hand us over."

"But we—*you*—are not really a Grant."

Rory rubbed his temple with the hand that wasn't holding the reins. "The Grants were one of the few clans brave enough to offer MacGregors protection during the worst of times. And we were allowed to use their name. 'Twill be honored."

"Well, if you think—"

"I *think*," he interrupted, "that ye had best go into that shop, purchase a dress, and tell your story instead of standing here in the street, blethering."

"I am not *blethering*."

"Ye are." He looped Baron's reins to a post and took her arm to lead her toward the door. "I will go in with ye to make sure the shopkeeper hears our tale, then I have a bit of business to attend to."

"Here?" Juliana looked around. "I thought you did not

want to linger."

"I doona. I am going to see about buying a horse for ye."

She glanced at Baron, then bit her lip. "The poor thing *has* been carrying both of us for two days."

"Aye, plus we will make better time if we are each on our own mount. But," he cautioned her as he opened the door, "I doona want ye to leave this shop until I return for ye."

She knit her brows. "Where would I go?"

"Nowhere. Ye will go nowhere."

He turned to greet the shopkeeper, leaving Juliana no time to retort. She assumed a pleasant smile as Rory related their sad plight, but she really did not like being told what to do.

. . .

*The woman is going to drive me completely barmy*, he thought as he made his way to the public stables. They'd spent most of the morning arguing—she called it *discussing*—what they were going to do. Then she made him repeat the gist of it as though *he* might have forgotten the plan. Did she really think him so daft?

He hoped the shopkeeper believed their story. He did have to admit that Juliana had been quite convincing, especially when it had actually looked like tears were welling in her eyes as she described her fear of being abducted and assaulted. Although that performance might have actually come from the truth of the ordeal she'd been through with Neal Cameron.

Rory snorted as he thought of what she'd done next. She'd turned sorrowful eyes at him, clutched his arm, and gushed about what a hero he had been to fight the highwaymen and get her away from them. She'd explained it so vividly that he'd almost believed they *had* been accosted by cutthroats.

Even worse, something primal had stirred, making him want to protect the lass. He shook his head as he approached the stables. The blasted woman was already driving him barmy.

He repeated the story they'd invented to the stable master, who didn't seem overly interested in what had befallen them. The man was much more interested in selling Rory a horse.

There was a time-honored tradition to horse wrangling—offering old or sway-backed mounts at high prices then negotiating down to more acceptable horses and prices. Obviously, the stable master had not had the opportunity to do so in quite a while, because he dragged out the process—or perhaps he was just bored and wanted company. Either way, Rory spent a good part of an hour purchasing a suitable mare at a fair price.

At least that meant Juliana had time to try on a dress or two. He'd left her with enough money to purchase whatever else she might need. Leading the horse back to the merchant's shop, he looped the reins next to Baron's and went inside.

Juliana was nowhere to be seen, although there were several wrapped purchases on the counter. He closed his eyes briefly, hoping she was in the back room trying on clothes, but he had a sinking feeling she was not. But when he inquired of the shopkeeper if she'd left, the man's words chilled him to the bone.

"Aye, she left a good quarter hour ago," he said, "with a dragoon."

# Chapter Six

When Juliana saw the dragoon outside the shopkeeper's window, a rather wild idea came to her. It might be a bit risky, but there was no guarantee that Neal Cameron would head straight to the Grant holdings. Wouldn't it be better to completely waylay him? Or, at least, cause him the inconvenience of being held and questioned, thereby giving herself and Rory some real time to get away? Rory would not approve since it was *her* idea, but he wasn't here. Besides, she'd probably be back before he returned.

Leaving her purchases on the counter, she hurried outside. "May I have a word with you, sir?"

The dragoon stopped, looking surprised. "You are English?"

"Yes. I am the sister of the Countess of Woodhaven, who was given the title to Strae Castle by King George himself." She waited for those words to sink in. "Is there someplace nearby where we could sit? I have some important information that you should know about."

"Of course. There is an inn just a block over that has a

public room." He looked around. "Are you in some kind of trouble?"

"Of a sort. I would prefer to tell you the whole story at the inn."

"This way, then," he said.

"You have so many medals on your uniform," she remarked once they were seated. "Are you the person in charge of the garrison here?" Juliana gave the dragoon her best imitation of Lorelei's flirtatious smile, although it felt completely strange.

The young man puffed up a bit, but shook his head. "No, my lady. I am just a lieutenant." He doffed his tricorne. "Lieutenant Townsend, at your service."

"How kind of you. I am ever so grateful." Juliana considered batting her eyelashes, but that was going too far. Besides, she had no experience in acting coquettish, so it would probably look as though she had something stuck in her eye. "Well, I will get right to it. My...betrothed and I were returning to Castle Grant from a celebration my sister gave at Strae Castle, and we were assaulted by highwaymen. I wanted to let the soldiers know."

He drew his brows together. "Where was this?"

"I am not familiar with the territory, but not far from here. We were able to get away, but I am afraid they might still be in pursuit."

"Can you give me a description? How many were there? What did they look like?"

She had no idea how many men Neal would bring. There had been six with him when he abducted her. But if she said six, the lieutenant might wonder how Rory had managed to fight them all off. "I am not really sure. A small number, I think. It all happened so fast, and it was dark. They seized the carriage—thankfully, my betrothed's horse broke loose—and we were able to get away."

"Why do you think they are still in pursuit? Highwaymen are known to accost and grab what they can and then run. If they confiscated the carriage, they would probably consider that enough booty."

"Well..." Juliana lowered her lashes as she'd seen Lorelei do and felt like an idiot. She hated simpering—and appearing helpless—but if she were going to convince the soldier that Neal was a danger and needed to be stopped, then circumstances warranted it. She glanced back up. "I do not want to sound immodest, but the leader seemed to be quite taken with me."

The lieutenant smiled. "Understandable, my lady."

Juliana blinked. Was he flirting? Men never flirted with her. Truthfully, she wouldn't believe flowery flippery anyway. She managed what she hoped was a demure smile. "He made some comment that since I was on Cameron land, he could claim me."

His eyebrow rose. "Did you get a name?"

She knew she was treading on boggy ground here and would have to be careful. She had no idea what kind of alliance the English dragoons had with the Camerons. The English were here to keep law and order, but it would behoove them not to make enemies of the surrounding clan. If she gave Neal's name, he'd be certain to be stopped. There was also the real probability that this soldier would recognize him as the laird's son, in which case he might not want to make an issue of it.

"No. But my...betrothed did say if it were Camerons who assaulted us, Clan Grant would not be happy to hear it." She widened her eyes like she'd seen Lorelei do. "Could that lead to clan war, Lieutenant?"

His mouth tightened. "The king would not be happy if it did."

"Then I pray that will not happen. Perhaps you could

be the one to prevent it. You might alert your captain that if a group of men ride into Fort William and start asking questions about us, they are going to start trouble with Clan Grant and they need to go home." She smiled at him again. "I am sure your captain would appreciate knowing."

He colored slightly, then nodded. "I will let him know at once."

"Thank you." Juliana rose, causing him to rise, too. "Since the news is somewhat urgent, there is no need to walk me back to the shop. My…betrothed will be waiting for me."

He bowed slightly. "I am off to talk to the captain, then."

As they parted ways, Juliana smiled to herself. That had been easier than she'd expected. And she had probably just alleviated a confrontation with the Camerons. Rory couldn't deny that.

. . .

"Which way did they go?" Rory asked the merchant and then ran out the door when the man pointed. Juliana wasn't *going* to drive him barmy, she already had.

He skittered to a stop halfway down the street, realizing he had no idea where the dragoon may have taken her. The garrison was not far away, but with twenty-foot stone walls, the only way in would be through the gate. An *armed* gate. The news of the MacGregors having been un-proscribed just this month might not have traveled this far. Even if it had, there were soldiers bloodthirsty enough to claim they hadn't heard. Besides which, Fort William was situated in the heart of Cameron country. Some of the soldiers who'd been here long enough might well favor the clan. Did he dare risk approaching as a Grant?

There was no sight of any Camerons, and he doubted they had already arrived, although he didn't think they were far behind. If he were caught—or worse, if Juliana was caught—inside the garrison when Neal got here, they were doomed.

Rory looked around. There were no dragoons around, nor did he see Juliana. How had the dragoon found her, anyhow? The ones they'd seen on the ridge were on patrol. Since there was nothing overtly suspicious about two people on horseback riding toward the town, they wouldn't have been inclined to follow immediately. Besides, they would not have had time to reach the fort before he and Juliana had.

Why would a dragoon have gone into a general merchandise store while on duty? Even if he did, why would he question Juliana? Their alibi should have been convincing enough, at least initially. Why would he have taken her away?

*Damnation. Where is she?*

He took a deep breath and started walking toward the garrison. What other choice did he have?

"Rory!"

He stopped and turned around to see a woman walking quickly toward him from a side street. For a moment, he didn't recognize her. She'd changed into one of the gowns she'd bought and managed to put her hair up under a lady's hat.

He sprinted across the street, grabbed her arm, then bent to pull her over his shoulder. Getting a firm grip on her thighs, he straightened and began to run.

Juliana pounded his back. "Put me down!" She tried to kick his groin, but he shifted his hands to her ankles, at the same time lifting her farther over his shoulder, and tried to ignore how close her intimate parts were to his face.

"Have you gone mad?" She pounded some more. "Put. Me. Down."

"Nae." He continued to run toward their horses. "I doona ken how ye escaped the dragoon, but we have to get away." He was a little short of breath by the time he finished the sentence, but they'd reached the horses, and he bent again to set Juliana on her feet.

When he stood, she was staring at him, for once not saying a word. Her bodice was askew, the laces loosened, revealing a bit of breast above the neckline. Her new hat dangled from a ribbon, and her hair had come undone. She looked thoroughly disheveled and he expected a reprimand, but none came. Instead she shook her head.

"You are completely daft."

"We doona have time to argue. Let me help ye mount."

"I left my packages on the counter."

"We have nae time for them. We must ride before ye get caught again."

"No one is chasing me."

"'Tis nae the point…" He stopped. "What do ye mean?"

"No. One. Is. Chasing. Me." She attempted to tidy her hair, then sighed. "At least I bought a comb."

"Forget the comb. What do ye mean, no one is chasing ye? The shopkeeper said ye left with a dragoon."

"Well, yes, but I sought him out."

*"Ye did what?"*

Juliana frowned. "He was passing by and I thought—"

"Ye obviously dinna think at all!" He cursed in Gaelic. "We have been trying to avoid the dragoons, lass, nae strike up a conversation."

"Well, it seemed to me this was an opportunity to reinforce our alibi." She plopped her hat on her head and retied the ribbon, albeit crookedly. "I thought it best if we got our version of what happened to the dragoons first."

He groaned. "What did ye say?"

"Simply that we were returning from a celebration at Strae Castle—"

"Ye told him we were returning from Strae Castle?" He somehow resisted the urge to throttle her. "Ye might just as well have declared us MacGregors."

She glared at him. "I made sure he knew that I was the sister of the Countess of Woodhaven and that—"

*"Ye identified yourself?"*

"Will you stop interrupting me? It is quite rude." She gave a sniff as she pushed a strand of hair back. "I told him we were betrothed and on our way to Castle Grant, so you need not worry about disclosing your identity."

"*Humph.*" The urge to give her a good shake was still there, but he'd never used violence on a woman. Not even one who drove him completely barmy. "Did he believe the alibi?"

"Well, I did change it a little."

Rory rubbed his temples, a headache beginning again. "Lass. If ye are going to lie, ye need to stick to the truth of the lie."

"The *truth* of the lie?" She gave him a look that said *he* was more than a little addled.

"Aye. If ye keep changing it, ye are bound to get caught in a spider's web."

"A spider's web..." She shook her head. "I told the dragoon we thought the ruffians might still be pursuing us since their leader seemed quite...er...taken with me." She looked defensive now. "Which is close to the truth."

"I'll nae argue the point."

"I did not mean to brag, of course." She looked a little unsettled. "I just wanted to establish that, if the Camerons do come here, it would be quite clear that I was not agreeable to whatever Neal might claim. I thought...that might keep the dragoons from believing him."

He raised his brows and waited for her to go on.

"And I also said, if it came to light that the Camerons were involved, Clan Grant would not be happy."

Rory groaned again. The lass was going to ignite a clan war without any help from anyone. He was almost afraid to ask, but he had to know. "What did the man say to that?"

"He agreed, of course. I suggested he alert his commander so the Camerons could be stopped here at Fort William and Clan Grant would not be involved." She lifted her chin, her voice stronger. "I think it was a rather brilliant idea."

He closed his eyes briefly, an absurd image of the Celtic warrior queen Boudicca leading her tribe against the Romans flitting through his mind. Hopefully, a red-haired Sassenach was not about to set the Highlands ablaze.

...

Men truly were exasperating creatures. Juliana glanced at Rory as they rode out of Fort William. He simply would not admit that her idea had been good. Not only had she set up a counterargument for whatever story Neal might tell, but she'd also insinuated that there might be trouble between clans if he continued his pursuit, which the English definitely did not want. *And* she had also given the lieutenant an opportunity to be the hero by alerting his commander. All in all, she was quite pleased with herself.

Obviously, Rory was not. He'd had no comment after her explanation. He'd only muttered something in Gaelic and then stomped into the store to retrieve her packages. When he'd come out, he'd introduced her to Misty, the dappled grey mare he'd purchased, then hoisted her up without so much as a by-your-leave, picked up her reins, and set off at a trot.

"I can take charge of my own horse."

He looked over to her and raised a brow.

"What? I can ride, you know."

His brow went fractionally higher. "How would ye handle the reins when ye are hanging on to the pommel as if your life depended on it?"

"My life depends on staying atop the horse, does it not?

How can I do that with all the jolting if I do not hang on? My teeth are rattling."

His mouth quirked. "Think of the poor horse, then."

"What do you mean?"

"I suspect the mare might appreciate it if ye dinna bounce up and down, jarring her at every step."

Juliana glared at him. "A trot is hard to ride."

"Would ye care to canter then?"

Cantering had a rocking-chair motion, which had been fairly comfortable when she'd ridden pillion with Rory, in no danger of falling off with his arms on either side of her. But she wasn't entirely sure she could hold on by herself at the faster pace. Not that she was going to admit that to Rory. "Can we not just walk?"

He shook his head. "I want to reach Spean before nightfall. Having to ride north first and then circle back is going to take time."

She gave him a suspicious look. "Are you saying that because it was *my* idea to ride in the direction of Grant Castle in case someone saw us and might remember which direction we went?"

"Nae. Actually, 'twas the best idea ye had."

"Thank you." She frowned. "I think."

He didn't answer but reined in both horses a few paces later.

"Why are we stopping?"

"I canna bear seeing ye torture that poor mare any longer."

Her brows drew together again. "I am not trying to torture Misty. She is a very nice horse." For emphasis, she leaned over to pat the sleek neck. "She likes me."

"Ye are lucky she has nae decided to deposit ye alongside the road, given the way ye ride." Rory grinned. "'Tis why I'm holding the reins."

"I cannot help..." She stopped and redirected the topic. "I am sure Misty understands that I am not an experienced rider. She is a girl, after all." When Rory gave her a blank look, she added, "Females are much more forgiving about such matters."

"Forgiving?" His grin widened. "I have nae noticed such a trait in ye. Are ye hiding it?"

She drew her brows down. "Did we stop so you can insult me?"

"Nae." He sobered. "I need to show ye how to ride the trot so your understanding horse will nae have a sore back by the time we reach Spean."

Juliana was about to retort but bit the words back. She truly did not want to injure the animal or make her sore. She'd never been the rider that Emily was, although she'd been all right with a sedate walk through Hyde Park. As much as she didn't want to admit incompetence, it was probably already obvious. And she certainly didn't want to torture poor Misty. "All right then."

Rory smirked a little as though he knew what she was thinking, but to his credit he made no comment.

"First, be sure your feet are firmly placed in the stirrups. Then, as the mare steps out, raise yourself in the saddle, hold the position while her second and third hoof come down, then lower yourself on the fourth hoof. Rise again on the first..." He leaned over and wrapped Misty's reins around the hook on the pommel. "Doona touch those," he warned. "Just watch me."

She was about to tell him what she thought of his orders, but Misty was standing perfectly still, so maybe she shouldn't spoil a good thing. "Go ahead."

He tapped his heels on his gelding's flank and demonstrated, then circled around. "Once ye get the feel of the rhythm, ye willna have to actually raise and lower. Ye will become one with the movement." He pointed to her reins. "Now unwrap those and try."

Juliana did so rather gingerly, realizing now, that after her brave talk, she'd really not had any control over this mare. Would the horse try to unseat her? Rory was watching, though, and she was not about to admit any fear in front of him. Cautiously, she nudged Misty forward as she'd seen Rory do. To her surprise, after a few wobbling attempts at standing and sitting, she was actually able to anticipate the mare's gait. And also to her surprise, Rory let her keep her reins as they rode on.

But she was sore when they finally arrived at the coaching inn at Spean and he helped her dismount. For a moment, she leaned against the horse while he steadied her. She managed to straighten.

"I am fine."

He nodded. "Why do ye nae go inside and wait while I see to the horses? Tell the innkeeper I will be along in a few minutes."

"I will." The idea of finally sitting in a chair that didn't move was really appealing. So was the thought of a good meal, a hot bath, and a soft bed.

A mail coach pulled up as Rory walked away with the horses. Several people got out, probably to stretch their legs and use the necessary. The man sitting on the bench hopped down and went inside the inn, while the driver started unhitching the horses to replace them. Juliana gave the first man a thoughtful look, then followed and watched as he picked up a leather satchel full of mail.

"Where are you headed, sir?"

The man looked her over. "Fort William, lady."

"If I give you a letter, can you make sure it gets to Strae Castle near Dalmally?"

"Aye." He looked offended. "'Tis me job."

"Thank you. I will just be a minute." She turned to the clerk behind the counter. "May I borrow some paper?" Then she added, "Can you tell me how far it is to Invergarry Castle?"

"About fifteen miles."

"Thank you." Hastily, she scribbled a note to her sisters telling them Rory had rescued her and they were headed to Invergarry to take a circuitous route home and not to worry. She folded the paper, put it in an envelope the clerk provided, and wrote the address on it. Then she handed it to the man along with an extra shilling—luckily she had change left over from her purchases—for his troubles.

"Thank you," she said as the man nodded, put the letter in the sack, and walked out. She breathed a sigh of relief.

Rory might not agree, but she knew her sisters were worried. Now they would know that she was safe.

# Chapter Seven

The warm scents of hay, horses, and leather enveloped Rory as he led the tired animals into the stable behind the inn.

"I need a stall for each and a portion of oats along with hay," he told the stable master.

The man shook his head. "I can do the food, but there's nae a stall available. Your nags will have to stay in the paddock."

He resisted an urge to inform the man his mounts were not nags, but coaching inns tended to treat horses as commodities because they leased and traded them on a regular basis. Nor was he about to leave them outside. The weather had already grown considerably colder while they'd ridden this afternoon, and he wasn't about to subject the animals to sleet or snow if he could help it.

He looked around, then pointed to an area filled with old harnesses and other discarded tack. "What about that corner over there? Can it be cleaned out?"

The man looked at him as though he'd requested tea service on china. "My two lads have all they can do to see to the four coaching horses that just came in."

Stifling a comment that the stable master himself appeared to have two usable hands, Rory produced a guinea and saw the man's eyes light. "Would this pay for the effort?"

The stable master grabbed the coin and pocketed it. "I can have it cleaned in a thrice."

Rory nodded and dropped the reins to both horses. He knew Baron would not move and he doubted the mare would, either, since she seemed to be comfortable following the gelding's lead. His mouth quirked as he went to examine the freshness of the hay. Too bad a certain other female was not inclined to follow a man's lead.

It probably was just as well to spend a bit of time in the stables, getting the horses settled. It would give him time to sort out the day or, more importantly, the company he had kept.

Riding pillion this morning to Fort William had been pure torture with Juliana bouncing her arse up and down against his groin. That arse had become more delectable and desirable as his cock had hardened. He wondered how she had not noticed. Surely even a virgin would recognize something that thick and hard... He shook his head. As poor a rider as she was, it was possible she had not. She hadn't mentioned it, and if there was one thing he could depend on her for, it was voicing her opinion.

The afternoon ride hadn't gone much better, he thought as he checked the quality of the oats in the bin. Once he'd relinquished her reins, she'd ridden alongside him instead of trailing behind, giving him a very nice view of her partially exposed leg since she'd hiked up her dress to ride astride. It was a nicely curved calf, not thin or chunky, and he'd had a sudden desire to know if her thigh was equally well portioned.

To make matters worse, she didn't even seem to be aware of the allure or its effect on him. Any other woman he knew would be issuing him an invitation by showing so much flesh or trying to entice him into a compromising situation that could have dire repercussions.

But Juliana had been oblivious and, obstinately, he had become more intrigued.

He grimaced as he led the horses to the now cleaned-out corner. He should have told her to buy some breeches for riding. His sister and even Emily wore them when they rode. The cloak Juliana had would have covered the feminine curves outlined by those breeches. They would purchase a pair in the morning, he decided. She would probably balk at the suggestion—since he was the one making it—but he'd simply say they were more practical and warmer heading north. Even someone as cantankerous as she was would see the logic in that.

He unsaddled the horses, slipped off their bridles, and loosely tethered them to hooks in the wall originally used for harnesses, making sure they could reach down for the hay. Then he borrowed a brush from the stable master and set to grooming them. He suspected he was procrastinating about returning to the inn—and Juliana would probably be in a fine temper for having to wait so long—but he needed to come to grips with his increasingly lustful thoughts.

Rory reminded himself—as he had done many times that day—that he had been sent to rescue Juliana from the Camerons. He was responsible for bringing her safely back to Strae Castle, and that meant he also needed to safeguard her virtue. Claiming to be handfasted was simply that. A claim. Not something that was actually going to be put in place. He had a duty to his brothers to bring pride and honor back to the MacGregors. That would require his full attention. His increasing thoughts of her lying lush and naked beneath him were not part of that plan. And he was sure lust was not what Juliana was thinking about, either.

But as full as the stable was, the inn was probably equally crowded. And if they had to share a room…

Well. He hoped the water in the horse trough was cold enough to douse the heat he felt rising.

• • •

"There is only one bed." Juliana frowned as Rory gave her an amused look, which she did not appreciate. He had just closed the door to the room the wife of the innkeeper had shown them to after they had eaten. "This will not do."

"'Tis generally only one bed to a room at an inn."

"I know that." Was he deliberately being obtuse? "Why did you not ask for *two* rooms?"

"If ye remember, we are supposed to be traveling as a handfasted couple," Rory replied. "Just in case Cameron makes his way to Spean."

"But that is just for outward appearances. Not"—she motioned vaguely in the direction of the bed—"this. Besides, did you not say handfasted meant betrothed? A betrothal does not give the man the right to…to…to spend a night *alone* with his intended."

One brow lifted. "We have already spent a night alone."

"That was different. We were both too tired to do more than drop to the ground and sleep." Strange that she hadn't even considered the possibility that Rory might have…might have… She pushed away the horrible recollection of the rape she'd endured. That man was dead, even if her memories weren't. She gave herself an inward shake. "And last night… we had no choice."

"We doona have a choice tonight, either."

"What do you mean?"

"Have ye nae noticed the inn is full? This is the only room left."

"But…" Juliana eyed the bed. It hardly looked large enough for two people. *Not* that the two of them would be sleeping in it. She couldn't. It did pose a problem, though. The only other furniture in the room was a small table with two straight-backed chairs. The floor would be uncomfortable with only a threadbare rug in front of the small hearth. She could hardly ask Rory to sleep there. The man, irritating as he was, had rescued her, after all. She owed him something for that. Hopefully, when they got to Invergarry, there would be a separate room available. She took a deep breath.

"Fine, then. You can have the bed."

Rory nearly dropped the saddlebag he was holding as he stared at her. "*What?*"

"I said you can have the bed—"

"I heard what ye said."

She knit her brows. "Then why did you ask?"

He shook his head as though to clear it. "Because 'tis the most daft idea ye have had yet."

"I do not have *daft* ideas." Juliana straightened her shoulders. "You admitted my idea to invent the story about the highwaymen accosting us was good."

"I dinna say *good*."

"You did not say it was *not*, either."

He blinked at her. "Sometimes when ye speak, ye doona make sense."

Juliana heaved a sigh. "Never mind. The point is that you agreed to spread the story in Fort William and I happened to come upon a dragoon who will corroborate the incident. And here we are, safe and sound."

A corner of his mouth quirked up as he glanced at the bed. "So ye feel safe and sound with me?"

She felt her face heat. With her fair skin, she was probably the color of a beet. "I…I was referring to escaping from the Camerons."

"Ah." He looked amused again. "And do ye plan on escaping from this room as well?"

Her mouth started to drop open, and she snapped it closed. "No. Since there is no other room available, we will have to share this one. I already said I will sleep on the floor. I trust you will not bother me."

All semblance of humor left him, and his face turned stony. "I have never forced myself on a woman, and I never will. Ye can be sure I willna *bother* ye."

Her eyes widened at his tone. "I did not mean to make you angry. I simply—"

"I am nae angry, but I am a man of my word. I have a responsibility to bring ye back to Strae Castle, and that is what I will do." He threw his saddlebag into a corner as a knock sounded at the door. "That will be for ye."

"For me?"

"Aye. I asked the innkeeper's wife to fetch a bath for ye." He turned toward the door. "Doona wait up for me." He pointed toward the bed. "And I will be the one sleeping on the floor."

He was gone before she could say a word, and she sighed softly. Rory MacGregor had to be the most infuriating man she'd ever met. And yet... He'd ordered a *bath* for her.

· · ·

Rory wanted to slam his fist into something as he made his way down the stairs to the public room of the inn. He'd have welcomed seeing Neal Cameron right then and punching the daylight out of him, but the room contained only weary travelers.

He signaled for a pint and took a table in a darkened corner where he could observe and not draw attention to himself. He didn't think they'd been followed. He hadn't seen any sign of Camerons when they'd left Fort William, so it was probably safe to assume they hadn't yet arrived by the time he and Juliana had left.

Juliana. The woman had the ability to vex him like no other female. She was as aggravating as she was tantalizing. Contrary and opinionated, unwilling to take his advice and all too ready to follow her own, yet there was something... He couldn't quite come up with the right word. She certainly wasn't fragile, nor was she easily intimidated, but... There was something *vulnerable* about her.

He started to laugh as he imagined what Juliana's reaction would be if he told her he thought she was *vulnerable*. No doubt her hair would blaze—it did seem to brighten when she was angry—and fiery words would spout from her mouth. The image of a flaming-haired Medusa came to mind, and he chortled.

The barmaid who'd just set down his mug gave him a wary look and took a safe step back. She probably thought he was some halfwit, so he managed to straighten his face. For good measure she tugged her bodice up over half-exposed breasts, clearly *not* extending an invitation. He began to grin at that, since it'd never happened to him before, but quickly stopped. He didn't need the barmaid telling the innkeeper they had a lunatic sitting at a table. Much as the floor of the bedchamber would be uncomfortable, he didn't want to be put outdoors. He placed an extra shilling on the table.

"Thank ye for your trouble."

He hardly noticed how quickly she grabbed the coin and disappeared as he returned to his thoughts. Then he quickly sobered as he remembered what Juliana had said.

*I trust you will not bother me.* He frowned. Did she really think he would *bother* her? He remembered that quick, panicked look before he'd kissed her in front of the Camerons and how she'd stiffened when he'd first touched her. He'd thought that was because they generally argued more than they agreed on anything, but she *had* softened and even parted her lips…actions that he was well aware were the first signs of arousal.

Rory took a healthy draft of the ale. The woman was perplexing, and he didn't like being confused, but if anything reconfirmed what he'd been preaching to himself about responsibility and duty, it was her statement. *I trust you will not bother me.* He took another hefty swig, nearly draining the mug.

Even now, as he sat there brooding, she was upstairs soaking in a hot tub. Soaking *naked* in a hot tub. He could picture her with her head tipped back, long hair spilling over the rim of the tub so it didn't get wet, her breasts poking out of the water, wet and glistening with soap suds as she moved the washcloth slowly over herself… His cock grew hard, and he resisted the urge to bolt up the stairs and finish washing her himself.

*I trust you will not bother me.* Damnation. He needed to stop thinking about Juliana. The woman was truly driving him to insanity. He slammed his empty mug down and looked around for the barmaid. When he didn't see her, he cursed again. The wench was probably cowering somewhere to avoid coming to his table. Perhaps he was already mad and she was smart enough to realize it.

Rory sighed and forced his thoughts back to the present situation. Not the one upstairs in the bedchamber, but the one that would get them back to Strae Castle as quickly as possible.

He still didn't like the idea that she'd actually hailed a dragoon and identified herself, even as an Englishwoman, but he really couldn't fault the rest of her plan. If Cameron took the bait and rode straight north to Grant Castle, they'd safely be at Invergarry before Neal realized he'd been sent on a fool's mission. There would be no reason for the man to stop at Invergarry on his return to Fort William since he'd have no cause to suspect they'd gone there, but even if he did, by the day after tomorrow they'd already be on their way to Drumochter Pass and then on to Blair Castle, home of Clan Murray. From there it would be another hard day's ride home. He grimaced. A hard day being close to fifteen hours in the saddle, but he didn't think Juliana would fight him on that since she clearly didn't want to spend any more time with him than she had to.

*I trust you will not bother me.* He clenched his jaw and stood. Whatever he might think or feel, he would make sure he didn't bother her. He was simply here to take her home.

But perhaps a dousing in the cold water of the horse trough would help him remember that.

...

"What do ye mean, they're gone?" Neal stared at Jamie, his second-in-command, and drew the collar of his coat closer to his ears, silently cursing the English for not allowing the tartan to be worn. He and five of his men had been huddled in the increasing cold next to Spean Bridge for nearly an hour. "I would have seen them."

"The clerk said they left before dawn."

"In this weather? It's starting to snow. More than likely a storm is coming."

The other man shrugged. "'Tis probably why they left early."

Neal cursed aloud this time, his temper rising because MacGregor and the wench had given him the slip a second time. That it had almost been the *third* time did nothing to quell his fury.

He and his men had arrived in Fort William late yesterday

afternoon as the gloaming was descending. He'd gone directly to the garrison to request help from the dragoons to return his captured bride-to-be, only to learn that the commander had already received quite a different version from his lieutenant. Devious little bitch to come up with that. He'd enjoy bringing Juliana to heel even more once he caught up to her.

And they'd have gone on a completely useless trip to Grant Castle as well if he and his men hadn't decided to have a hot meal at the coaching inn in Fort William first. It was there that he'd overheard a female from the mail coach that had just arrived talking with a companion about a woman with beautiful red hair at the inn at Spean. That comment had alerted him like a hound scenting a fox. Instead of questioning her—which would have been highly irregular, since he was a stranger—he went off to find the driver instead.

That's when he found out from the mail carrier that the red-haired woman had inquired about the distance to Invergarry and that she'd given him a letter to deliver to Strae Castle. After buying the man several drams of whisky—and bribing him with two silver crowns—he was able to get a look at the letter. She'd written of their plans to go north first and then southeasterly to Blair Castle and take a circuitous route home. He'd given the letter back to the carrier to deliver since he didn't need more MacGregors searching for her.

By that time it had been near midnight, and he and his men decided to get a few hours' sleep, since he knew his prey was only ten miles away. They'd risen early and ridden out shortly after breaking their fast this morning.

He uttered another curse. What kind of woman got up before dawn? Juliana Caldwell seemed to defy him at every turn, and he did not like being bested by anyone. Especially a woman.

"What are we going to do?" his man asked.

Neal looked up at the leaden sky. "We ride for Invergarry."

The man's eyes widened. "In this weather? We're like to have a blizzard."

Neal gave him an annoyed look. He didn't like to be questioned. "'Tis better to catch MacGregor on the open road rather than let him get to the castle."

And if they were lucky, MacGregor's frozen body wouldn't be found for weeks…long after he'd made Juliana Caldwell his woman.

# Chapter Eight

Juliana glanced over at Rory as they rode north in the dim predawn light. As exhausted as she'd been from two eternal days in the saddle and only a few hours' sleep on hard ground, she had not heard him return to the room last night. The hot water of her bath had soothed aching muscles, and she'd nearly fallen asleep in the copper tub. She vaguely remembered pulling the night rail she'd purchased over her head and had no recollection of her head even touching the pillow.

She wasn't even sure if Rory *had* returned to the room. When he'd shaken her awake an hour ago, he'd been fully dressed. Had he spent the night elsewhere? He'd said there were no more rooms to let, but she'd seen the way one of the serving maids in the public room had eyed him while they'd eaten last evening. Juliana frowned. The girl had been a pretty young thing with flaxen hair and a generous bosom that spilled over the neckline of her bodice. Surely he'd noticed. Had she offered to share the comfort of her bed while Juliana had denied him theirs? She grimaced. The bed hadn't been "theirs." She'd offered to sleep on the floor, but he'd refused. If Rory MacGregor wanted to sleep in a warm bed—with someone—that was his business.

"I ken 'tis cold."

"I am fine." He'd obviously mistaken her gloomy countenance for dislike of the weather, which was probably better than him knowing what her real thoughts had been. "Will we ride all the way to Invergarry today?"

"Aye. 'Tis nae villages between here and there."

She didn't have to ask how far it was, because she knew. By her own calculations and given that the terrain was getting rockier, it meant another full day of riding. She groaned silently. Or perhaps not so silently, because Rory gave her a contemplative look.

"Are ye that sore, lass?"

*Yes*, she wanted to scream. Every ache and pain had returned this morning, magnified, it seemed, to punish her for enjoying a soft bed last night. Her thighs were rubbed raw, her back hurt, her shoulder muscles bunched tightly, and even her fingers felt numb from holding on to the saddle while they climbed up and slid down winding trails. But Rory was riding with the relaxed posture of one long accustomed to the saddle. She wasn't about to let him think she was a fragile flower, or worse, a ninnyhammer who expected coddling. She gritted her teeth.

"I am fine." She pulled her cloak closer with her free hand, then grabbed for the saddle again, causing the cloak to flap as Misty stumbled on a rock.

"Ye are cold," Rory said as if he hadn't heard her.

"I…I will be all right…" She hoped her chattering teeth couldn't be heard over the horse's hooves. "…once the sun comes up."

Rory looked up at the still near-dark sky. "I hate to tell ye, but I doona think we'll be seeing the sun today." He raised his head and sniffed the air. "It smells like snow."

She looked at him, wondering if the cold had affected his brain and he didn't know it. "Snow smells?"

"Aye." He nodded as though it were perfectly clear. "'Tis a certain crispness to the air. A bit like the clean smell of earth after a rain, ye ken?" He lifted a shoulder in a half shrug when she stared at him. "The cold feels different, not quite so biting, before the snow falls."

As she was thinking how to respond to that—or perhaps it was best not to, since she had no idea what he meant— the first flakes landed on her cheeks. An odd chill that had nothing to do with cold ran down her spine as she looked up to see more flakes floating down. "How did you…" She let her voice fade away since he was grinning at her.

"I told ye I could smell it, especially since it was so close." He glanced up at the sky and then sobered. "But I fear we may be in for a storm."

She eyed him. "You can smell that, too?"

He shook his head. "'Tis common sense. The clouds are lowering; the air is growing heavier. Ye ken how still it is?"

She hadn't been aware until he mentioned it, but it was strangely quiet, the only sound that of the horses plodding along. No hardy birds flapped their wings in the air; no animals scurried through the bushes, no rustling sounds of the wind through the bare branches of trees. Only silence. "I do, but why?"

"'Tis what the sailing folk call the calm before the storm. On the water, the seas will lie, they may even flatten, the wind drops, the sails flap in the lull. A good captain kens to batten down the hatches then, because the wind is about to shift and come roaring back." He looked around. "The same thing happens on land, although ye canna see it so easily."

Juliana glanced back at the sky. The snow was definitely getting heavier now, the flakes making her cheeks wet.

"Should we turn back and wait for the storm to pass?"

"Normally, I would," Rory answered, "but we doona ken where the Camerons are."

"Will it not take them a day to get to Grant Castle and then another day back?" Juliana asked. "Besides, they will not know where we went."

"We hope they doona, but Cameron is a suspicious one. Depending on how many men he has, he might split his party and send scouts out."

She hadn't thought of that. "Well, if they get caught in the storm, he will not get any news until he gets back to Fort William."

"We canna count on that. Sometimes the storms pass quickly through."

"Then we will keep going?"

"Aye, lass, but nae on land."

She gave him a questioning look. "How are we going to get to Invergarry, then?"

"Loch Lochy goes practically to the gates of Invergarry," he replied. "There is a boat landing where River Spean connects with the loch. We can catch a sailing ship from there."

"Sail? In a storm? Is that not more dangerous than continuing on horseback?"

"Nae. These gales blow in from the west. We will be heading north. The wind will give the ship a good beam reach…" He paused at her obvious confusion and explained. "That means the wind will be coming over the side of the boat and filling the sails. 'Twill be a fast journey."

She must have still looked wary, because he added, "And ye willna have to sit on a horse. Ye'll be warm and dry below deck."

That sounded wonderful. Out of the wind and cold and able to rest sore muscles… She drew a sigh of relief. "Let us do it, then."

He nodded. "We will be at Invergarry in nae time at all."

• • •

As they turned their horses toward the landing, Rory looked up at the sky again. Dawn had definitely broken, but the sky was still almost dark as night. The complete stillness of the wind did not bode well. He and his brothers and sister had grown up sailing on Loch Awe, and anyone who spent time on the water knew the calmer the wind before a storm, the stronger it would be when the gale struck.

He glanced at Juliana, who was still grimacing as she tried to find a comfortable position on Misty. No doubt she'd be glad to be out of the saddle, but he wasn't sure she'd be happy with the boat journey, either. He'd told her it would be fast, but he'd not mentioned that the ship would be sharply heeled over, its rail in the water most likely the entire time.

Sailing up the loch was still the best option, though. Returning to the inn at Spean was too risky. He wasn't at all sure Neal Cameron would accept the story of their heading toward Grant Castle or even if he would talk to the people at Fort William that they'd told the tale to. If he didn't, he was likely to follow the river east toward the Pass of Drumochter, and Spean Bridge was directly on that route. Rory had no idea how many men rode with Neal, but fending off a half dozen or more was something he didn't want to contend with. Especially since they were still near the border of Cameron lands.

Continuing to ride north with the approaching storm was not a wise decision, either. Blizzard conditions could form within minutes, and it would be easy to lose the trail. Nor was Juliana accustomed to traveling in such weather. London might get snow and cold temperatures, but it was nothing to the wind howling at gale force off the Cuillin Sound like a piercing knife of ice to chill a person's bones.

Rory glanced over to Juliana. "We are almost there."

"Are you sure a ship will be available?"

"Aye. Postal packets travel daily up and down the lochs. They doona leave the dock until the crews break their fasts."

"That makes sense, I suppose."

He nodded. "'Tis usually the only meal they can count on, since most vessels sail with a minimal crew and all hands are needed on deck."

A wary expression crossed her face. "With so few men, will it be safe if the storm hits us?"

"They ken what to do."

She still looked unsure, but she pressed her lips together and said nothing. He wasn't sure if she was being prudent—which wasn't exactly her strong suit—or if it was because her teeth chattered when she spoke.

He glanced at her again. Even though she now wore breeches under her skirts, only her cloak was wool and her gloves were thin cotton, appropriate for the dress, but hardly warm in a Highland winter. He didn't need her half-frozen by the time they reached Invergarry, or worse, to come down with a fever that would keep them from continuing on once the storm passed. He wanted this journey over so he could collaborate with his brothers on strategy. Already he'd been thinking of getting back the adjoining lands the Campbells had taken during their proscription. He was wasting valuable time wandering about the Highlands.

Last night had been among the most miserable he could remember. He could tolerate lying on cold, hard ground as he had the first night, but denial of yesterday's anticipation of a warm, soft bed that he'd fantasized about sharing—*eejit* that he was—had nearly done him in.

He'd dipped his head into the horse trough, hoping that

the cold water to his head would send some sense to his *other* head, but to no avail. It only left him with wet hair. The buxom barmaid—not the one who'd scurried away from him earlier—had hurried over to him with a dry towel when he went inside and invited him to her bed. For a moment, he'd considered the offer. It would be a soft, warm bed with a soft, warm woman… Then he'd realized, to his dismay, that his cock didn't even twitch at the thought. And, with growing alarm, he didn't think his lack of reaction had anything to do with cold water.

He'd spent the night sleeping in the stable with his horse. If his brothers ever got wind of it—which they *wouldn't*—he'd never hear the end of it. He gave Juliana a covert glance.

His conscience niggled at him, too. Although Juliana didn't realize it, declaring them to be handfasted was the same as *being* married in the Highlands. And, while they had the option of ending the union at the end of one year, it still *was* a union. All of the responsibilities of marriage came with that, including being faithful, even if he didn't get to share the marriage bed. Not that he was about to explain any of that to Juliana. Her reaction wouldn't be a simple tempest in a teapot. He envisioned a full-force storm.

He just hoped that when he got the vexing woman home, things could return to normal.

· · ·

Rory's version of *no time at all* to reach Invergarry felt like an eternity. Juliana clenched the raised wooden fiddle along the edge of the bunk that kept her from rolling off it as the boat tipped dangerously to one side again. He'd called it "heeling" and said the motion was normal due to the strength of the wind filling the sail, but she didn't really care what it was called. Every time the boat leaned over, panic rose in her stomach.

She just prayed she wouldn't be sick. The cargo hold—where the berth was—wasn't large and also held their horses. The scent rising from their damp coats permeated the close space, along with odors of various other livestock that had been passengers at some time. There was also the stench of tar from the pitch smeared into the hull planking, as well as the smoky smell of oil from the gimbaled lamp providing light belowdecks. The effect, along with the constant heaving motion of the boat, made her stomach roil.

There was an empty brass chamber pot next to the berth, and Juliana wondered if it had been put there for some other use than its original purpose, possibly for passengers who were going to cast up their accounts? She swallowed several times, willing herself not to let nausea take over. Rory already knew she wasn't a competent horsewoman from how stiff and sore she was from riding. She wasn't about to let him know she wasn't given to sailing, either. It was already embarrassing that she'd chosen to come below where it was dry and somewhat warm, while two hale and hearty Scots women were staying on deck, facing the elements.

The hatch above her lifted, and Rory climbed down the ladder. She swallowed quickly and fought the bile that was rising in her throat.

He took the lamp off its swinging hook. "I've come down to check the horses."

She nodded, afraid that if she tried to speak, something other than words would spew forth.

Thankfully, Rory didn't appear to notice. He turned toward the stern of the boat, where four half stalls took up the width. The stalls were narrow, barely allowing enough room for a man to squeeze by a horse to tether it. The wooden panels between were well padded so that when the boat tipped—*heeled*—the animals bumped against something soft, and there was a good foot of straw beneath their hooves for traction. They were probably not minding the ride as much as she was.

"They're doing fine," he confirmed as he came forward and started to hang the lamp back on its gimbaled hook. As he did, the light hit her face, and he paused and peered at her.

"Ye are a bit green-looking, lass."

She swallowed again, not daring to open her mouth. Rory frowned, hung the lamp, and reached down to take her arms and pull her to her feet.

"Ye need to go up on deck and get some fresh air."

There was no point in arguing, not that she had the energy to do so. She turned toward the ladder and put a foot on the lower rung. Unfortunately, the boat lurched sideways at the same time, and she fell back on Rory. Then his strong arms encircled her, holding her steady as he half lifted, half carried her up the ladder. For an instant, her body molded against him, the feeling of his granite chest a source of comfort. And then she had the most unusual clenching in her lower belly as his fingers inadvertently swept across her abdomen as he moved his hands to her sides.

"Grab on to the stanchions—the railings—right beside the hatch and hang on to them."

She suddenly realized she was practically lying prone in his arms. Good heavens! The last thing she wanted... Scrambling to a more dignified position, she saw a railing on either side of the opening. With an effort she righted herself, all too aware that Rory's hands were cradling her bottom as he hoisted her up onto the deck and climbed up after her.

Wind-driven rain, as sharp as sleet, struck her face. She swept the wetness from her cheeks. Strangely enough, in spite of the bitter cold, it was invigorating, and her stomach began to settle. Then the boat heeled again. She lost her balance and began to slide across the slick deck. Arms of steel slipped around her waist, righting her once more.

"I told ye to hold on."

"I did." She trusted herself to speak now that the urge to spill the contents of her stomach had subsided. "You did not say for how long."

He muttered something in Gaelic, and she thought it might be useful to learn a few words, although she suspected what he was saying wouldn't be called respectable vocabulary. "You can let me go now. I am hanging on."

His hands didn't move. "Ye need to let go."

She frowned at him. "You just told me to hold on. Now you tell me to let go. Do you not to know what to do with me?"

One brow rose. "Ye probably doona want to ken that answer."

She lifted her chin. "Are you going to curse at me again?"

He blinked. "Nae. I need ye to release your hands so I can guide ye to the stern where the other women are."

She was about to retort that she could walk the short distance, but the deck rolled under her feet, and she decided that it might be wise to acquiesce, just this once. "Fine."

"Ye need to hold on to me."

When she placed her hand near his elbow, he took it and drew her arm around his waist beneath the coat he wore. She started to pull back and felt the solid muscles of his back. He stayed her hand.

"This is not proper."

His brow rose again. "It is if ye doona want to slide overboard."

Before she could protest, he wrapped his arm around her waist like a steel vise. She looked down at the water, not that far away since the rail of the boat kept disappearing into it, making them stand at an odd angle to stay upright. Perhaps it would be wise to acquiesce on this, too.

Rory kept his free hand on the wood railing attached to the deck house as they made their way aft. Once on the stern, she saw what looked like a big, wooden locker behind the wheel the captain was manning. The lid was propped open, and the two young women she'd seen earlier were bundled inside. They looked at each other when they saw her and smiled.

"We were wondering how long it would take the Sassenach to figure it out," one of them said to Rory.

"She did last longer than most," the second one added.

"What are they talking about?" Juliana asked.

"Och," the first one said before he had time to answer. "Everyone kens 'tis hell to stay below when the boat is bucking like a horse new to saddle."

"'Tis much better to be on the open deck where ye can see land." The second one squinted at her. "Did ye get sick down there?"

"Nae, she didna," Rory answered as he led her toward the women. "And I'll thank ye to stop talking about it." When neither of them looked abashed, he shook his head and turned to Juliana. "Ye'll have time to make their acquaintance while ye huddle together for warmth, but these are MacDonnells."

"Aye." The first one looked a bit mischievous. "And we hear ye are to be our guest for a bit."

"Well, ye had best climb in then." The second one moved over to make room in the locker. "And we'll have a bit of gossip as we go."

Juliana somehow managed to smile as Rory helped her into what looked more like a coffin, and she wondered if she'd just traded one hell for another.

# Chapter Nine

"I am Aileen," the first one said as she made space in the sail locker.

"And I am her sister Greer." The other one lifted a plaid blanket. "Get in."

"Juliana." She wiggled into the cramped area, trying not to take up too much room. The warmth was immediate, the wool tartan incredibly warm. She knit her brows as she fingered the material. "I thought these were outlawed."

Aileen grinned. "Only by the English."

"Aye," Greer said with a smirk. "They may have forbidden *wearing* the plaid, but 'tis a blanket we're using."

She glanced from one to the other. They looked to be about her age, perhaps a bit older. Both of them had light reddish-blond hair, but Aileen's eyes were brown and Greer's were green.

"I should thank you for taking us in as guests at your castle."

"Well, 'tis our uncle's keep, but our father and mother and brothers live there, too," Aileen replied.

"And other kin," Greer added. "I suspect it will be a surprise to all of them when we bring a Sassenach home."

"Well, Cousin Morag will nae like it for sure."

Juliana frowned. "Your cousin hates the English that much?"

Aileen shrugged. "'Tis more that she likes Rory."

Juliana managed not to groan. She hadn't considered that. Of course, Rory would have socialized with the MacDonnells and one of the females felt an attachment to him. She should have known. The MacGregor men were all a good-looking lot, she had to admit, and they seemed to attract women with little effort. Ian's ward, Glenda, had fancied herself in love with him and had resented Emily. Neal's sister Margaret had a lusty interest in Devon. And even Lorelei enjoyed flirting with Alasdair, although in her sister's case, it was as much practicing for London's Season as it was for real interest. At least, that's what Juliana thought. No matter. She definitely did not need a MacDonnell woman jealous of her.

She also remembered too well the not overly warm welcome her sisters and she had received when they'd arrived at Strae Castle. She wouldn't have her sisters for reinforcement if the reception here was the same. She'd be entirely dependent on Rory. A thought that did not sit well under any circumstances, but most especially when she would be the only English person for who knew how many miles around. *Especially* if Cousin Morag had set her sights on him.

He had not said much when he'd woken her this morning. She hadn't asked if he'd had a comfortable night—she couldn't even think how to word that question without it sounding like prying—and he hadn't offered the information. Other than making the decision to take the postal packet, he hadn't been inclined to conversation on the way to the landing, either. And their latest exchange had nearly turned into an argument.

Aileen's sister gave her a curious look. "Why is Rory

bringing ye north?"

"Greer," her sister warned. "Maither says we shouldna ask such questions."

"Well, he wouldna tell us anything."

"Mayhap he is wanting to speak to our uncle first."

"About what? She is nae Rory's hostage, 'ere she'd still be below." She turned to Juliana. "He dinna steal ye, did he?"

It seemed as though Aileen were going to reprimand her sister again, but then her expression changed, and she gave Juliana an expectant look.

So he hadn't told them, at least not about the handfasting. Which was probably a good thing. Or had he remained silent because of Cousin Morag? Juliana gave herself an inward shake. She was creating problems that didn't need to exist. Rory had probably not explained the situation because of the crew being able to hear everything. But how much should she say? The captain appeared to be concentrating on steering the vessel, but he wasn't that far away. And Rory had gone forward to help the men on the bow.

Perhaps it was best to stick with the highwaymen story, at least for now.

"So Rory thought it best if we went north and took a circuitous route home to avoid running into them again," she finished.

Apparently convincing Scottish women of such a tale was harder than appealing to an English lieutenant and a couple of merchants. Both Greer and Aileen looked skeptical. She'd left out the part of whom they "suspected" the highwaymen were for now.

"I doona ken how Cousin Morag will take this," Greer said.

Aileen gave her a stern look. "It doesna sound like Rory had a choice now, does it?"

"Aye, but—" Greer clamped her mouth shut as Rory

came into view.

Juliana didn't think she'd ever been so glad to see him. *Not* that she'd admit such.

He probably saw her as a burden he was saddled with, even though she had to admit he'd felt wonderfully solid and strong when he'd insisted she hang on to him while he held her firmly against him. She chided herself for those thoughts. Rory certainly hadn't been flirtatious in the least, only civil. And, she reminded herself, there was Cousin Morag, whom he'd evidently paid some attention to.

Rory was simply making sure he got his burden home safely, that was all. Juliana grimaced. He'd have too much explaining to do if she washed overboard.

...

She'd nearly gone overboard. Juliana's stumble on the slippery deck had unnerved him more than he'd cared to admit, and he went forward to help haul in the jib to work off the shakiness that he felt. With the churning water in the loch making the boat pitch and roll, along with near blizzard conditions, she'd have been lost if he hadn't grabbed her.

He'd *told* the daft woman to hang on. *Then*, when he told her to let go so he could lead her to safety, she'd started to argue with him. Again. Why did this particular female have to contradict every single thing he said? Even his sister, Fiona, who didn't take kindly to anyone telling her what to do, had common sense. Had Juliana not realized how perilously close to death she'd been?

Rory sighed. He was going to have grey hair by the time they returned home.

And then there was the *other* problem that continued to niggle at him. In spite of repeatedly telling himself that Miss Juliana Caldwell was nothing but trouble—he was seriously beginning to believe that he'd done something to anger the fae and dealing with her was the faeries' retribution—he still couldn't seem to keep lustful thoughts of her out of his head. She was both opinionated and quarrelsome and they rarely agreed on *anything*, as had just been proven a few minutes ago, but somehow that cantankerousness aroused him. He enjoyed matching wits with her. Not that he would admit such.

There was also the small fact that he knew he was lawfully handfasted to her, even if Juliana didn't. That gave him the right to take her to his bed, according to Scottish tradition. He'd never forced a woman, and he never would. Still, knowing he was entitled to claim her only gave way to more lustful fantasies, damn it.

Rory slowed his pace as he approached the deck locker where all three women sat huddled inside, looking at him. The hair rose at his nape, an indication that danger was imminent. He glanced up at the rigging to make sure he wasn't in harm's way, but all appeared to be secure. Sheets were wrapped around cleats; none were loose or flailing in the air. The reefed mainsail was well off to starboard, its boom not a problem. No lines lay strewn about the deck, and sailors were attending their posts. Nothing posed a danger from the ship. That left only the women.

He turned his gaze back to them. Deer-like brown eyes blinked back at him and green eyes twinkled in amusement, but it was Juliana's eyes, flashing like fire, that made him uneasy. What in the name of creation could he have done *now* to make her angry? He'd been helping the men up on the bow, for God's sake, and hadn't taken part in whatever conversation the women had been having...

He paused. What had they been talking about? He'd left Juliana with Greer and Aileen because he had no other choice. She'd been green as a summer vegetable garden when he'd gone below and probably only moments away from retching. Once that process started, the victim was in for sheer misery until back on solid land. With their reduced sail due to the wind, mixed snow, and sleet, it was going to take twice as long to reach the dock at Invergarry. He'd had to bring her up on deck. Once topside, conditions certainly didn't allow for her to wander about. She was obviously no more used to a ship's movement than a horse's, so he'd led her to the one safe and warm place. And occupied by the two MacDonnell women, who had a penchant for mischief.

Rory proceeded forward—actually, *aft*, since he was moving toward the stern, which just indicated what a tangled mess his mind was in—and decided a casual question might be in order to establish Juliana's mood.

"Do ye need another tartan for warmth?"

"We're warm enough," Greer said.

"Toasty as oatcakes," Aileen added.

He looked at Juliana, who hadn't spoken. "What about ye? I ken the weather—"

"I am fine."

Her tone was chillier than the air. He glanced uneasily at Greer and Aileen, who were now looking innocent as bairns. Juliana didn't seem to be angry with them. Instead, she was staring at him, sparks flashing from her eyes. As if he had committed some grievous crime. What had they said to her? Their clans were allies, coming together at gatherings several times a year...

And then he knew. The MacDonnell women must have mentioned their cousin Morag.

The bane of his existence. Or, at least, she had been at the last gathering, more than a year ago. She was the laird's only child and he doted on her, especially since her mother had died of fever. Rory had made a point of being kind to the lass. Morag had just turned six and ten and, unfortunately, had fixated on him, much to his brothers' delight—making him the butt of their jokes for months. He'd danced with her several times that first night, listening to her prattle with only half an ear, and had thought nothing of her seating herself beside him the next morning when they broke their fast. He hadn't really taken notice, either, when she'd brought her horse alongside his when they'd hunted boar, intent as he'd been on finding one. It hadn't been until that night, at the feast, when she'd sat close enough to rub thighs, that he'd gotten an inkling as to where her thoughts were turning.

He'd avoided dancing that night, claiming a sprained foot, and the MacGregors had headed home to Strae Castle the following morning. He'd given no more thought to the situation, thinking it was mostly a young girl's attempts at flirtation. He certainly didn't think she still cared.

And maybe she didn't. Maybe he was conjecturing nonsense. After all, more than a year had passed, and there had been no contact. She was a winsome lass, a bit too determined to be deemed biddable, but with her father being laird, she had no shortage of suitors.

Rory gave Juliana an overt glance. Was she worried that Morag would not take kindly to her presence? He didn't know what—if anything—the MacDonnells had said regarding the whole thing. He certainly didn't want to launch into an explanation if the subject hadn't even come up. Juliana would probably accuse him of being arrogant and that would launch another argument.

Better to remain quiet, watch, and wait.

...

Juliana had grown quite warm under the tartan, and she didn't think it was because of the wool or the bodies crammed into the locker. The heat was radiating from within, no doubt because her temper was past simmering and threatening to boil over. For the sake of not wanting to create a horribly bad impression on Greer and Aileen, she held her peace, which only made her temperature rise higher.

How dare Rory not have told her that he had a…a paramour, or whatever they called such in Scotland, waiting at Invergarry. Was that why he had been so agreeable to her plan to head north? She narrowed her eyes. Come to think on it, *he* had been the one to suggest they not go to Grant Castle but, instead, to Invergarry.

He probably wanted to see *Cousin Morag* again.

Not that she was upset about his having a…a paramour. She was not. Definitely *not*. What angered her was that he hadn't told her. He hadn't mentioned *Cousin Morag* once. Not one single time throughout their discussion of the plan, or on the ride to Spean, or even after they'd gotten on this ship. He certainly could have made mention of the fact. He could have said, "By the way, I have a special lady friend at Invergarry…" or something to that effect. She might at least have been warned, maybe even tried to convince him to go to Grant Castle instead. But no. He had not bothered to mention the liaison that awaited him. Not. One. Single. Time.

When was he planning to? Or wasn't he? Had the thought even occurred to him? Had he not considered that *Cousin Morag* might not welcome his bringing another woman to Invergarry?

Not that Juliana was attached to him. She wasn't. He certainly wouldn't announce that business of being handfasted, since *Cousin Morag* awaited him. In any case, that claim was meant only to allow them to escape the Camerons and would serve no purpose now. She and Rory were both free. And he was probably looking forward to sharing a warm bed with *Cousin Morag*. Juliana sniffed and tossed her hair back. Well, that was just fine. It was.

# Chapter Ten

The storm had turned into a full-fledged blizzard by the time the postal packet docked just south of Invergarry Castle. The wind, already gale force, had picked up and now screamed like a banshee. Pellets of sleet mixed with the near-blinding snow, stinging Rory's face as he led the horses down the plank to solid ground. Baron flattened his ears, letting Rory know his disapproval of the weather, while Misty tossed her head and pranced sideways, nearly sliding off the ramp. Luckily, the mare was sure-footed enough to scramble to safety. The gelding seemed to remember his manners when she joined him and gave her an inquisitive nudge with his muzzle, as if checking to make sure she was all right.

There was no such caring gesture from Juliana. She had barely deigned to look at him the last half of the trip and had spoken even less. Now she stood with Greer and Aileen, the three of them wrapped in a tartan that they'd pulled over their heads; the only things visible were their stark faces with wet strings of matted hair clinging to their cheeks.

Rory thought about making a jest of how lovely the day

was to lighten the mood, but quickly reconsidered. While Greer and Aileen might appreciate the attempt and come back with their own retorts, he was pretty sure Juliana would not, judging from the stony expression on her face.

He looked around, not seeing any men or horses waiting for the MacDonnell women. There was a small cottage, hardly more than a shack, that served as a collection site for mail to be taken on. Usually these places had a man available who also served as the mail collector and distributor, but they'd had to tie up to the docks by themselves this afternoon. There was a ramshackle lean-to beside the cottage that could house a horse or two, but it was empty and there wasn't any smoke coming out of the chimney.

He frowned. "Why are there nae men here to meet ye?"

"There seems to be some inclement weather," Juliana said.

Rory almost grinned. Her voice may have been a bit frostier than the weather, but it seemed the lass had a sense of humor lurking beneath her scowl.

"I was nae sure ye noticed," he replied. One of her eyebrows rose, and he decided not to push his luck. "This landing is less than a mile from the castle gate, and the men would ken the trail well, even with the snow blowing. They would nae have left these lasses to fend for themselves." He turned back to them. "Do ye ken any reason why they are nae here?"

Aileen exchanged a look with Greer. "Mayhap they dinna ken we were coming today."

*"What?"*

Greer shrugged. "We cut short our visit to kinfolk in Fort William and decided to come home. We figured we could walk the distance with nae trouble."

"The weather hadna turned when we boarded," Aileen added.

"Well, it certainly has now." Rory dropped the horses' reins and walked to the door of the cottage to find it locked. For a moment he contemplated breaking down the door and lighting a fire to keep them warm until the storm blew over, but he quickly abandoned the idea after he looked in the window. The place had one room and housed a table and a single chair. There was no bed, nor could he see any cabinets that might hold cooking utensils or food. It appeared that it was used strictly as a drop-off point.

He glanced up at the sky. He could barely make out dark-grey, leaden clouds beyond the still-swirling snow. The storm wasn't going to abate anytime soon.

"Can we stay on the boat?" Juliana asked with about as much enthusiasm as one asking if a surgeon was available to remove a tooth.

He shook his head. "The ship's already slapping against the dock with the wave actions. The captain will be untying the lines in a minute or two and anchoring it in the safety of deeper water. The boat will roll and pitch all night, and ye'll be sick for sure." She looked as though she were going to argue, so he added, "Besides, there is nae room for the four of us and the eight crewmen below."

Greer giggled. "I doona think our da will be pleased if we spend the night with sailors."

He wanted to tell her he was pretty sure MacDonnell would not be pleased to find out what his daughters had done in the first place, but this was not the time to bring that up.

"What are we going to do, then?" Juliana asked.

Aileen grinned as if she didn't have a care in the world. "I would suggest we go home."

"An excellent suggestion," Rory replied. "And the sooner we get started, the better."

Juliana drew her brows together. "We only have two horses."

Both MacDonnells blinked at her.

"We can ride one of your horses," Aileen said.

"And ye can ride with Rory," Greer added with a smirk.

Rory held his breath, waiting for the explosion that would no doubt erupt from Juliana. He still wasn't sure what had gotten her temper roiling, but he suspected it had not calmed down. Riding pillion with him was probably the last thing she wanted to do.

And, diabolically, his cock decided it would be very nice indeed.

...

Juliana had always thought hell would be hot. The clergy described it as a continually burning fire pit into which the condemned were thrown to suffer but never die.

Now, Juliana had discovered the truth. Hell was a frozen world with bone-chilling winds and biting pellets of ice lashing at her exposed face.

Or maybe not. Maybe *true* hell was being held firmly against Rory's hard body by arms that felt like steel, while her own insides were turning to mush. He had looped the reins loosely around the pommel since there was no fear that Baron was about to gallop off, given that both horses were hanging their heads to avoid the blowing snow and moving at the pace of three-legged turtles. That left Rory's hands free to grasp her upper arms, which he was now stroking beneath the plaid that he'd wrapped both of them in. That movement was causing a pleasant tingle to spike through her arms to odd parts of her body. If she turned her head to rebuke him, she'd wind up with her mouth inches from his, and he might interpret that as... Well. She certainly didn't intend for him to think she wanted a kiss. She hadn't quite been able to put the first one out of her mind, not that it had meant anything to him. Oddly, it had felt warm and firm, but not harsh like that time... She pushed that thought firmly away. In any case, it probably wasn't wise to try to speak. Inhaling too much of the bitterly cold air could lead to the ague or lung fever.

"Are ye getting warmer?"

She felt his breath against her ear as he asked the question and realized that his chin was tucked on her shoulder. Thank goodness she hadn't turned around or their lips really would have been touching. *Would they be warm?* She chided herself. She didn't need to be thinking about kissing Rory MacGregor. Again. Hadn't she just told herself that she didn't need to be remembering his kiss at the Camerons', either? That had been done out of necessity, even if it had been unexpectedly pleasant. She'd admit that he certainly knew *how* to kiss. He had made her tingle... No. His rubbing her arms was making her tingle. She managed to refrain from giving an unladylike snort. Of course the man knew how to kiss. He'd probably had lots and lots of experience. She needn't even question that premise, since *Cousin Morag* was obviously still pining for him. No doubt she'd be warming his bed this evening.

"I am fine." What else could she say? *The weather is lovely?*

However, Juliana was beginning to feel too warm, in spite of the miserable storm raging around them. The oily wool of the tartan kept the wet cold out and kept the warmth in. She could feel Rory's body heat now, surrounding her like a warm blanket and seeping through to her very bones. Then came the realization that him rubbing her arms was bringing circulation back. She felt herself blush, glad that he couldn't see her face and equally glad she hadn't rebuked him for trying to take advantage of the situation. There was no situation other than they were in the midst of a blizzard and he was more than likely trying to keep her from freezing—literally. Still... She made a soft mewling sound at how good it felt.

Perhaps she had been a bit harsh in her judgment of him. Even if his paramour awaited him at Invergarry, he was still being considerate and making sure that she would arrive without frozen appendages. She was actually beginning to feel comfortable and finally relaxed against him, enveloped in a safe cocoon of warmth and the scent that was uniquely him. She let her breath out slowly. Did she dare trust him? She was confused. She'd never allowed any man to be this close to her, and yet, her mind wasn't shrieking warnings and her body was pressing against his.

Now an entirely different kind of storm began to rage inside her.

• • •

When Rory felt Juliana relax against him, he sighed with relief. The obstinate woman had sat as stiff and upright as a damn English general leading the troops. She'd looked as though she wanted to argue about even getting into the saddle, but since the MacDonnells had swiftly mounted Misty—he wasn't entirely sure of their motives for that, since he'd caught Greer's smirk—it left Juliana with no choice other than walking. Stubborn as she was, he'd wondered if she would choose that option. Not that it would have mattered. He'd simply have picked her up and placed her in the saddle anyway, although likely he would have been in for a tirade. Common sense must have prevailed, though, because she'd finally given a curt nod somewhere in his general direction and allowed herself to be helped into the saddle.

She'd pulled her cloak tight as he swirled the tartan over them in a protective wraparound. Then she'd tried to bat at his arms when he'd encircled her waist and pulled her against him. He'd instinctively done that to trap their body heat, but soon realized it was a grave tactical error, at least on his part.

No sooner had he settled her rounded arse firmly in front of him than his wayward cock decided it should react. He'd subtly adjusted his own position so she wouldn't notice, but it had been a rather painful ride since.

Nor was riding with his arms wrapped around her waist particularly helpful to his rapidly increasing libido. The placement offered a delightful opportunity to extend his hands and let his thumbs graze the underside of her breasts while his fingers fondled their soft roundness. To keep himself from receiving a well-deserved slap, he'd taken to rubbing her arms instead. At least there was a purpose for that, should she complain.

But, rather surprisingly, she hadn't. Instead, she'd made a sound rather like the purr of a contented kitten. Gradually, she made that sound again as she capitulated and lost her rigid posture to *finally* let herself slump against him.

Rory bit back a grin. Perhaps she wasn't so immune to him.

...

Neal cursed and pulled his plaid farther over his head. The sleet pellets were sharp as knives, and the blowing snow made it hard to see more than a few feet ahead.

"Mayhap we should turn back," Jamie said.

It was lucky for his second-in-command that they were all bundled in layers, or else he would have tackled the man and trounced him thoroughly. Since he had no wish to expose flesh to the weather, he merely glowered at him.

"Nae."

"The storm is worsening," another said. "'Tis getting harder to see the road."

"Aye," a third chimed in. "'Twould be easy to lose our way—"

"We keep on going!" Neal bellowed. "MacGregor has my woman!"

That silenced his men, although a moment later he realized it was because they were all looking at him speculatively. None seemed particularly daunted by his outburst, but then, most were used to his temper. Still, he didn't want a rebellion on his hands, since he'd need his men to handle MacGregor when they caught up. All the MacGregors were fighters, but Rory harbored a personal vendetta against him because of the MacFarlane slut.

"They canna be far ahead," he said to pacify them. "When we reach them, ye make quick work of MacGregor and we hie away with my bride. We'll be back at Spean by nightfall. The whisky will be on me." That proclamation drew no response, either, other than silent looks. He reined in. "What? Ye might as well speak up."

"We canna be sure they are ahead," one man said as they all stopped.

"They dinna turn back," Neal retorted. "They'd have met us."

"We ken they had at least an hour head start," another said.

"Which means they canna be far ahead." Neal sighed hard. The fact should be obvious. "The Sassenach is nae a good rider. She will slow them down."

"We have nae seen tracks."

Neal glared at him. "With the wind blowing and the snow swirling, we canna see our own horses' tracks, ye eejit."

"Aye," the first man replied, "which means they could verra well have gone off the road and gotten lost."

"Lost? Are ye forgetting that MacGregor managed to track us all the way to the MacLean? The road follows the loch. He willna be daft enough to leave it."

"The loch…" The man paused.

Neal frowned. "Aye, we've kept it in sight. What of it?"

The man hesitated. "Well, I saw a packet boat pass by earlier. Is it possible MacGregor decided to take passage on it and nae attempt the road at all?"

Neal cursed roundly in Gaelic and then again in English. It certainly made sense, since they had not caught up with the pair and by now, they should have. He'd been a fool not to think of that, although by the time they'd have gotten to the landing, the ship would already have sailed.

He clenched his jaw and contemplated. Under good conditions, the packet would already have arrived at the Invergarry, but given the strong winds and choppy sea, they'd have had to take down sail, which meant they would still be on the water.

"We need to catch them when they land and before they get to the castle." He lifted the reins and nudged his horse forward. In a moment, his men fell in behind. "Drowning MacGregor is as easy as any way to kill him. Then we take the wench, board the packet, and sail back without the MacDonnells ever being the wiser that they were to have guests." He looked at his men. "A fine plan, eh? And a dry ride home."

A few chuckles ensued as they moved on, but Neal's good humor faded when they got to the landing. Sailors were dropping anchor in the loch, well away from the dock, and no one else was to be seen.

"They must have just come in. We may still overtake them on the way to the castle."

"Aye." Neal spurred his horse to a canter, not caring how rutted the trail might be. This was their last chance to make quick work of the situation. But it was too late.

He drew his lathered mount to a stop behind a copse of trees as two horses with four riders went over the drawbridge, and then he watched as the gate closed behind them.

# Chapter Eleven

Juliana's first impression of Invergarry Castle was that it rose like a ghostly specter out of the swirling snow. Situated on a rise above a loch, it loomed five stories with a tower that disappeared and reappeared in the low-hanging clouds.

The wind, as if furious that it had no frothing sea to stir up, howled like a pack of wolves giving chase and turned the heavy mist into tiny needles stinging her face.

As the horses clattered across the cobblestones of the bailey, she wasn't sure she wanted to leave the warm nest that the thick wool tartan and Rory's body heat had created. Not that it was something she cared to admit, even to herself. It was of no benefit to give in to such thoughts. *He* was probably thinking of the Scottish girl who awaited him.

"We were nae expectin' ye!" A middle-aged woman with a trace of grey in her reddish-blond hair burst out the door to the keep and hurtled down the steps with no shawl, in spite of the cold. The resemblance to Greer and Aileen was strong, so this was probably their mother, although Juliana wasn't sure if the woman was addressing her daughters or Rory and herself. "We'd have sent the carriage."

She wondered how a carriage could have maneuvered on the road, if it could be called that. It seemed little more than a rutted trail, but perhaps the snowdrifts had concealed part of it.

"We decided to come home early," Aileen said nonchalantly as she dismounted and handed the reins to a stable boy who'd come running.

"And we found Rory MacGregor, too." Greer spoke equally as casually, as if they'd picked up an interesting item at market. She glanced up at Juliana. "And he seems to have rescued a lady."

The woman turned her attention to the two of them. "Well, whatever brings ye here, 'tis better we go inside to discuss it."

"Aye."

Rory slid off the back of the horse, leaving Juliana suddenly bereft and feeling cold at his absence. She chided herself. She really had to stop these mad thoughts. Then he reached out for her, and she felt his strong hands encircle her waist and lift her down from the saddle. She inhaled his scent and allowed herself another second or two to savor the feeling of being cared for, and then she straightened.

"I can walk."

He dropped his hands immediately. A little too quickly, Juliana thought, but then, *Cousin Morag* might be watching from some window. She turned to the older woman.

"I am Juliana Caldwell."

"I'm Sima MacDonnell," the woman said. "Let us go in before we freeze into pillars of ice out here."

Rory handed over Baron's reins and followed them inside. It didn't take long before they were all seated before a blazing fire in what probably functioned as a library, although there were few books, and a huge desk occupied the space along one wall. They'd been joined by Calum, Greer and Aileen's father, along with their uncle the laird. Several serving girls had quickly brought in hot cider and warm buttered scones, but Juliana hadn't seen anyone who might be the cousin.

"Lady Caldwell was accosted on the road!" Greer said as soon as everyone had a drink. "'Tis the most exciting tale!"

Rory arched an eyebrow at Juliana, but she pretended not to see. She hoped he'd go along with the story they'd used while in Fort William, but before she could decide on how to approach that without blundering, the laird spoke.

"*Lady* Caldwell? Ye are English?"

"Yes, but my father was just a baron, so I am not addressed as 'lady,'" she replied.

"But her sister is the English countess that married Ian MacGregor," Aileen explained.

The laird looked surprised. "MacGregor got himself married?"

Juliana wasn't sure if he considered it an insult that he hadn't known. In English Society, not receiving an invitation to a major event certainly would be deemed so. "Actually, it took place five days ago without much fanfare. The MacGregors were celebrating the king's proclamation that their clan's standing was returned"—she paused, wondering if the MacDonnells had been slighted about that—"and it just seemed the natural time for them to wed."

The laird nodded, not seeming upset. "'Twas time for the proscription to be lifted. We couldna journey down to Strae Castle for the celebration since the Frasers had taken to reiving some of our cattle."

That explained the absence, then, even if she didn't quite understand the whole concept of reiving. Why anyone would try—or even want to—steal sheep or cattle from their neighbors made no sense to her, but apparently it was some sort of odd, time-honored tradition in the Highlands.

"So how did ye come to be here?" Calum asked.

Juliana gave Rory a quick glance. "We were accosted by highwaymen on the road, and Mr. MacGregor rescued me." The man raised a brow, as did Rory.

"Ye were on the road this far north?" the laird asked.

"Well..." She glanced at Rory again, but he remained stoically silent. Evidently, he was going to leave the lying up to her. "The ruffians blocked our way to return home, so we headed in the opposite direction. Which was north, of course. And..." Good heavens, she was babbling. "Well, here we are."

"And where did this happen?"

"Ah...on the road...near Fort William, I think."

Both of the MacDonnell men looked skeptical.

"If ye reached Fort William, why did ye not seek help from the dragoons to escort ye back?" the laird asked. "As an Englishwoman, they wouldna have turned ye down."

"Yes, but..." Juliana looked toward Rory once more and frowned when she saw he was looking rather amused. She lifted her chin. "Mr. MacGregor suspected the ruffians were Camerons, and since the fort is in the midst of their holdings, we did not know if we could depend on support from there." She really wanted to glare at Rory for not helping her out, but since everyone was watching her, she had to maintain a neutral demeanor.

"Camerons?" Calum asked. "Why would they be attacking travelers on the road?"

"Aye. 'Tis nae like their laird to condone such a thing."

"Perhaps he did not know," Juliana answered. "They might have been renegades or some such."

The MacDonnell laird frowned. "If there be Cameron men turned outlaws, their laird needs to ken about it. I'll send a messenger as soon as the snow clears—"

"—and we can also send a letter to Strae Castle," Sima added, "so they ken ye are safe."

"I already did that when we stopped at Spean," Juliana replied. "There was a mail coach stopped there."

That earned her a look from Rory that promised there would be a discussion later. *Fine.* "So there is no need to send a message to the Camerons—"

"'Twas Neal Cameron who led the party," Rory interrupted.

Heads swiveled toward him at that news.

"Neal?" the laird asked. "The man has a temper and everyone kens he likes to have his own way of things, but what would possess him to take to robbery? He is nae so stupid."

"He dinna intend to rob, at least, not our coin." Rory ignored Juliana's warning look. "What he intended to steal was a bride."

Sima blinked. "A bride?" She looked at Juliana. "Ye?"

She could cheerfully have kicked Rory—hard—in the shins, except her feet were just beginning to thaw out and he wore high boots. "I have no idea why he would want to do such a thing, but it seems he did."

The laird frowned. "Neal Cameron abducted ye?"

"Aye," Rory answered for her. "And I was sent to fetch her back."

"Which is what he did while we were on the road," Juliana said quickly before anyone would ask how he had accomplished that. She certainly didn't want him bringing up that whole business of being handfasted. The embarrassment of being rejected when he embraced his paramour—wherever the cousin was—would be too humiliating. Of course, she wouldn't really be *rejected*, since he'd only made that claim to get them away from Neal and hadn't *meant* it. All the same, if either of them tried to explain the circumstances, it would still *feel* like rejection. Which didn't really make any sense— why should she care?—but perhaps her brain was half-frozen, too. "So," she quickly concluded, "we decided to ride north since Neal Cameron might be pursuing us."

"The man is hardheaded," the laird acknowledged, "but the storm will nae doubt make him turn back."

"He'd be a fool to try and follow ye on horseback," Calum added. "'Tis too easy to lose the trail with the snow blinding ye."

"Aye, 'tis the reason I decided it best to sail up the loch," Rory said.

"Since only one packet sails north each day, he willna have followed ye by sea, either."

Rory nodded. "And the captain decided to anchor for the night rather than try to sail south during the blow, so if Cameron thought to follow by ship, he'd have to wait another day."

"More likely, he'll hole up at Spean and, if the snow hasna stopped, his men will want to turn around and head home."

"Meanwhile, ye'll be safe here at Invergarry," Sima said. "I've already had two chambers prepared for ye."

*Two* chambers. Juliana gave her a grateful look, glad she wasn't going to have go through another debate about sharing a bed. Or rather, *not* sharing a bed. Of course, Greer and Aileen's mother might have made sure Rory had his own chamber because he'd be entertaining Cousin Morag later.

She just hoped his chamber wasn't close to hers if he did.

...

Juliana woke the next morning to a soft knock on her door, and a moment later, two cheerful-looking young girls entered, one carrying a tin pitcher and the other a pile of clothing.

"I'm Caitlin," the one with the clothing said, "and this is my twin, Calin."

"I've brought ye hot water to wash with." Calin placed the pitcher on the dresser near the door. "And some heather soap, too."

Juliana swept the covers back and sat up. "Thank you."

"And Sima thought some of this clothing might fit ye." Caitlin placed the pile at the foot of the bed. "We were told to ask if ye want anything else, since ye are English."

She was very much aware that Scots considered English ladies to be pampered and spoiled, and she certainly didn't want to prove them right. "I will be fine. Just tell me where I should go once I am dressed."

"There's a small room off the kitchen where most of the household breaks the fast," Calin said. "Someone should be about."

Juliana thanked them again and maintained a straight face as the twins bobbed awkward curtsies. It looked more like both of them had gotten a sudden cramp in their legs, but she suspected they'd never attempted a curtsy before. Last evening she'd realized that Greer and Aileen's mother functioned as the housekeeper and, since these young maids had called her by her Christian name, she obviously didn't set too much store in formalities, especially not curtsies.

She shivered when her feet touched the cold stone floor. The coal in the brazier had gone out during the night, and the maids hadn't bothered to relight it. Probably because—as Juliana had discovered shortly after arriving at Strae Castle—people were not expected to stay abed in the mornings. She hurried over to the dresser, poured the still-warm water into the basin, and made fast work of her ablutions. It wouldn't do to have the MacDonnells think she was lazy. She had no idea of how early—or late—it was, since the sky outside her window was a slate grey that promised more snow.

Moving to the stack of clothing on the bed, she took a moment to run her hand over the fine texture of the wool. Scots were known to be some of the best weavers in the world, and the gown, while plain blue wool, was of good quality. She shed the night rail she'd been lent the night before and donned a fresh chemise, then slipped the gown over. The Scots were practical, too, having the laces in front and keeping the skirts to a simple amount of material that didn't require hoops or petticoats. Not that she had either. She'd discarded her torn and ruined ball gown along with its necessities when she'd purchased the traveling dress, which had been a practical garment, too. She sat down on the bed and quickly pulled on heavenly warm wool socks and then found her half boots. Quickly braiding her hair into a thick plait that swung down her back, she smoothed her skirts and took a deep breath as she opened the bedchamber door.

Today, she'd no doubt meet Cousin Morag. Had the girl spent the night with Rory?

...

Rory had gotten up at dawn, or as near dawn as he could surmise, given the leaden sky. Juliana would probably not be pleased that they were going to have to stay another day or two until the weather cleared. He wasn't especially happy about it, either, since he wasn't as sure as the MacDonnells that Neal Cameron had given up. In addition to a ferocious temper, when his pride was pricked, he would not give up seeking revenge. The ploy that Rory had used to dupe him certainly met that mark, as did their escape. The sooner they could head east toward Drumochter Pass and reach Blair Castle, the better he'd feel.

He looked up from the table as Juliana entered the breakfast room and managed to curb a sharp intake of air. Sima had worked magic—or perhaps the fae had been following them and decided to intervene out of boredom—but Juliana looked breathtaking. The blue of the gown brought out the color in her eyes and made her hair seem on fire. The soft wool clung to her, showing dips and curves that weren't usually visible in her regular clothes. The neckline was modestly low, only hinting at the fullness of her breasts…a much more tempting illusion than some of the fashionable gowns where bosoms nearly popped out. It made a man want to dip a finger between cloth and skin and pull the material down. He pushed that thought away.

"Did ye sleep well?"

"Yes. It felt wonderful to sleep in a feather bed again."

A picture of her snuggled into that bed, covers drawn up over her naked body, did nothing to banish his previous thought. Damnation. If he didn't stop thinking like this, he was going to have to take himself in hand, something he hadn't done since he was a green lad. Something he hadn't *had* to do, although he wondered now if he could last the entire year of a handfasting staying celibate.

He gestured toward the sideboard. "We are nae waited on here, but I can fix ye a plate."

She gave him a look as though he were daft. "I think I am capable of putting food on a plate."

He grinned. She'd actually sounded affronted. Perhaps if he teased her a bit, it would get his mind off his lust. "'Tis quite a decision ye'll have to make. There's shirred eggs and boiled, porridge, bacon, herring, black pudding, scones, and oatcakes. Jam, butter, and clotted cream as well. And," he added for emphasis, "ye'll also have to make a choice between coffee or tea and then decide on the sugar and milk. Are ye sure I should nae just take care of it for ye so ye willna tax your mind?"

Her expression turned to one that might be used when observing someone not quite sane. He suppressed another grin as her eyes began to spark blue fire.

"I am sure I can handle such a demanding task."

For a moment, he contemplated following her to the

sideboard and helpfully pointing out each dish. That would be sure to rile her. He could even suggest how big or small a portion she should have, which would truly cause her to dissemble…which could be interesting in itself. But he held himself in check. He'd accomplished his mission. His lecherous thoughts had subsided. For now.

...

Juliana cast a wary glance at Rory as she brought her plate back from the sideboard. Had the trek up the loch yesterday in the icy cold affected his thinking? Or perhaps he'd overindulged in bed sport last night? Not that she was going to ask about *that*, but she had overheard a rather risqué widow in London talking about *la petite mort* once. The lady claimed she'd actually lost consciousness during the act, and it had sounded like it was a good experience. At the time, Juliana had just stared at the woman, wondering how anyone could possibly find it pleasurable to pass out. But maybe that had happened to Rory, and lack of oxygen had marred his thinking. Why else would he have rambled on about making selections and listing every item available? It was quite strange.

"Have the others already eaten?" she asked and hoped he wouldn't start a recitation of the food items again.

"I doona ken. I suspect Greer and Aileen might still be abed."

And Cousin Morag? Was she still snuggled in the warmth of Rory's bed? But then, why would he be down here? Juliana frowned and pinched herself under the table. She had to stop thinking about his paramour. Not. Her. Business.

"Is something wrong with the food?"

She looked up from her plate. "No. Why do you ask?"

"Ye are grimacing like ye took a bite of something gone bad."

The only thing that had gone bad was her thinking. Maybe she was the one whose brain had been affected by the chilling storm. Plus, she'd pinched herself a bit harder than she'd intended.

"Actually, the food is quite good." She took a spoonful of porridge. "The cinnamon adds wonderful flavor."

"The cream and butter probably help, too."

She gave him a covert glance. Was he going to start talking about the food again? Perhaps a change of subject was in order.

"It is not snowing this morning. Do you think we can leave?"

Rory shook his head. "With as low as the clouds are, I doona want to take a chance on getting caught in another snowstorm. We'll have to cross the Monadhliath mountain range to reach the pass to Blair Castle."

Juliana was about to take a sip of tea, but she put the cup down. "We have to climb mountains?"

"We can stay to the foothills, but even they will be treacherous right now."

"Do we have to go to Blair Castle? Is there no other way we can go?"

"The only other way is to cross over the loch and go to Grant Castle." A corner of his mouth quirked up. "Which is exactly where ye hoped Cameron went."

*Is he making fun of my plan?* She bristled. "It was a good idea."

"I am nae arguing the point, but…" He paused to take a swallow of his coffee. "Even if we went there, we'd still have to get through Cameron country to get home."

"Going back the way we came is not an option, I suppose?"

Rory lifted an eyebrow. "Only if ye want to make sure ye run into Neal."

She shuddered. "I do not want to ever lay eyes on that man again."

"I wouldna mind doing the same."

Juliana remembered something his sister had said about some girl. Was it Morag? "Fiona mentioned that the two of you had a falling-out?"

"I guess ye could put it like that. The man took advantage of a MacFarlane lass and then wouldna own up to it."

MacFarlane. Not MacDonnell. She should have remembered that. So she was still nowhere closer to discovering who the mysterious cousin was. Or where she was. It was not something she could ask Rory, since he didn't even know that she knew.

Her thoughts were interrupted by the stomping of boots in the hall. A moment later, the laird came in.

"'Tis starting to snow again."

She bit back a groan. "Maybe it will not last long?"

"I canna say, but the glass is falling."

"What does that mean?"

"'Tis a barometer. Every ship has one, and every castle close to a loch has a sailing vessel or two, so 'tis wise to keep a storm glass on hand," Rory replied. "What it means is we are in for more stormy weather."

"We do not wish to impose on you for long," Juliana replied. "If the storm ends today, can we be on our way tomorrow?"

The men exchanged looks, and the laird shook his head.

"We've already had snow here, and this storm is one of the strongest I've seen this early in the year. Trekking through the hills will be hard, if nae impossible. Drumochter Pass will be closed for certain. Ye'll be lucky if ye can leave sometime after Yule."

"Yule? But…" She paused. "You are saying we may not be able to leave until the end of the month?"

"Aye. If nae longer."

Juliana tried to school her face into what she hoped was a bland expression. She and Rory were going to be stuck here for days? *Maybe weeks...* How was she going to abide it?

# Chapter Twelve

Rory went off with the laird and his brother, leaving Juliana to finish her breakfast alone. She wasn't hungry after that last bit of news, but she was grateful for the solitude so she could collect her thoughts.

That privacy didn't last long, however. A few minutes later, Greer and Aileen burst into the room, both of them seeming a little surprised to see her.

"Ye are up."

It sounded more like a statement than a question, but Juliana answered it anyway. "I like to rise early."

That comment was followed by looks of astonishment.

"Ye do?" Aileen asked. "I thought all Englishwomen liked to lie abed."

"Especially the fancy ladies from London," Greer added.

"I am not a fancy lady. Just a miss, although I would like for you to call me Juliana." She could practically hear her sisters laughing at the image of her staying in bed until noon.

"But doona all ladies go to balls and parties and nae get home until the sun rises?"

Aileen nodded. "That's what we heard."

"You are referring to the *haute ton*—"

"The what?"

"*Haute ton* literally means 'high fashion' or to 'set the tone,' but basically it refers to the rich social set in London," Juliana explained.

The sisters exchanged confused looks. "But your sister—the one that married Ian—was a part of that, nae?" Aileen asked.

"Yes and, of course, she was invited to many social doings, but she often chose not to go."

"Why nae?"

She could hardly say because often Emily had bruises or was too sore. Her sister's marriage to the damn earl—who had a fondness for opium and gambling—had been horrible and part of the reason Juliana didn't want to get married. The other reason was… Juliana pushed the thought of that horrible night out of her head. It certainly wasn't something she planned to share. "Those parties and balls are often terribly boring."

"Boring?" Greer looked intrigued.

Juliana shrugged. "Everyone gossips. Most of it is lies, or half-truths, at the very least. The *ton* likes to make up stories about everyone and everything. It gives them something to do."

"But…" Greer wrinkled her forehead again. "With all the money they have, they can do anything they like."

"Not exactly anything. Women are very limited in what they're allowed to do."

Aileen narrowed her eyes. "Allowed?"

Juliana had to smile at her reaction. It was very similar to hers. Yet another reason she didn't desire marriage. "Their husbands can tell them what they can or cannot do and, since husbands also control the money, wives have little choice but to do as they are bid."

"Scots men may try ordering us about, too." Aileen grinned. "But they doona get far with it."

"Aye, our men can be a bragging lot, but they ken how to treat their women," Greer said.

Juliana considered Rory. The man was bossy. They rarely agreed on anything. He hated admitting when she was right—like about their plan—but...he *had* treated her well. Even if Rory considered rescuing her his duty, he'd still treated her well. He had let her have the room at the inn to herself. He'd gotten them passage aboard the packet so she wouldn't have to endure riding in the frigid cold, and then he'd known to get her on deck before she became violently ill *and* had made sure she would stay relatively warm. And this morning, he hadn't even cursed about being snowed in.

She frowned. Maybe that was because of *Cousin Morag*?

"I suppose your cousin holds Mr. MacGregor in that regard?"

Greer giggled. "Ye could say that. Morag would walk around like a mooncalf whenever Rory was about."

Not exactly what she wanted to hear. The dear cousin had probably gone right to his bedchamber last night when she found out they'd arrived.

Aileen nodded. "Morag will be angry as a disturbed hornet if she doesna get back before ye leave."

Juliana's ears perked. "She is not here?"

"Our maither said she left a week ago to visit the MacKenzies at Eilean Donan Castle," Aileen said. "She'll have to wait until the snow melts to get back."

"Even then, it will be a three-day ride," Greer said.

Juliana breathed a sigh of relief. At least the girl wasn't here, and she wouldn't be subject to a romantic interlude. By the time the snow melted, they'd be gone and on their way long before Morag got home.

But her elation was short-lived.

"Of course, the snow melts fast at Eilean Donan with all that water around it," Aileen said, "and they doona usually get as much as we do farther inland."

Greer giggled again. "She may be back in time to make calf eyes at Rory again."

Juliana schooled her face once more. Those were words she definitely did not want to hear. Definitely *not*.

...

"Did ye see any sign of the Camerons?" Rory asked the MacDonnell laird once they were in the library behind closed doors, along with Calum.

He shook his head. "The blowin' snow would have covered the tracks, if there were any. What makes ye think Cameron may have come this way? From the story ye put out, 'tis likely he would go on to Grant Castle."

"'Tis a…feeling. A thought flying through my head."

A side of the laird's mouth quirked up. "Did the fae grant ye magical powers, then?"

"There may be more truth to what ye say than ye think." The laird's eyebrow went up in question, and Rory continued, "I had trouble tracking Cameron because there were three trails he could have taken. I wasted time on the first two. Ye ken how the faeries like to meddle and make trouble."

"Aye," Calum said. "'Tis best to give the fae their due, just in case."

Rory nodded. "I finally caught up to Cameron, but was nae until after he arrived at the MacLean's holdings."

The laird frowned. "Ye didna catch up on the road like the lass said?"

"Nae." Rory shrugged. "She didna want me to go into detail about what happened."

"Was there trouble?"

"Nae at first. I told the laird I was handfasted to Juliana and Neal had nae right to claim her."

Both MacDonnells stared at him. "Ye did *what*?"

"I ken! I ken!" Rory held up a hand. "'Twill mean I canna tumble a lass for a year—"

"Ye can tumble the one ye are handfasted to," Calum said.

"Nae." Although Rory had been entertaining far too many lustful thoughts about Juliana, he knew how well—how *not* well—the idea would go over with her.

"Nae? Ye have rights since ye are handfasted."

Rory shrugged, hoping he looked nonchalant. "The lass doesna exactly understand the whole thing."

The laird grinned. "I would think *explaining* it all would be a wee bit of fun."

"I can have Sima move the lass's things to your bedchamber," Calum said.

"Nae!" He'd already endured one night of supposedly sharing a room at Spean. If Juliana were forced to share his bedchamber here, he'd be sleeping on the floor for sure. Not what he wanted to do. "She thinks it more of an English betrothal, which keeps the bride pure."

Calum waved a hand dismissively. "Ye can also explain that in *Scotland* we do things differently. When a man claims a lass and she doesna object..." He paused. "She didna object, did she?"

"She couldna. We would nae have been able to leave."

"There ye have it, then," the laird said. "The lass is rightfully yours, at least for a year."

Rory shook his head. "She thinks 'twas a way to leave and that it means nothing."

The laird studied him. "But ye ken it *does* mean something."

"I ken, and I'll nae break my word to keep faith with her, but I'll nae force her to share my bed."

Neither of the MacDonnells spoke, but the laird finally nodded. "Aye. 'Tis the honorable thing to do."

"I suppose 'tis," Calum agreed, "but if everyone believed ye, why did ye nae go back to Strae Castle?"

Rory rubbed his temples before answering. "Well, ye may nae have noticed—*yet*—that the lass is strong-willed and doesna mind sharing her opinion on anything. She told Margaret Cameron she had nae desire to marry Neal or any other man."

"And Margaret told her father?"

Rory nodded. "Just as we were riding away, the men came out shouting. I kenned we would nae be able to get away riding pillion, so I headed north."

"A practical decision," the laird said.

"I didna have a choice."

"I can see why ye think the fae had a hand in this," Calum said. "Ye now have a bride who doesn't ken she is one."

"Aye, and it needs to stay that way. I doona want her thinking I tricked her into anything."

"Ye can expect us to keep your secret," Calum said, "although I think ye might reconsider. A year is a long time to go without bed sport."

"I'll manage." *Somehow.*

The laird changed the subject. "I can see why ye think Cameron wants to pursue ye but, assuming the fae are nae really involved, what makes ye think he didna believe your story to go to Grant Castle? 'Tis logical enough."

"Aye, but so is coming to Invergarry," Rory replied, "since your castle is farther east and easier to return home from. If we'd gone to Grant Castle, we'd still have had to make our way back. Either across Loch Ness and then down to Drumochter Pass or attempt to return through Fort William and be back in Cameron lands."

"Um, I suppose ye could be right."

"Cameron is nae stupid, even if he is hotheaded and single-minded." Rory frowned. "He probably sent some men to the Grants and took himself to Spean. If he did that, the innkeeper would have told him we were there. 'Twould nae be hard to figure out where we were headed, especially with the storm."

"Even if he did get to Spean Bridge, do ye really think Cameron daft enough to follow ye with the blizzard raging?" Calum asked.

"He would try," Rory said grimly. "He wants Juliana Caldwell, but he wants revenge more. I made him look like a fool."

"Aye. 'Tis a pity the lass talked to Margaret. His pride could have been salvaged, at least, if no one kenned he'd been duped."

Nobody needed to tell him that. Whether Juliana realized it or not, she'd started something that wouldn't be finished until Neal called Rory out…and that might very well start a clan war.

He rather doubted the fae had meddled in this. Even collectively, they probably would be no match for one Juliana Caldwell. Then again, perhaps he shouldn't be so quick to dismiss the fae. The faeries could very well have had their hands in this mess, because he legally had a bride he could not have.

...

"What are ye planning to do? We are freezing our arses off."

Neal took his eyes off the closed castle gate he was focusing on from the safety of the tree line and looked at his second-in-command. "Are ye complaining?"

Jamie frowned. "'Twas nae the best of accommodations last night."

That brought laughs from the other men, which were quickly squelched when Neal glared at them.

"Are ye nae Camerons? Ye complain about spending a night in the woods? We were out of the wind and had our tartans, for love of the devil!"

Jamie straightened his shoulders. "Even a plaid gets soaked through with snow on the ground."

"*Contrachd ort!*" He let his glance sweep over his men. "Curses on the lot of ye for acting like bairns."

Jamie had the audacity to raise a skeptical eyebrow, and Neal knew the man well enough to read the look. He thought Neal was the one acting like a bairn. And his second knew *him* well enough not to voice that opinion. Still, it rankled.

"There was naewhere to go. We wouldna have made it back to Spean before dark."

"Nothing is stopping us now." One of his other men spoke up. "Dawn broke near two hours ago."

"We could be having a hot bowl of stew by midday if we leave now."

"Aye, and a bit of whisky to warm us up as well."

"Ye have whisky in your flasks, nae?" Neal asked absently, refocusing on the castle in the distance.

"We went through most of that last night."

"And we have nae provisions, either."

Annoyed, Neal looked back at them. "Ye are all blethering like a bunch of women. Ye'll nae starve this morning."

"We dinna think we would be doing surveillance, either."

"The plan was to overtake the wench on the road."

"Enough!" Neal shouted. It was a good thing he wasn't laird yet, or these men would be turned out for daring to speak to him so. But as long as his father was alive, he didn't have that option. "I ken what the plan was! How was I to ken

MacGregor would take the packet instead of the trail?"

"Well, he is behind the safety of Invergarry's walls now." Jamie refused to be cowed. "We can hardly launch an attack with so few men."

"And your father doesna want to start a war with MacDonnells."

Neal gritted his teeth. He didn't need to be reminded of how his father preferred to keep the peace. "My intended bride is inside those walls."

"And likely to stay there," Jamie replied.

"We doona ken that. The wench is likely to want to get home as soon as she can."

"Have ye looked at the sky? 'Tis more snow coming. The pass will be blocked for days. MacGregor would be a fool to start out with her."

It was what else MacGregor might do with her that upset Neal. Even though Margaret had told him that Juliana had no interest in the man, it didn't mean MacGregor didn't have an interest in *her*. And Neal had been looking forward to being the one who would plow her fields the first time. To show her how strong and powerful a man could be. To bring her to submission through pain so she would not defy him again. If she were not a virgin when he finally took her, MacGregor would pay with his life.

Until then, though, his men were right, much as he hated to admit it. They were not prepared to lay siege to Invergarry. Beyond not having enough men, they had no supplies to maintain themselves. They could hardly ride into the village outside the walls and show themselves. Word would get to the MacDonnell laird within minutes.

For now, he would turn back. But he wasn't giving up. Miss Juliana Caldwell would be his.

# Chapter Thirteen

"Since ye didna see the castle yesterday, would ye like us to show ye around?" Aileen asked as they finished breakfast.

"Yes, thank you." She hadn't really had a chance to get her bearings yesterday. They'd arrived late, spent some time in the library explaining their situation, and then she'd been shown to her chamber on the second floor. Sima had ordered a hot bath for her—which had thawed out her bones and felt heavenly after the cold they'd endured—and had a tray sent up. Juliana had been almost too tired to eat and had gone to sleep within minutes.

"Come along, then."

Juliana followed the sisters out of the small family dining room at the back of the castle and down the hall to the main entrance. She remembered climbing the steps to it yesterday, although pretty much everything else had been a blur. Now she noticed narrow slits on either side of the heavy oak door.

"What are those?"

"Shot holes for arrows," Aileen answered. "This is the old part of the castle that wasn't blown up by the Duke of

Cumberland after Culloden."

She didn't remember seeing anything like that at Strae Castle, although it had an old section, too. She wasn't sure how old, though.

"When was this built?"

Aileen shrugged. "I think about one hundred seventy-five years ago. There were two other castles before this one."

"There are shot holes in the tower wall as well as in the staircases below," Greer added.

As was common, the main floor was elevated above the ground floor that housed the kitchens, pantries, laundry, and such. "The servants were trained in weaponry?" Juliana asked.

"Aye. To hear our uncle tell it, and our *seanair* before him—"

"Who?"

"Grandfather," Greer filled in.

"To hear them tell it," Aileen continued, "every servant was trained to use a bow."

"Even the women?"

She nodded. "And any girl old enough to help in the kitchen."

"The boys were trained even earlier," Greer said.

"Every pair of hands had to be counted on in the days when the English would attack or even when rival clans would declare war." Aileen wiggled her own fingers. "Everyone had to know how to defend the castle."

Juliana thought of how different her own childhood had been. Her father had been an eccentric baron, pretty much throwing the family fortune away on worthless inventions. While he may have been able to load and fire a musket, he was by nature a gentle, peaceful soul. They had teetered on the edges of genteel poverty more than once, but Papa had always protected his daughters. She couldn't imagine him expecting his daughters to defend themselves, let alone teaching them how to do it. Juliana grimaced. Perhaps if he had, she wouldn't have been raped.

Aileen must have noted her expression, because she lifted an eyebrow. "Ye doona approve of women handling weapons?"

Juliana quickly shook her head. "No. I mean, yes. I do not think women should be defenseless. In fact, I would like to learn how to do just that. Defend myself, that is."

Greer smiled. "Ye could ask Rory to teach ye. All the MacGregors are grand fighters."

Aileen nodded. "They've had to be."

Juliana had already gathered that from living at Strae Castle these past six months. Their proscription had just been lifted by the king two weeks ago. Before that, the MacGregor name had been banned and they'd been banished, their lands forfeit. At one time, other clans had even been forbidden to help them upon threat of hanging. They'd been forced into hiding and scavenging and came to be known as Children of the Mist for their ability to disappear as quickly as they appeared. They had to fend for themselves. She could well imagine the women and girls being trained, just to survive.

"I do have a knife."

"Do ye ken how to use it?" Greer asked.

"Well..." She remembered how easily Rory had taken away the knife she'd purloined off the Cameron table. "Not very well, I admit."

"Since ye willna be going anywhere for a bit, we could arrange some training sessions," Aileen said.

Greer nodded. "And it will give Rory something to do. He already looked restless when he left the room earlier."

He was probably restless because he wanted to get her back to Strae Castle as fast as possible. Not that she didn't want the same thing. Or, maybe, he was restless because

Morag was not here and he had hoped to see her. Juliana tsked at that. She needed to turn her thoughts elsewhere.

"We can discuss that later. I really would like to see the castle."

Greer gave her a curious look, then opened a door to the left of the entryway. "This is the great hall."

They stepped inside, and Juliana looked around. As with Strae Castle, the room was a large rectangle with a raised dais at the far end and a wooden family crest on the wall behind it. Large hearths were centered along both sides, and an array of weapons was displayed on the stone walls. Perpendicular to the dais were long trestle tables with benches that could easily be moved to the sides to clear the room for clan celebrations. Iron chandeliers hung suspended from the ceiling, and sconces protruded out from between the various weapons on the walls. In contrast with the fancy ballrooms of Mayfair town houses with their glittering crystal chandeliers, silk-lined walls, and brocaded satin chairs, a Scottish great hall was a simple but very practical room.

Juliana walked toward the dais and looked up at the crest. A black bird sat atop a rock and the Gaelic inscription. "What do the words say?"

"*Cragan an Fhithich* means 'Rock of the Raven,'" Aileen replied. "'Tis the name of the rock the castle is built on."

"Interesting. I didn't get to see much of the outside yesterday, but I did notice we climbed a high hill." She smiled. "I guess it was this rock."

"Most castles are built on the highest point of land possible, so the enemy can be seen approaching," Greer said, "but now 'tis just a beautiful view, especially from the tower."

"Can we go up there?"

Aileen nodded and pulled a torch out of one of the wall sconces and moved to light it from the fire in the hearth. "Follow me."

She led the way down another hall, and Juliana realized that this castle was actually laid out in an L shape rather than a simple rectangle like Strae Castle. A heavy wooden door opened into the base of the tower, and as Aileen closed it behind them, she pointed to the stout braces on either side of the frame.

"In the old days, a heavy bolt would ensure raiders couldna access the tower. The women and children could hide in the stairwell while the men fought from the battlement."

As they climbed the spiraling stairs in the dank darkness of the tower, Juliana wondered how many of those attackers had been English. Her knowledge of history wasn't the best, but she knew most Highlanders had sided with the Jacobite movement against the present king's grandfather. She noticed the shot holes along the way as well and wondered if some of those hidden women—and maybe children—had fired arrows from them.

By the time they reached the sixth story, her thoughts had turned somewhat morbid, and she was glad when Aileen opened the door that led out into the open air. Unfortunately, there wasn't much of a view since the heavy clouds scudded so low she felt like she could reach out and touch them.

"The snow seems to be falling a lot heavier," Greer said.

Juliana blinked as she felt large flakes strike her face. "I was hoping the skies would clear."

Aileen glanced at her. "Our da says we're likely in for days of this."

That's what he'd said at breakfast, although Juliana had held out hope he was wrong. Still, it might be worth getting a second opinion. "How long, do you think?"

She lifted one shoulder. "This time of year, storms start building all the way across the ocean. By the time they reach here, 'tis just one after another that often follows."

Juliana sighed. Apparently, they were going to be stuck

at Invergarry for a while. But, if it was snowing, that should mean that Morag would also be delayed returning. She hoped.

"'Tis cold out here. We didna bring shawls," Greer said. "Let's go back."

Juliana didn't argue with her. The wind was picking up, and she didn't want to experience yesterday's cold conditions again. She reached out and pulled the door latch. The handle loosened unexpectedly, and Juliana nearly lost her balance as she staggered backward. For a moment she stared at the brass knob in her hand, and then she looked at the closed door.

There was no longer a way to open it from their side.

# Chapter Fourteen

The breakfast room was empty as Rory left the library, and he supposed she'd gone back to her chamber, or maybe she was off exploring the castle, since he'd heard Aileen and Greer coming down the stairs when he'd been going to meet with the MacDonnells. Either way, it was probably better the room was empty. His blethering on like an eejit about the breakfast selection had only temporarily distracted his thoughts.

The talk with the MacDonnell brothers hadn't helped. Neither of them would think less of him for moving Juliana into his bedchamber. Handfasting meant they were considered married, at least for a year and a day, until they decided to make the arrangement permanent. And every right of matrimony—including bedding—went along with that.

His lower head stirred eagerly at the thought while the one on his shoulders tried to remain firmly lodged in logic. At the moment, he wasn't sure it would prevail. Seeing how wretched she had been on the ship yesterday had evoked empathy from him, since as a lad, he'd been a bit greenish on more than one occasion himself. And he'd even added a bit of admiration to that when she hadn't complained about feeling ill *or* the weather conditions. Having her seated in front of him with her rounded arse rubbing against his cock had not exactly helped matters, nor had blanketing themselves together for warmth. He had felt the soft weight of her breasts on his forearms as he'd held the reins. And then this morning, she'd appeared in that formfitting gown with her hair like a halo of fire.

He sighed. A Scottish lass would understand the custom of handfasting and, even if they'd used it as a ruse to escape the Camerons, *might* allow him the privilege of sharing her bed. But Juliana was English and, in her mind, it was simply a false betrothal that she could easily call off, should rumor of it start circulating. Not that he expected that news to spread. Every Cameron present three days ago when he'd duped them knew of Neal's pride and temper and would hold their peace. Rory suspected the MacLean would instruct his people to consider it a misunderstanding, since he'd not want to anger either Camerons or MacGregors. He'd asked the MacDonnells not to mention it as well.

Still. Rory knew he'd taken an oath, even if it meant nothing to Juliana and, much as his manhood wanted fulfillment, he would have to refrain. Besides, he wasn't ready for a real marriage—not with all that needed to be done for his clan—and certainly not to someone as hot-tempered as Juliana.

He moved on to the entryway and grabbed the nondescript plaid from the boat's captain off a hook by the door. As he wrapped it around himself, he wondered when— if ever—the English king would see fit to allow the clans to wear their colors once more. Although the MacGregors had been banned from using their tartans as well as anything else associated with them, the other clans had only been forbidden the use of their true plaids since Culloden. He grimaced. King George—the second one—had seemed as determined as Edward the Hammer in squelching the Scots for good. As if that would ever be the case. Rory opened the door and went down the steps. Perhaps the current George might be persuaded… He had lifted the proscription, after all. It was a thought to pursue.

Right now, though, he was going to pursue something much more tangible. He was going to find out if Neal Cameron had followed them.

...

"*Tha sinn a 'dol a bhàsachadh!*" Greer cried.

Before Juliana could ask what that meant—she wasn't sure she wanted to know—Aileen shook her head.

"We are nae going to die."

Her sister stared at her. "Are ye an *eejit*? Nae a soul kens we are up here! And we nae have shawls!"

Aileen tightened her mouth, and Juliana quickly spoke. "We can yell. Surely someone will hear us."

Greer shook her head. "We doona keep guards posted these days, so there is nae one on the battlements. And with the snow, nae one will venture out unless they have to."

"But surely someone can hear us!" Juliana repeated.

"Even if someone were out, with the wind blowing, 'tis nae likely," Aileen said.

Juliana didn't like the grim look on their faces. "But what about inside? If we stand at the door and all of us shout at once, will it not be heard inside?"

"Ye may nae have noticed, but the door to the tower is a good foot thick so raiders couldna break it down. And," Greer added, "we are six stories up."

"But..." Juliana hated feeling helpless. "There must be something we can do."

Aileen straightened her shoulders. "We will think on it. Meanwhile, let us get out of the wind and huddle together like we did on the boat."

Except there they'd had a wool blanket or whatever they called it. Still, Juliana didn't argue as Aileen led the way around the corner of the tower and away from the wind. It did feel incrementally warmer without its biting force. Or maybe her mind was only wishing it so. She looked at the handle she still held.

"Why did this come loose in the first place?"

Both sisters stared at it, and Greer shook her head. "I doona ken."

Aileen took the handle from Juliana and examined the broken end. "'Tis corroded."

Greer ran a finger along the rough edges. "Hardly anyone ever comes up here, so who kens when it was last looked at."

"I thought you said you liked the view from here," Juliana said. "Would you not have noticed rust or something?"

"We only come up here when the weather is warm, and then we just prop the door open." Greer pointed to a large rock that looked like it could be rolled. "With that."

"Which we should have done this time," Aileen said.

Juliana shook her head. "I should not have suggested it in the first place."

"'Tis nae your fault," Greer replied.

"That doesna matter now." Aileen stepped toward the door and tried to fit the broken end of the knob back into the door. "Mayhap if I can get this to hold..." She pushed the broken end in as far as she could and twisted it, but it didn't catch.

Greer muttered something else in Gaelic under her breath, and Juliana didn't even ask what it meant. It was better she didn't understand the language. No matter what they said, she still felt this was entirely her fault. Then she remembered the knife.

"Wait! How about this?" She lifted her skirt and pulled out the stolen knife from her boot. She'd felt a little silly putting it there, but Rory had said it was always good to be armed. She held it up now. "Could this work?"

"Aye!" Aileen grabbed it and attempted to slide it between the door and the frame. It barely slipped between the door and frame because of the tight fit, but at last she got part of it in. "Now, all I have to do is wiggle it and maybe I can get the latch pushed back..." She concentrated on her effort. "I think I can feel it moving..."

Juliana moved beside her and managed to stick two fingertips into the opening where the knob had broken. "If you feel the latch give way, I'll try and pull the door open."

Aileen nodded and maneuvered the knife. "Just a little more... I think I have it..."

And then there was a loud snap as the knife's handle broke off. For a long moment all three of them stared at it.

"Bloody hell," Juliana finally said. "*Bloody* hell."

• • •

Rory fashioned a hood with part of the plaid and wrapped the remains over and around his shoulders several times, grateful he was wearing doeskin breeches and didn't have to bother with pleating the thing into a kilt. The wool was raw, the natural lanolin from the sheep left in the material. Not surprising since the plaid had been used on a ship and everything that could be waterproofed was. The oily substance also provided further insulation, for which he was grateful. The wind was increasing, making the cold air and swirling snow feel like icy talons striking him. They'd probably be in a full-fledged blizzard by noontime.

He hurried out the gate, not bothering with a horse, because he didn't intend to stick to the road. Calum had already told him there was no evidence of tracks there. He doubted that Neal would have stayed out in the open once the castle came into view, because he could have been spotted. More likely, he'd have taken cover inside the tree line just before the road curved into plain sight of the castle.

The curve was but a quarter mile from the gates, but Rory counted his paces before he turned off and again as he made his way to the trees. If the snow increased while he was out, he wanted to be able to find his way back.

Once among the thick trunks, the wind diminished considerably. Rory pushed back the hood and attuned his ears for sound. The creatures of the forest were silent, mostly likely taking refuge in nests and burrows and any crevice that provided shelter. He heard only the pines rustling above him. Lifting his head, he scented the air. No trace of smoke or peat ash lingered. That didn't mean Neal hadn't been here, though. This close to the castle, he might not have taken the chance of lighting a fire. Then, too, everything around was wet.

Rory grimaced as he moved farther into the woods. It would have made for a cold night outside, but a man bent on revenge would have the heat of his anger to warm him up.

The light was growing dimmer, and for a moment he thought he might have wandered too deep into the forest, but then he realized he could still see where the trees ended. That meant the weather was getting worse fast. The storm was closing in, so he didn't have much time if he didn't want to be caught out in it. He looked around and decided to follow a half-frozen burn just a bit farther. If the man had spent the night out here, he'd have wanted water for his horses.

That instinct paid off. Three dozen paces later, a small

clearing appeared past a set of boulders. It wasn't big enough to be called a glade, but it was large enough to hobble several horses. Rory looked at the ground, already covered with an inch or two of new snow, and he slowly moved forward as he brushed it away with his boot.

And that's when he saw it. A pile of horse dung, the crust hardened by the frigid weather. Picking up a small, fallen branch, he poked it. The crust gave way to a soft mess underneath. Fresh then, not thoroughly frozen. And it still smelled. Rory brushed more snow away with the stick. While there were no clear tracks, the dead grass had been churned up.

He noticed a deer trail that Cameron had probably used. Since it wound between clumps of bramble, the snow hadn't completely covered it. Moving closer, he crouched down. He could make out a few small deer prints and then some partial tracks that were much larger. Horses. Several of them. He straightened.

Someone had spent last night here. He was fairly certain it had been Neal Cameron. Anyone else would have sought Highlander hospitality and come to the castle on such a bitter cold night. And he had not been alone.

There was no sign of them now. Perhaps his men had talked some sense into him and they'd gone back to Spean. But would they go back to their holdings or attempt to return once the weather cleared? It was something he needed to discuss with the MacDonnells.

He hurried back, arriving at the castle just as the wind decided to unleash its wrath in full fury. A mug of hot cider would be heaven while he talked to the laird and Calum.

But all hell appeared to have broken loose when he entered the castle. Servants were scurrying everywhere. Sima was wringing her hands, and her husband and his brother looked grim.

"What's wrong?" he asked, unwinding the plaid.

"Aileen, Greer, and Juliana are gone," Sima said.

"Gone?"

"Aye." She was trying not to cry. "Disappeared. We canna find them anywhere."

# Chapter Fifteen

Rory stopped unwinding the plaid. "Where have ye looked?"

"Everywhere." Sima gestured to servants still coming and going behind her. "We've had everyone looking into every room, closet, and crevice in the castle."

"And the grounds outside?" Though he couldn't imagine why three women would even venture out with the wind howling and the air rapidly growing colder.

Sima pointed to the row of hooks lining the wall beside the great hall. "They dinna take their cloaks or even shawls."

A thought struck him that chilled him to the bone, and it had nothing to do with the inclement weather. Could Neal Cameron have possibly gotten into the castle and abducted Juliana? There were no guards posted on the battlements, especially in the winter months. He looked to the laird.

"Is your postern gate kept locked?"

"Aye." He frowned. "Why do ye ask?"

"I found signs of a makeshift camp," Rory said. "I think the Camerons were here."

Sima's eyes widened. "Ye think they stole our lasses?"

"I doona ken." He knew Cameron wanted Juliana, as much for salvaging his pride as anything else. From what he'd seen of the tracks, there had probably been half a dozen horses. If Neal had caught her—somewhere—with Greer and Aileen, it would have been easy to overpower all of them. And less messy to take all of them than leaving two bodies to be found. Not that Rory was going to suggest that. He didn't even want to think it. "Is it possible Cameron could have gained entrance?"

"I doona see how. Someone would have seen him," Calum said.

"Mayhap not if he was in full sight."

"What do ye mean?"

"Have ye asked the guard in the barbican if a small group came to the gate, posing as beggars? He might have been able to slip in whilst waiting for bread."

The laird narrowed his eyes, then gestured to one of the male servants and whispered in his ear. The man's eyes widened, and he took off at a run.

"We will soon find out."

"Any possibility that Cameron could have scaled the walls? Mayhap with a grappling hook?" That theory was farfetched since there would have been no need for Neal to be traveling with one and Rory doubted he'd have had time—or forethought—to secure one, since he'd pursued them on horseback, no doubt hoping to catch them *before* they reached the castle. From the way Calum and his brother were staring at him, they evidently thought the idea ludicrous as well.

"The walls are only the first line of defense," the laird said, as if explaining the concepts of castle building to a halfwit. "Ye may have noticed that Invergarry Castle perches on a rock with a steep incline to the door. There are nae windows close enough to the ground for someone to get in, let alone carry three lasses out."

"'Tis a well-designed castle." Rory hoped his next question wasn't going to infuriate the laird. "What about the servants' entrance at the kitchens?"

"Nae one came in that way...or left," Sima said. "I asked the cook and her helpers myself."

"How about hidden passages?" Rory asked. Nearly all old castles had them. Strae Castle had several that led from bedchambers to a tunnel, allowing escape in times of siege.

"The entrance to those have been blocked off with rocks since Culloden," Calum answered. "We dinna want unexpected guests finding their way in."

Rory nodded in understanding. Old King George had been determined to wipe out every remnant of Bonnie Prince Charlie's supporters, even if it meant turning one Scot against another by paying them to spy. Before he could continue, the man the laird had sent out returned and shook his head as he came toward them.

"Nae a soul approached the gate since MacGregor brought the lasses home," he said to the laird and turned to Rory. "And ye were the only one to leave."

That answered his next question of whether anyone had seen Juliana or the sisters leaving. Not that he thought they would have, since their cloaks were hanging on the wall. But still. If Cameron hadn't abducted them, where could they be? He looked again at the wall to make sure none of the hooks were bare. And then he noticed a torch missing from a sconce. He pointed to it.

"Could Greer and Aileen have taken Juliana exploring the passageways?" She hadn't indicated an interest in exploring the ones at Strae Castle, but that didn't mean that either sister might not have suggested it. "Mayhap they are still in one of them."

He didn't want to add *and injured*. Some of the boards could have rotted, and it would also have been easy to slip on the narrow, winding stairs since the stones would be slippery with the dank wetness that clung to those passages. Even though he didn't voice those thoughts, he saw the alarm on Sima's face.

"I had nae thought of that."

"Neither did I." The laird's voice was grim as he took two more torches out of sconces and handed one to his brother. "We will take a look at each of them."

"If ye'll give me a third torch and show me a passage, it can save some time," Rory said.

"And I as well," Sima said.

Calum looked like he was about to protest, but something flashed in his wife's eyes, similar to the glare Juliana gave *him* when she thought he'd made a stupid remark. Instead, Calum handed her his torch and retrieved another.

If the situation wasn't so dire, Rory would have smiled. Juliana had more than a bit of tenaciousness in her soul. He just hoped she was using it now.

• • •

"Bloody hell," Juliana said again as the wind whipped blowing snow across her face. The three of them were sitting huddled together on the rooftop, braced against the tower wall. "We certainly could use a bit of cooperation from the weather."

"The only thing ye can count on with Scottish weather is that it keeps changing," Aileen said between chattering teeth.

"And this time of the year it only gets worse." Greer's voice was muffled since her nose was buried in her sleeve for warmth. "Ye can go from cold and wet to wet and cold."

"Aye, and add miserable to the mix." Aileen shivered. "We were stupid to nae even bring shawls."

Guilt washed over Juliana. "It was I who suggested coming up here in the middle of a snowstorm, so I think that makes me the stupid one."

"Och, 'twas just beginning to snow, and ye wanted to see the view," Aileen replied. "We were nae planning to stay but a minute."

"And 'twas nae all that cold before the wind picked up," Greer said.

"True." Aileen nodded. "We oft go from the castle to the granary or vegetable shed in the winter without putting on cloaks and such."

Juliana knew they were trying to make her feel better, but she still felt like an idiot—Rory would call her an *eejit*—for suggesting such foolishness. Now she had put all three of them in peril since she was *also* the one who'd pulled the handle off the door.

She stared at the loose knob and broken knife lying beside them. They'd almost succeeded before it had snapped in two. They'd tried to use the broken half to push the latch back again, but that had only resulted in Aileen getting her thumb cut. Juliana glanced at the injured hand. The cold air had kept it from bleeding too much, but the blood that had surfaced had an icy crust to it. The sight of that made her see just how serious their situation had become. Greer may have been right. They could well freeze to death before they were found.

How long before someone realized they were missing? After that strange conversation at breakfast, Rory had gone off with the laird and the girls' father to the library. If the MacDonnell men were like the MacGregors, they could be in there for hours, discussing options about what to do. Even if Rory came out sooner, he wouldn't necessarily think anything of not seeing her or the sisters. Most men just assumed women spent their time in the solar or in their chambers. Sima was busy running the household. She probably wouldn't even wonder where they were.

Juliana took a deep breath and immediately regretted it, since the cold air burned her lungs. Even if Rory—or Sima— took notice that they were gone and started searching, why would anyone even think of the tower? Aileen had closed the heavy door behind them before they'd started ascending the stairs.

They could literally be up on the roof for hours, and that might well be too long.

"I think we should try shouting again."

"We already did that and are nearly hoarse," Greer managed to mumble. "And nae one heard us."

"And with the snow falling this hard, nae one can see us this high up, either," Aileen said. "'Tis better we stay as warm as we can by huddling together, rather than stand by the embrasures again."

Juliana saw the sense in that, but the icy crust on Aileen's cut was a reminder of just how cold it was, and she didn't know how much more time they had. "You two stay here and keep warm. I am going to try one more time."

They both looked up, and she saw how pale their faces were and how bloodless their lips.

"Doona take too long," Greer said.

Juliana nodded as she rose and then stumbled as her legs almost gave way. They were numb, and she awkwardly shuffled forward. She hoped it was from sitting crouched as long as they had and not because of frostbite... She pushed the thought away. *No.* They were not going to die up here.

As she reached the crenellations along the perimeter of the tower, she reluctantly withdrew her hands that had been wrapped inside her sleeves. She could hardly feel them, either, but she needed to brace herself on the merlons on either side of her.

She could see nothing but swirling whiteness, and for a moment she felt disoriented and dizzy. The rough feel of stone on each side of her steadied her a bit. She took a breath, trying not to breathe in too much cold air and yet have enough to be able to shout and then thrust her head and shoulders over the edge of the embrasure.

"Help!" she called. "Help me! Help *us*!"

· · ·

Rory emerged from the passageway he'd been searching, immersed in cobwebs and with enough mice—more likely rat—droppings covering his boots to know that no one had been in that passage for years, possibly decades. Nor had there been any lingering smell of pitch or smoke from a torch other than his own. He'd not seen any priest-holes or walkways that went off in other directions, either.

He took a wash cloth from beside the basin on the dresser and took a moment to scrape the mess from his boots. Then he looked around, recognizing the dress Juliana had purchased folded over a chair. So this was the guest chamber she'd been given then. Instinctively, he glanced over to the bed.

Her night rail lay neatly folded across the counterpane. Without thinking, his feet led him to the bed. The night rail was made of rather heavy, unbleached linen without adornments, save for the ribbon that tied it closed at the neckline. A garment meant for Highland winter nights that she'd probably purchased while they were in Fort William. He picked it up, catching the faint scent of heather soap as he held it to his nose. She had used the same soap at Strae Castle, so the scent was familiar, but he thought he also caught a whiff of something that was uniquely her.

He looked back at the bed. It was definitely large enough for two, although an entwined couple didn't need that much room. How did she sleep? On her side curled up like a bairn? Or on her stomach like a babe? Or perhaps on her back, making it easy for him to slide a leg over... He pushed the thought away abruptly. This was not the time to be entertaining lecherous thoughts of her sprawled naked under him, night rail tossed aside. He looked at the garment as though it were the cause for his lust and laid it back on the bed. Then he glanced around once more.

The open wardrobe—through the back of which he'd entered the hidden passageway—held only the breeches and oversize shirt she'd worn to ride in. Her sturdy half boots were neatly placed side by side next to the chair, which meant she must be wearing slippers and had not intended to go outside. The only things on the dresser besides the pitcher and basin were a hairbrush and the wash cloth he'd just used. None of the furniture seemed out of place, and there was no sign of a struggle anywhere.

So where in the hell was she? And where were the MacDonnell lasses? They certainly wouldn't have gotten lost in their own home.

He left Juliana's chamber and went down the stairs to the library, where they'd all agreed to meet once they'd finished searching their individual passages. Perhaps someone else had found them.

But he knew he was wrong when he caught sight of the laird's and his brother's faces. He shook his head at their unspoken question.

"Mayhap Sima's found..." Calum began and then stopped as his wife walked into the room. No one needed to ask if she'd been successful, either.

"They canna have just disappeared," Rory said. "Ye are sure every room has been searched?"

Sima nodded tearfully. "I gave the instructions myself."

"And I ordered the stable lads to check every outbuilding as well," Calum said.

"Then the only thing that makes sense is Cameron

somehow managed to abduct them," Rory said slowly, not wanting to even think of the possibility. "He gained entrance at Strae Castle by bribing one of the new maids—"

"We have nae new servants," Sima replied.

"And if anyone is disloyal, he or she kens well the consequences," the laird added.

"Aye, but the fact is that Cameron and his men are gone. Did they leave because of the weather or because they had gotten what they came for?" Rory turned toward the door. "I am going back outside. There may be something I missed outside the walls."

"Tracks will have been covered with this blowing snow," Calum said.

"It doesna matter," Rory replied. "I may still find something."

He grabbed his plaid from the hook near the door and grimaced as he noted Juliana's cloak still there. If that damn bastard had taken her wearing just a gown... He cursed profoundly as he opened the door and strode out.

The snow was falling so heavily he could hardly see the barbican from the castle steps. Calum had been right. There would be no trace of tracks, but there were other things to look for. If there were a trace of evidence that Cameron had been at the walls—fresh scratches on the stone from climbing, a rock or two that had come loose, a bit of earth loosened and not yet frozen solid—he would find them. But first, he would question the man at the gate and find out who else had done duty.

He was nearly to the steps that led up to the barbican when he thought he heard something. It was faint, and for a moment he thought it was simply the sound of the wind. And then he heard it again. An odd lament that floated high above him.

He looked up, his hand shielding his eyes from the

swirling snow, but he could see nothing. Shaking his head, he started climbing the steps. What was he thinking? That a ghostie was floating about, wailing in distress? Then he heard it once more. And this time he could faintly make out words.

*"Help me! Help us!"*

He jerked around, staring upward once more. Was that something moving high on the tower battlement? He couldn't make it out clearly, but he heard the call once more.

Leaping from the steps, he raced back into the castle.

# Chapter Sixteen

Rory burst into the library, startling Calum and the laird.

"The tower! They're in the tower!"

"What?" The laird rose from behind his desk.

Calum stopped pacing. "Why would they—"

"I doona ken, but I heard Juliana calling for help. With this weather we doona have time to waste. Where's the entrance to—"

"This way." The laird strode past him before he'd finished speaking. Rory followed him, Calum hard on his heels.

They went down a corridor off the main hallway. It was narrower, with no doors opening to rooms. Only one wall sconce had a torch lit, so he assumed this led only to the tower. The laird made a sharp turn, momentarily disappearing from sight, but when Rory came around the corner, he saw the entrance door only a few feet away. Why the women would want to go up there on such a blustery day was a mystery, but one that could wait to be solved. Right now, they needed to get to them.

The laird reached for the latch, and Rory prayed they had

not bolted it from the inside. To his relief, the door creaked open, and that's when he noticed that the dust on the floor had been disturbed before. There was a clear line where the bottom of the door had scraped against the stone. None of the servants searching the rooms would probably have thought to come this way. Rory swore beneath his breath. If he'd inspected the castle himself, he would have seen this. Instead, he'd wasted time elsewhere. How long had the women been up there in the freezing cold?

Rory sprinted up the spiraling stairs, nearly running over MacDonnell, who had come to a stop at the top. A narrow platform in front of the door was barely large enough for the two of them. Rory knew from the way the old part of Strae Castle had been built that such a small space was meant to keep enemies from gathering to join forces to break down the door. It opened outward and most likely could be bolted shut from outside as well. He prayed again that it wasn't stuck on the other side.

"Is it locked?" he asked as the laird rattled the handle.

"I doona think so." He pushed at the latch. "It seems to be loose, though."

"Loose? Let me try."

The other man lifted a brow but stepped aside. Rory knew he had practically insulted him with his demand, but he'd make amends later.

"Juliana!" he yelled, hoping she could hear him through the thick door as he rattled the handle, too. It did indeed feel loose. And then he heard her faint voice.

"Rory? Is that you?"

"Aye. I'm here. We'll have ye out in nae time." At least he hoped they would. What in hell was wrong with the handle? It felt like it wasn't attached. "Juliana?" he called again.

"Yes?" Her voice was very faint.

"What happened on your side of the door that ye canna

get it open?"

"The...handle...came...off."

He could barely make out the words. She was probably so numb with cold that she was having trouble talking. He looked at the laird.

"Tell her to hold it in place and nae to let go when she feels it move. 'Tis the only way to force the latch back."

Rory repeated the words, hoping she'd understand. He thought he heard a muffled "I won't," but he wasn't sure. He made himself count slowly to five to give her time, but it felt as though he were wasting minutes. Then he shoved the handle on his side of the door hard and, holding it tightly in place, he began to turn it. For a moment he didn't know if it would catch, and then he felt a moment of resistance as it came in contact with the other piece. He pressed his shoulder against the door for extra strength, and the laird did the same. With yet another prayer, he finished turning the handle, and the door swung open with their added weight.

Rory stumbled to catch his balance, managing to right himself as Juliana toppled into his arms. The laird and Calum rushed past him to help Greer and Aileen up, and they bustled them quickly down the stairs.

Juliana looked up at him, her lips bluish and her skin tinged blue, too. She felt as cold as a block of ice, and her gown and hair were dripping wet. "You found..." she managed to say and then slumped against him into oblivion. He panicked for a moment but then felt her breath softly against his neck.

Bending slightly, he scooped her into his arms and swept a kiss across her icy forehead as he turned toward the steps. "Aye, lass. I found ye."

Rory kicked open the door to Juliana's bedchamber and strode to the bed, then hesitated before placing her on it. Her clothing was soaking wet and would only dampen the sheets. The gown definitely needed to be removed, and she would not appreciate finding out he'd been the one to undress her, even if she were currently not aware. He looked around and opted for the armchair near the hearth. Pulling it closer to the small fire with his boot, he lowered Juliana into it, then went to the door and shouted for a maid. When he heard no footsteps, he shouted again. Sima would be attending to her daughters, but surely that didn't require the whole staff.

He waited for what seemed like half an eternity with still no response and then grimaced as he remembered that Invergarry only housed a handful of servants. The rest came up daily from the village or surrounding crofts. With the storm raging, many had stayed home. It was entirely possible that everyone who was here was helping Sima at the moment. Furthermore, the castle was built in an *L* shape, and the family's quarters were on the other end, away from the guest chambers, so he could probably bellow like a bull and not be heard.

Turning back into the room, he considered the situation. It wasn't like he had never undressed a lass before, but the circumstances had been vastly different. For one, the lass was usually conscious. Secondly, the lass was a willing participant. Neither applied to Juliana. Still, he had to do something. The longer she stayed in those wet clothes, the more likely she'd become fevered.

He stoked the fire with two more logs and poked at it until he had a good blaze going, then rose to pull the counterpane and sheets back on the bed. He returned to kneel beside her and remove her sodden slippers and stockings. At any other time he would have appreciated the comely curve of her calf, but now he could only think her legs felt more like cold marble than human flesh. He took a moment to massage her toes, thankful they were not blue. Getting some circulation back was a start.

The gown that Sima had lent her was a simple affair with

the laces in front, but the configuration also had his fingers brushing Juliana's breasts as he loosened the bodice. In spite of trying not to think about female anatomy—her breasts were just the right size to fill his hands—his cock half rose in eager anticipation. For the first time in his life, Rory wondered if men really were complete eejits ruled by the smaller of their heads. That theory became more plausible when he hardened even more as he peeled the gown off Juliana and lifted her against him to push it down her back. Luckily for him she remained unconscious, and he eased her back on the chair while he tugged the gown completely off, leaving her in her chemise. Thankfully, it was a practical one made of heavy muslin that she must have purchased at Fort William and not of thin lawn that would be transparent.

Placing a hand to her side to determine how damp the chemise was, he breathed a sigh of relief that the wool of the gown had kept it from getting wet. What he definitely did not need right now was to see her naked—especially her nipples or the curls at the juncture of her thighs—even if his wayward cock tried to stand at attention.

He carried her to the bed and laid her on it, then pulled the covers up. He stood there for a moment, not liking how cold she still felt. She needed heated bricks in the bed to raise her body temperature, but his shouting for help earlier hadn't brought anyone here, and heating those bricks would take some time if they were to last long enough to be effective.

He was plenty warm. Near sweating from the fire and the clothing he wore. His body heat could warm her faster than waiting for bricks. He hesitated, though. Given how Juliana had reacted to sharing the bed—or *not* sharing it—at the inn in Spean, she would not take kindly to sharing *this* bed. Kindly *would be an understatement*, he thought wryly. Without a doubt, Juliana would be furious. He could almost see her eyes sparking and her red hair blazing in anger. He could also hear her tirade, some of which he didn't think ladies even knew.

But...she had not regained consciousness, so she might never know, although the fact that she had not awoken also bothered him. Had the freezing weather affected her brain? He touched her forehead, which was still nearly as cold as when he'd carried her in. That decided him.

Kicking off his boots, he stripped his shirt and vest and then stopped at his breeches. Taking them off would be dangerous. She certainly wouldn't understand, and having them off would only make his damn desire harder to control. Better to stay half-dressed for both their sakes.

Lifting the cover, he slipped beneath the sheets, then turned Juliana so her back was against his bare chest. He encircled her waist, drawing her close. The undersides of her breasts fell softly on his arm, and he bit back a groan. This was going to be pure hell, and he'd take his leave just as soon as she felt warm enough.

He just prayed Juliana would not wake until then.

...

Juliana drifted, her body floating free in the snowy cold. There was no feeling anywhere. She was weightless, rising and falling whichever way the wind swept her. There was nothing. Nothing but swirling whiteness around her.

And then, suddenly, something solid restricted her movements, and for a moment she wanted to struggle against whatever was keeping her from her peaceful oblivion, but it took too much effort to push against her bonds. She just wanted to go back to that placid, serene place...

Her mind gradually sensed that something had changed, but she was too exhausted to try and decipher what was happening. It was easier to stay in that faraway place instead of trying to think.

Slowly, she became aware that the cold no longer surrounded her. She could feel her limbs again, as though they had been detached and were only now returning to her body. There was the most delicious feeling of warmth in her toes, as though they were stuck in woolen socks that had been placed near a fire. Except the socks were moving, circling, pressing, and kneading… How could that be? Silly socks. She must be dreaming.

Yes, she was dreaming. Now she felt hands brush her breasts. That really was something she shouldn't be dreaming about at all. She needed to swat them away. She tried to raise her arm, but it felt too heavy to move. And…well, the sensation wasn't all that bad. It felt rather good. The hands moved down her arms, baring her skin in gentle strokes. A rather nice sensation, too. Maybe she should let it continue… *mmm*.

She felt her body shift. This time it didn't feel weightless as she flopped forward over something solid. Now those hands were sliding down her back, causing odd little tingles along their path. Something heavy was being stripped away, leaving her feeling free once more as she leaned back, wanting to burrow into the depths of wherever she was. She had never dreamed like this before.

And then she felt herself lifted. She struggled to open her eyes, but all she could manage was a flutter. Her mind stirred, flustered. Was that Rory's face she'd seen? She tried once more to open her eyes, but it was too hard. What in the world would Rory be doing in her dream? Her foggy mind tried to reason through it. He'd be horrified if he thought she was *dreaming* of him. Another thought broke through as her thinking started to clear. Maybe her mind was putting him there to spoil her dream, which she probably shouldn't be having. That was more likely. At least it was *her* dream and he'd never know.

She retreated into near oblivion again as she sank into a soft mattress. Maybe she was dreaming this, too. What she needed was sleep. She'd almost fallen asleep while she was floating in the swirling whiteness...only this was much warmer.

Much, *much* warmer. Suddenly it felt like her back was against a warm stove. Heat engulfed her. Heat was wrapping itself around her, pulling her closer to the source.

And then she caught the familiar scent of soap and leather. Her eyes sprang open as all remnants of dream swept from her brain like fog dissolving in front of a brisk wind. A strong, muscled arm encircled her waist. A *bare*, strongly muscled arm.

She didn't have to turn to look. Rory MacGregor had been no dream.

# Chapter Seventeen

Rory sensed the instant Juliana became fully aware of where she was. Although she didn't move, everything about her started to tense. He felt her lungs expand beneath his arm as she took a quick intake of breath. Her body became rigid. Even her hair seemed to stand on end. Or maybe that was because her temper was most probably rising.

"Ye are awake?"

There was silence, and for a moment, he didn't think she'd answer. Finally, without turning around, she spoke, her voice as icy as she had felt only moments ago.

"What are you doing naked in my bed?"

*Ah. That's the Juliana I know.* It was interesting, though, that she hadn't tried to move away from him. He smiled, in spite of the situation.

"I am nae naked, although I can oblige ye, if it will help ye get warm."

*That* got her moving. She scooted away from him faster than a bairn who'd just learned how to crawl and then sat up.

"I do not need that kind of help!"

Her eyes widened slightly as she took notice of him shirtless. Rory resisted the urge to flex any muscles but regretted that he'd left his breeches on. It would have been interesting to see where her gaze went if he'd inched the sheet below his waist a few inches.

Maybe she read his thoughts, because she did glance at the edge of the sheet, and he thought she blushed. He managed not to grin.

"I was only warming you with my body heat." He couldn't resist teasing a bit, just to see how she'd react. "It would have been easier if we'd both been naked, ye ken."

Her eyes rounded like an owl's, and she looked down as if to assure herself she was clothed. He bit back another grin, and a tiny devil prodded him. "I did ponder taking *everything* off ye."

Clenching the chemise to her, she scowled at him. "That would have been totally indecent." She looked to where her gown and stockings lay in a heap on the floor. "Did you remove my gown?"

"I did. 'Twas wet."

Juliana glared at him. "You could not have called a maid?"

"I tried, but no one came."

Her face flushed bright red. "It was still improper."

He shrugged, managing to stifle another grin. He couldn't remember Juliana ever acting so flustered. It was an interesting phenomenon. "Better improper than dead, lass. Ye were near frozen when I found ye."

Her brow furrowed. "You found me?"

He sobered. She didn't remember? "Aye. I heard ye call when I went outside to search for ye."

"Outside. In the storm…" Her voice trailed off.

An alarm started to sound in his head. "Ye were on the tower battlement. Do ye nae recall?" She looked at him quizzically, then slowly nodded, much to his relief.

"We went up there to see the view."

He frowned. That didn't make sense. "In a storm? Without your cloaks or even a shawl?"

"It had hardly begun to snow. We were just going to take a quick look."

Her face turned red again, and he chided himself for berating her. Greer and Aileen should have had more sense than to go up there, even if she hadn't. At least she remembered she had been up there.

"What happened? How did ye get locked out?"

"I... The handle on the door just came off." She wrapped her arms around herself and shivered. "It was so cold..."

"Aye. It was, and ye are still cold. Best ye get back under the covers." He got out of the bed on his side and held the covers up for her. "I'll get ye some warm bricks."

She shook her head and suddenly started shaking the fabric of her chemise. "I am not cold. In fact, I feel very hot."

Rory blinked, then looked closer. Her face was flushed again, and he hadn't said anything to embarrass her this time. Swiftly, he walked around to the bed to her side and laid his hand to her forehead. She felt like she was on fire, and the room was only minimally warm. And she hadn't been pressed against him for nearly ten minutes.

"Ye have a fever."

She shook her head, then stopped and put out a hand on the mattress to steady herself. "I feel fine, just a bit warm." She shivered again. "Or maybe not. Is it chilly in here?"

"Nae, lass. Ye need to lie down."

She looked up at him, her eyes overly bright. "Are you going to join me?"

His cock jerked, even though he knew she didn't mean the words as an invitation. Of any sort. Delirium could very well be setting in. He'd seen it before with high fevers. "Lie down now, lass. I…"

But he didn't need to finish the sentence. She'd already fallen back on the pillow.

"Ye should get some sleep, Mr. MacGregor."

Rory roused himself from the chair where he'd been dozing sporadically, waking himself up when his head nodded too far to one side or the other. He looked at Sima now, standing in the doorway to Juliana's bedchamber, holding a candle.

"I could say the same for ye."

She smiled, and he saw how tired she looked even in the light of the fire that had nearly gone out. He pushed himself out of the chair, gesturing for her to take it while he stoked the fire. He chided himself for letting it die down to near embers.

He glanced at the bed where Juliana lay. It didn't look like she'd moved at all, but what if she'd needed him? Some responsible caretaker he was if he couldn't even stay awake.

Sima had ignored his invitation to take the chair and gone over to check on Juliana. Both Greer and Aileen had come down with fevers, too, and he knew she'd been on her feet since yesterday morning taking care of them. He followed quickly.

"How is she?"

"About the same, I think." Sima rearranged the sheets over Juliana. "Her night rail is wet with sweat from the fever, but I doona see a reason to change it. She'll only dampen the second one, and exposing her skin to the air might make it worse."

"Are your daughters as bad off, too?"

"Aye. The fever still runs high with both of them."

"Mayhap we need to get a physician?"

"The closest one is in Fort Augustus." Sima's face set. "He probably wouldna come with the storm, even if one of our men could get through."

Rory felt a muscle twitch in his own jaw. Sima was right. The damn English dragoons would probably not deem it worthwhile to send their physician to help out a Scot. Although… "Juliana is nae only a Sassenach, she's sister to the Countess of Woodhaven. Would that nae make a difference?"

She shrugged. "It might, if the weather were fair, but they'll nae risk themselves or their horses in a blizzard."

Rory knew how easy it was to get lost in those conditions. Someone could become disoriented and travel in circles, even with excellent tracking skills. Still, he'd take his chances and ride the seven or eight miles to the fort.

"I am going to go."

"No…"

The sound had come from the bed. He and Sima both bent over Juliana. "Are ye awake?"

"No…do not…" Her eyelids fluttered. *"No…do not."* She took a shuddery breath and drifted back off to sleep.

Rory straightened. "I am—"

"No." This time the word came from Sima. "Ye heard the lass. She doesna want ye to go."

He looked back at Juliana, slumbering oblivious to the world again. "We doona ken if she even heard us."

"Whether she did or dinna, the message is still the same."

"Message?"

Sima gave him a level look. "A message. Mayhap from the fae if nae from her. Doona question from where, just heed the advice."

"But…" He couldn't totally dispute Sima's theory when even he'd suspected the fae in having a hand in this whole debacle of rescuing Juliana. A man might not openly admit to believing in their existence, but a prudent Scot wouldn't tempt the faeries, either. "I canna just sit here and do nothing."

"Ye *are* doing something." Sima patted his hand and picked up the candle she'd put on the bedside table and walked to the door. "The lass seems to sense your presence. 'Tis why ye need to stay."

He looked at Juliana again after Sima had gone. Did she really know he was here? Or had she been mumbling in a dream she was having? He hated feeling helpless.

He moved to the window, where dawn was breaking. Outside, the storm continued to rage, but there was also a storm raging inside him. He'd been an idiot to tease Juliana, enjoying making her blush while it had been the fever spiking that was making her face red. He truly was an eejit.

He walked back to the bed and took her hand, which felt like she'd just held it over the fire. "I doona ken what I can do for ye, but I am here, lass. Doona die on me."

...

Juliana continued to fade in and out of consciousness. Sometimes her eyes would flutter open and the brightness of the day would cause her to close them. When she'd open them again, the room would be dark, save for the flicker of a candle and the banked fire in the hearth. But always, she saw Rory sitting in a chair nearby. Once, at night, she wanted to ask him why he was there, but the effort to speak was too much, and she'd drifted into oblivion once more.

But her fever made the nightmare of two years past return.

Once again, she was six and ten and back at the Earl of Woodhaven's country estate. Her sister Emily—the countess then—had gone to visit a neighbor. Leaving Juliana and Lorelei at home should have been perfectly safe. The earl was snoring away the effects of opium he'd purchased from one of the dens in London, but no one had thought one of his gaming hell cronies would arrive at the door that afternoon.

*Baron Bistrow pushed past the elderly butler and demanded to see the earl. Juliana stupidly fancied herself the lady of the manor, since Emily was gone, and told the baron he could speak with her. Lorelei, just a year younger, peered down from the banister and caught the baron's attention. Knowing that the earl's friends were all unsavory sorts, Juliana told Lorelei to go back upstairs. Surprisingly, for once, her sister didn't argue.*

*Juliana led the baron into the library, thinking it would be a better place to conduct whatever business he wanted to discuss than the front parlor. Unfortunately, the library door had a bolt. She tried to scream when he locked it, but he was too fast. He clamped a hand over her mouth and ripped the bodice of her gown before she fully realized what was happening.*

*"I came to collect the gambling debt Woodhaven owes me," he said, "but I'll take you in exchange for it."*

*She bit his hand, which only resulted in a backhanded slap from him that made her world go hazy. He grabbed one breast roughly and squeezed hard while he stuck his tongue down her throat so far she gagged. She fought, flailing at him with her fists and kicking until finally he yanked a handful of hair and pulled her head back.*

*"If ye keep fighting, I will take that pretty little sister of yours next."*

*When she looked into his eyes, she knew he meant it. "If I stop fighting, do you promise me you will not harm her?"*

*He laughed, but he finally nodded. She went limp after that and let him do what he wanted. Afterward, she lay on the floor, bruised and bleeding and no longer a virgin.*

"No. No..." She sensed another presence in the room.

Was it the baron? Dear Lord! She had to escape! She tried to force her eyes open. "No...!"

And then she felt someone take her hand. It was a gentle, soothing touch, as was the voice. Not the baron, then. Whoever it was, she felt no danger. Perhaps there were guardian angels after all. With a sigh, she slept.

When Juliana woke again, the sun was streaming through the partially closed curtains on the window. She squinted against the brightness, letting her eyes adjust, then opened them once more and gazed at the ceiling. Memories came flooding back. Going to the tower. The door handle breaking off. The cold—the horrible, bitter, icy cold—and then Rory finding her. She had a vague recollection of him carrying her. She thought he might have undressed her as well, but she wasn't sure. It could have been a fever dream. She might have imagined the whole thing, since there was no reason for him, of all people, to remove her clothes. There were maids. Still, it had seemed so real. And *pleasant*. Unlike the nightmare.

Slowly, she turned her head on the pillow to look around and felt her eyes widen at the sight of Rory asleep, slumped in a chair near the bed. So that part had been real. She had seen him when she briefly awoke. Had the other part—his taking her clothes off—been real, too? A strange little tingle coursed through her.

Maybe it hadn't been a fever dream.

# Chapter Eighteen

Rory opened his eyes to find Juliana lying on her side, head propped on her arm, watching him. He pushed himself upright in his chair.

"Ye are awake!"

"Yes." She started to sit up, then fell back. "Oh."

"Careful." He was up in an instant and beside the bed. With a by-now practiced hand, he felt her forehead. Her skin was much cooler. "I think your fever has broken."

"I hope so." She tried to sit again and fell back once more. "I feel dizzy."

"'Tis nae surprising." He took an extra pillow and plumped it up, then started to lean over her. She gave him a wary look.

"What are you doing?"

He stared at her. *Does she think I'm going to take advantage of her? Now? Like this?* He frowned. He'd just spent…but no, she wouldn't know that he had been sitting by her bedside throughout this ordeal. "I am going to help ye sit up. Ye are weak as an unwhelped pup."

Her brow furrowed. "You are comparing me to a dog?"

"Nae. Well…aye, but I doona mean an insult." He leaned over once more and put a hand under each of her elbows to prop her against the headboard. Then, to lighten the moment—or perhaps to squelch the instant desire that rose at their closeness—he added, "I am quite fond of dogs, ye ken."

He saw a spark flare in her eyes and couldn't help but grin in relief. If he was already riling her, she must be feeling much better. Although there was no reason to cause her strain by arguing. "Are ye thirsty?"

She looked as though she were going to argue anyway, then simply nodded. He poured water from the pitcher into a glass. "Do ye want help?"

She gave him an arch look and held out her hand. "I think I can manage to drink by myself."

"If ye wish." He put the glass into her hand and folded her fingers around it. He could feel her hand tremble beneath his and tried not to think of how often he'd stroked that soft, small hand while she lay fevered. He held on, guiding the glass to her lips.

"I can do this. I am not a child."

He didn't need to be told. Everything male in him was aware of everything female in her. Ever since undressing Juliana and then getting into bed with her half-naked, he'd been able to think of little else. Except her possibly dying of fever. Now that she had come back to life, he needed to push all those fanciful thoughts aside.

"I ken ye are nae a bairn, but Sima would prefer nae to have to change the sheets if ye spill the water everywhere." He held on to the glass firmly. She managed a feeble glare, but apparently thirst won out over sparring with him. She started to drink in big gulps.

"Nae so fast." He eased the glass away. "Ye doona want it all to come back up."

Her brows drew together again, but she didn't argue. "Where is Sima? I need to thank her for her help."

"She's been taking care of Greer and Aileen. They've been fevered, too."

She gave him a strange look that he couldn't quite decipher. "How long have I been abed?"

"'Tis the beginning of the fourth day."

Her eyes widened. "Fourth day?"

"Aye." He tilted his head to study her, wondering if she'd been aware of him at all. "What do ye remember?"

"I remember being on the roof by the tower. I remember that you found us..." She closed her eyes briefly, then opened them and looked at him. "I should thank you for that. You saved my life—"

"I was almost too late."

"You had no way of knowing where we were. No one did." She grimaced. "It was all my fault. I was really stupid."

To hear Juliana be so humble and self-blaming was a bit disconcerting and made him oddly uncomfortable. "Ye couldna have kenned the handle would break off."

"It was still an asinine thing to do."

"'Tis past. Do ye remember anything else?"

She grew thoughtful. "I remember you carrying me, I think."

"I did. Ye swooned."

"I do not swoon!" For a moment she looked indignant then sighed. "Well, I suppose I did at that. It was so cold."

"Ye were near half-frozen." He really wanted to know if she remembered anything else. She'd had that brief period of consciousness when she'd awakened to find him pressed against her. He should explain that now that she was lucid again. But if she didn't remember, maybe he shouldn't bring it up. "Is that all ye remember?"

She looked away from him and stared into the fire

burning in the hearth. For a long moment, she didn't speak. He was beginning to wonder if the flames had mesmerized her when she finally turned to him.

"You undressed me and crawled into bed with me, didn't you? It was not a dream, was it?"

Rory took a deep breath. He might as well get this over with. "I did, but—"

"There is no need to explain." She smiled suddenly. "I was afraid I had been delusional."

He wasn't sure if he'd heard correctly. Juliana wasn't angry? Had she just said…? His bewildered brain was just fathoming its way around her words when the door opened and Sima poked her head in.

"Oh, good! Ye are finally awake," she said.

"I am. Please come in," Juliana answered.

Rory bit back a groan. Damn it. Now he'd never find out what she'd meant.

...

By the next morning, Juliana was feeling well enough to join Greer and Aileen in the solar. The blizzard had finally blown through and sunshine shone through the windows, making the room bright and cheerful. And *warm*. Juliana looked at the flames burning merrily in the hearth. She didn't think she'd ever take a warm fire for granted again.

"'Tis good to see all three of ye up and about," Sima said as she brought in scones fresh from the oven, along with strawberry jam and clotted cream. She set the tray down on the low table between the settees and took a chair. "Mayhap now I can get some rest myself."

Juliana looked at the sisters. "Did you both sleep through three full days like I did?"

"For the first day," Aileen answered, "but then Greer

started having nightmares and kept waking me up."

"What were they about?"

Greer shrugged. "Being frozen. We couldn't get the door open."

"Well, that seems reasonable, considering our circumstances." Juliana wasn't about to reveal the contents of her own horrible nightmare. "I guess I was lucky not to relive that."

"Aye. And lucky ye dinna keep getting woken up," Aileen said.

Greer glowered at her. "Ye caused enough noise on your own, blawing like ye did."

"And ye were both acting like crabbits by yesterday." Sima put an end to the conversation that sounded like it would escalate into an argument. She looked at Juliana. "I am just glad Rory was willing to look after ye."

Juliana felt herself blush as all eyes turned on her. So she hadn't been delusional when she kept waking up and seeing him there. Something warm fluttered through her belly at the thought that he had stayed with her, which she tried to ignore. He was kind and thoughtful, but it didn't mean he cared about her personally. He had told her shortly after their escape from the Camerons that he'd sworn to bring her home. Presumably, that meant alive and healthy. She'd spent enough time with Rory to know he was a man who kept his word, and that was important to her. But, in his mind, she was a responsibility. Something that had to be delivered to Strae Castle. And, she reminded herself, since her stomach had turned all mushy and warm thinking about him, there was the matter of Morag. Now that the snow had finally stopped falling, she would be returning, and he would honor whatever bond was between them. He was probably looking forward to that now that Juliana was mending.

"He probably did not want me to be more of an imposition

on you than we already have been."

"Ye are nae an imposition, lass," Sima said.

Greer giggled. "And I doona think *Rory* thinks of ye as one, either."

Juliana frowned slightly. "What do you mean?"

Aileen arched a brow. "He is verra protective of ye."

"He promised his brother and my sister he'd bring me home after I got abducted," Juliana replied. "He probably acts like a guard so I do not get into another situation that he has to rescue me from again."

The sisters exchanged glances, and both of them grinned.

"If that is what ye want to call him," Aileen said.

"He certainly seems to take his *guarding* ye seriously." Greer giggled again. "'Tis a wonder he didna crawl into the bed with ye."

Juliana felt her face warm again. Luckily, no one had walked in on them when he *had* crawled into bed to get her warm. A totally different kind of warmth flooded through her as she remembered, settling into a strange pulsing between her thighs. "That would not have been proper."

"Aye, it would have been," Sima said. "Ye are handfasted, nae?"

"Handfasted?" Greer stared at her.

"Ye didn't tell us that." Aileen's voice sounded accusing.

Juliana blinked. Rory must have told the laird and his brother—and Sima—the whole story about their ruse. "He only said that to convince the Camerons to let us go. He did not *mean* it."

The sisters exchanged glances again, and this time neither of them smiled. Juliana looked from one to the other. "What? Maybe saying we were handfasted was a lie, but it worked to help us get away. It is not like I am actually going to hold Rory to it. He knows I do not intend to marry."

"But ye agreed to it, aye?" Sima asked.

"I...I... Yes, I did." Juliana frowned. "But I did not have a choice. Not if we were going to be believed."

Aileen and Greer glanced at each other again.

"Did Rory just tell Neal Cameron?" Greer asked.

Juliana frowned. "No. His father was there, too."

Aileen looked thoughtful. "Anyone else?"

"Well...yes. We were in the great hall, so I imagine a whole lot of people—at least the ones nearby—heard it. But that still does not mean anything."

"I am afraid it does," Sima said.

"*What?*" Juliana shook her head. "Rory was not actually proposing to me."

"'Twould have been easier if he had."

Juliana stared at her. "Why?"

Sima studied her for a moment before answering, as if she were trying to choose her words carefully. "In Scotland, a handfasting is as binding as marriage. At least, for a year and a day. After that, either of ye may decide to leave."

"Yes, I understand that is a somewhat common practice," Juliana replied, "but only if both parties meant what they said at the time. This was simply a ploy to get us away."

"'Tis still binding," Greer said.

"*Especially* since there were witnesses," Aileen added. "The Camerons and the MacLeans all heard Rory declare ye to be handfasted. And ye said ye agreed. That makes it real, whether ye like it or not."

"That cannot be true! In England, a woman—or a man—can cry off a betrothal. Especially when nothing...nothing... *carnal* has happened." Juliana lifted her chin. "That is what we will do."

That remark was met with total silence. Juliana looked from one woman to another, an odd prickling of trepidation beginning at her nape. "What is it?"

"Ye cannot simply 'cry off,' as ye say. Ye are both honor-bound to uphold your oaths," Sima finally replied. "By Scottish law, ye are legally married."

"But...but that would mean..."

Greer giggled, and Aileen looked amused. Juliana didn't see anything funny in it at all. They didn't understand that she never intended to let another man near her again. Not in *that* way. She caught Sima watching her and struggled to maintain composure. This could not be happening. "I would be Rory's wife?"

"Ye *are* Rory's wife," the older woman answered. "In every sense of the word."

Why had Rory not explained what handfasting really meant? Juliana had asked herself that question dozens of times over the last several hours since she'd returned to her bedchamber to rest.

Not that she was getting any rest. Her mind was galloping full speed, like a horse bolting from an open stable door. Except *her* door was closed, not open. Actually locked, from what Sima had said. There was no escape—at least for a year and a day—so perhaps banging her head against a wall would more aptly fit how she presently felt.

If she had thought, for even one small second, that agreeing to be handfasted was *truly* binding, would she still have done it? Juliana rolled over and curled into a fetal position. The truth was, she probably would have gone along with anything to escape Neal Cameron. There was no doubt what the conclusion of her abduction would have been if Rory had not shown up. Neal had made his intention to bed her quite clear.

But Rory knew that declaring them handfasted was lawful in Scotland. So why had he chosen to claim her? She'd thought it was simply the easiest way to leave without a brawl. He was only one man against dozens of Camerons. But could he not have called Neal out simply for taking her from Strae Castle? It wouldn't even have had to be a duel. Fisticuffs probably would have worked, since men seemed to find some kind of strange honor from fighting. Then she remembered something he'd said about not wanting to draw the ire of King George by having a MacGregor start a clan skirmish so soon after they'd been un-proscribed.

That left her with another dilemma. She lifted her head so she could punch her pillow and then plopped back on it. According to Sima, handfasting meant Rory was within his rights to demand her presence in his bed. That thought sent a cold chill down her spine, while at the same time heat coursed through her body. She never, ever again wanted to endure anything like she'd experienced that horrible afternoon in the Woodhaven library. *Never. Ever.* That's why she didn't intend to marry.

And yet... She recalled the kiss Rory had given her after Neal had demanded it. The kiss had been gentle, almost inquisitive. Definitely indulgent and unhurried, as though he had hours of time. When she'd gasped involuntarily at the unexpectedly pleasant sensation, he hadn't stuck his tongue down her throat and choked her.

She rolled to her other side. Rory hadn't taken advantage of claiming his rights, either, not even the night at Spean when there had been only one bed. Or when she'd told him he could have the bed. He'd not so much as *mentioned* that he had any rights. Not once since they'd escaped from Neal. Even when she woke up to find him half-naked in her bed, he'd had a logical explanation for that. She felt her face warm as she remembered how he'd appeared with the sheet down to his waist. How broad his shoulders were, how muscular his arms, how tight the ridges of his belly... Then more heat infused her face as she recalled her rather brusque admonishment. Perhaps she had been a bit harsh. Rory had done nothing untoward. He could have lawfully done as he wished with her, but he had not attempted to even kiss her again. She flopped unto her back. She had no explanation for his behavior, especially when he *knew* what handfasting meant.

Her body suddenly went cold, as a thought washed over her like a pail of icy water. There was an explanation. Actually, it was probably the only explanation. He didn't want her because he didn't *desire* her. While that probably wouldn't matter to most men, she'd gotten to know Rory well enough to realize he wasn't one of those men. He would want a woman who *wanted* him, one who would respond to him with passion. Who wouldn't hold back. He'd spent enough time with her—she and her sisters had been at Strae Castle for nearly six months—to know she wasn't that woman.

That she was only his responsibility because he had sworn to return her could not have been made more clear than by the fact that he had not said a word about his rights. She couldn't very well bring the subject up, either, since he hadn't. Besides, she didn't want to hear a rejection, no matter how gently he might phrase it. If she asked him, he wouldn't lie.

With a sigh, she sat up and pushed the covers back. She wasn't going to get any rest this afternoon, and she might as well go back downstairs and help prepare dinner. It was the least she could do after lying abed for nearly four days.

She stepped out into the hall, about to go downstairs, when she heard feminine voices drifting up from the foyer. And then she heard a name she'd been dreading.

Morag had returned home.

# Chapter Nineteen

Juliana followed the sound of the female voices to the sitting room across from the great hall and then paused a few steps away from the door. A part of her wanted to retreat back up the stairs, stay sheltered in her room, and pretend that Morag had not returned. Almost as quickly as that thought entered her mind, she dismissed it. She was not a coward. She was going to have to meet the girl sometime. It might as well be now. Juliana took a deep breath, lifted her chin, and squared her shoulders. Then she marched into the parlor.

And nearly tripped over her toes as she abruptly stopped and tried not to stare. The delicate creature perched on the edge of the settee could only be Morag, since Aileen and Greer were the only two others in the room. Her stomach suddenly felt like she'd swallowed lead. She had assumed Morag would be pretty—Rory was a handsome man—but she hadn't expected...*this*.

The girl was petite, with alabaster skin that looked like porcelain. Long, glossy black hair—so inky it shimmered blue in the parlor light—curled itself around her shoulders like a shawl and flowed down her back, but it was her eyes that were intriguing. A pale shade of grey that was almost silvery, fringed with thick, dark lashes that gave her an otherworldly look. She was, Juliana had to admit, beautiful. Any man with one working eye would agree.

The girl turned and smiled at her, revealing perfectly straight white teeth along with a slight dimple that made her face even more engaging.

"And who might ye be?"

Juliana cast a surreptitious glance at Aileen and Greer. As friendly as Morag seemed to be, they probably hadn't told her yet. At least not about the handfasting. Well, *she* certainly was not going to be the one to break the news. Perhaps it could truly remain a secret.

"I am Juliana Caldwell—"

"Ye are English?"

She hadn't wanted to point that out, although she supposed it was inevitable once she spoke. "Yes. My sister Emily recently married Ian MacGregor."

"Ian? *Ian* got married?"

The girl started to laugh, a soft tinkling, like distant bells that sounded a little otherworldly, too. Juliana did not believe in faeries—other than the made-up ones in the tales she'd been told as a child—but in Scotland, people did seem to harbor the notion that such creatures might exist. What was it they called the ones who appeared as human? Changelings? She scoffed at herself. The girl—Morag—was human. As if to attest to that fact, Morag removed the pelisse she still wore, revealing a *quite* buxom bosom. She wouldn't need any help from faeries attracting a man.

Juliana shook her head to clear it. It didn't matter. "Ian and my sister got married a little over a week ago." Goodness. Had it not even been two weeks since she'd been happily—more or less—ensconced at Strae Castle? So much had happened in such a short time.

Morag looked puzzled. "So did Ian bring his wife and ye to Invergarry?"

"No. I...er, I was traveling..." Juliana wasn't sure how much she should say. Since Aileen and Greer hadn't told Morag the real story, perhaps it would be best to stick with the invented one. "I was nearly accosted on the road, and Rory MacGregor happened along—"

"Rory is here?" Morag nearly bounced off the settee as she turned to Aileen and Greer. "Rory is here?"

"Aye," Greer said, "but—"

"'Tis a long story," Aileen interrupted, "and can be told later."

Juliana shot her a grateful look. "I am afraid the storm that came through caused us to seek shelter here. He—Mr. MacGregor—did not know where else to bring me."

Morag smiled again. "Well, I am glad the storm brought ye here. I canna imagine how put out I would be to find Rory had stopped by and I was gone." She looked around as though he might be lurking in a corner somewhere. "Where is he?"

"I do not know," Juliana answered, thankful it was the truth. He and Calum and the laird had gone somewhere that morning and hadn't returned.

"Well, that will give me time to freshen up, then." Morag stood. "I willna take long. I want to be waiting when he gets back."

Unfortunately, she wasn't going to have to wait at all. Juliana heard the large front door open and then the tramp of boots that halted just outside the parlor.

Rory poked his head in, but before he could say anything, Morag shrieked and ran to him, throwing her arms around his neck. "How nice that ye've come to see me, Rory MacGregor!"

• • •

Rory unwrapped the tentacle-like arms from around his neck and managed a smile as he stepped back. He had hoped Morag had gotten over whatever infatuation she'd had last year, but apparently not. And why would she think he'd come to Invergarry to see *her* when Juliana was with him? He glanced from her to Aileen and Greer, who both looked at him speculatively. Juliana seemed to be studying a painting on the wall rather intensely. He grimaced inwardly. Morag hadn't been told anything about how they'd come to be here. Her next words proved his assumption.

"Ye are just the Christmas present I've wished for!"

A strange strangling sound came from Juliana, although she was still concentrating on the painting. Greer started to giggle, only to have it turn into an "oomph" when Aileen elbowed her.

He shook his head. "As intriguing as that sounds, I doona think we will be staying that long. Once the road clears—"

"Nonsense! Yule is but five days away!" Morag ran her hand along his sleeve. "Ye can help me find the mistletoe."

Another strange sound from Juliana, but this time she turned to face them. "I would really like to get back to Strae Castle in time for the holiday."

Morag glanced at her. "Of course. My father can arrange for an escort. Ye might be able to leave tomorrow morning."

"I…" Juliana paused, then pasted a smile on her face. "That would—"

"—not be possible," Rory finished for her. *Juliana isn't going anywhere without me.* "My brother would be furious if I didna bring his sister-by-marriage home myself." Then he added for effect, "…and ye ken what Ian's temper can be like."

Morag furrowed her brow. "How would he ken ye found

her? Juliana said ye just happened by when she was accosted on the road."

Juliana wasn't looking at him again, but she must have told Morag a part of the story she'd used in Fort William and not mentioned the Camerons or the abduction. Perhaps just as well for now. Still. He had to come up with something. "Actually, Ian sent me to find her."

Juliana turned startled eyes to him, and he gave her a barely discernible shake of his head, hoping she'd not contradict him, which, unfortunately, she loved to do.

Morag's furrow turned into a frown. "Why would he send ye?"

"Ye wound me, lass." Rory gave her a lazy smile. "Ye do ken I am the best tracker the MacGregors have?"

Juliana rolled her eyes—luckily Morag had her back to her—but at least she didn't *say* anything. Then, just as he was about to relax a bit with the direction things were going, Morag turned to Juliana.

"Did ye get lost? And where were ye going anyway? Invergarry is nae close to Strae Castle."

"Well, ye see, it—"

"I did not get lost." Juliana cut him off. "I…um…joined a small group of people traveling north after the wedding and my sister didn't approve, so Ian sent Rory to find me and take me back."

Rory arched a brow. It was a rather clever twist of the truth, he'd give Juliana that.

Morag looked at him skeptically. "How long did it take ye to find her?"

He wasn't sure if she was insulting his ability to track or if she was fishing for something else. Before he could come up with an explanation, Juliana spoke again.

"Mr. MacGregor caught up to us outside Fort William, but our…assailants…had singled me out, and to get away from them, Rory thought it best we ride west."

He appraised Juliana again. She had quite a talent for embellishment. They'd been *miles* outside Fort William, and she'd been "singled out" while she was still at Strae Castle, but the story wasn't complete fabrication. He *had* thought it best they rode west.

"Rather than risk being waylaid again by going back the way I'd come," he said, "I thought if we came north, we could find refuge here."

That seemed to pacify Morag, although Juliana narrowed her eyes slightly. He wasn't sure why, but at least he was telling the truth.

"Ye were right to come here." Morag patted his arm again. "'Tis as if the fae sent ye to me after all."

Rory bit back a groan, wondering if she might be right. The faeries took delight in meddling...and the present situation was becoming muddled.

...

Juliana listened to the exchange of words as she pretended to study a painting on the wall. If anyone asked her later, she probably wouldn't be able to describe it, but her ears were working quite well at the moment.

Morag thought Rory was a Christmas present? And *he* thought it was an *intriguing* idea? He probably thought gathering mistletoe with Morag was intriguing, too, but Juliana hadn't wanted to hear that, so she'd interrupted, saying that she'd really like to get back to Strae Castle in time for the holiday.

She and her sisters had always celebrated Christmas together. Well, "celebrated" might be putting too much of a glorification to it. When Papa and Mama had been alive, there had always been presents, although not expensive ones, since Papa too often invested in inventions that were not successful. Still, they'd always had a tree, decorated with strings of cranberries and popcorn, and Mama would roast a goose that would be shared with the two or three servants that remained loyal to her father, the baron. That had all changed after their parents had died and Emily had been forced to marry the earl to keep a roof over their heads. *Those* Christmases had more often been spent huddled in Emily's bedchamber with the door bolted, hoping the earl would sleep off the effects of opium from his gaming hell or, better yet, not come home at all.

But what had mattered was that the three sisters had been together. Of course, Emily's marriage to Ian had changed that. For certain, there would be no reason to stay hidden in a locked room.

She turned her attention to Morag and tried to appear nonchalant at the offer of an escort for her the next morning. *Her.* Not *them.* There was no doubt Morag was determined to keep Rory at Invergarry for Yule. What did surprise her, though, was Rory's answer. And then, of course, the subterfuge had begun.

Once she'd started talking, she couldn't seem to stop. She felt like she was digging a hole with each semitruthful explanation she gave. And Rory simply stood there, staring at her, letting her fall deeper into the pit of her dubious creativity. She'd been racking her brain for some logical reason they'd ridden all the way here when he'd finally seen fit to take over the conversation.

At least he hadn't mentioned the Camerons, although claiming to seek refuge at Invergarry was all Morag apparently needed to convince herself he'd chosen the place because of her. Juliana stifled a snort. The fae hadn't sent him—*them*—here at all. Bloody Neal Cameron had. A man who was only too human. And Rory hadn't bothered to correct Morag before he'd made an excuse to leave.

Aileen and Greer were watching her expectantly, and Morag looked as though she wanted to ask more questions. Juliana didn't want to get any more tangled in the web she had just woven. It wouldn't take too long before Morag started thinking about how long it had taken them to get to Invergarry and where they'd spent the nights. Best to turn the conversation to another topic entirely. She pasted a smile on her face.

"It seems I will be indulging in your hospitality for Christmas, after all. What traditions do you follow?"

"We call it Yule here," Aileen said. "'Tis a mixture of English, Norse, and Celt mingled together."

"It lasts several days, not just one," Greer added, "and it ends with a bonfire that everyone from the glen is invited to attend."

At least it wasn't a ball like the one the Campbells had given. The one where she'd met the infernal Neal Cameron.

Her mind went back to the brief conversation in the parlor. She was grateful nothing had been said about being handfasted, but the thought niggled at her brain as to why Rory had not informed her of the implication of those words.

*Is it because he's looking forward to spending the Yule festivities with Morag?*

# Chapter Twenty

Since the storm had passed, it seemed the entire household at Invergarry rose with new vigor, like hibernating bears awakening and hungry for food. Juliana hadn't slept well, and she hadn't seen even a glimpse of Rory since he'd disappeared from the parlor yesterday afternoon. He and the MacDonnell men had been huddled behind closed doors in the library, and dinner had consisted of bread, dried beef, and cheese left out on platters. The kitchen staff was too busy to prepare a real meal, since the Yule holiday feast approached and they'd been delayed by the blizzard in making preparations.

Everyone certainly seemed to be making up for it now. Juliana helped herself to morning porridge from the sideboard—at least it was hot—and looked for a place to sit. Not that there wasn't space. She was the only one in the smaller dining room off the kitchen, but empty plates had been left behind and, it seemed, most of the servants had taken off as well.

She pondered that as she added sugar to the semiwarm tea still in a pot on the table. Scots really didn't see their help as servants, possibly because some of them, maybe even most, were kin, due to the clan system. Even though old King George had banned the clans and taken away legal power from their lairds, the ties were still strong.

The MacGregors had been slow to accept the three of them, especially since Emily had been given a special dispensation by the king to the title of Strae Castle *and* she came with the title of Countess of Woodhaven. It was something of a minor miracle that Emily and Ian had fallen in love.

While she and Rory had argued. About everything. She couldn't remember when they'd agreed about anything. It was probably a miracle that he'd come after her at all. Juliana pushed her half-eaten porridge away. *That* was the crux of her problem. Rory had come after her and, because they hadn't actually argued over every single thing, she'd let herself get lulled into thinking… Well. She wasn't sure what exactly her thoughts were, but she knew her feelings about him were changing. She knew the kiss at the MacLean home had been forced. She knew Rory took his responsibility to bring her home seriously. He hadn't taken advantage of their situation when he could have, especially now that she knew he was her husband according to Scottish law. He'd acted the gentlemen and treated her with respect. That should have given her a great sense of relief. Yet… Somehow, it didn't.

She took another sip of tea—cold now—and made a face as she rose, wishing she knew what was wrong with her.

...

Rory had gotten up before dawn to break his fast and then headed to the stables, not bothering to wake the stable lad who was supposed to be keeping watch. He remembered all too well how tedious that job could be, especially on a cold night when the stable was nice and warm and fresh hay offered a good pallet on which to sleep.

He smiled as he led Baron out of his stall and then stopped as he saw shadowy figures waver near the stable door. Before he could reach for his sword, Calum emerged out of the still-dark night. Rory glanced behind him but saw no one else. He raised an eyebrow.

"What brings ye out so early?"

"I could ask ye the same thing," Calum replied.

Rory shrugged. "I thought I might ride out and see if I can find tracks in the new snow."

"Ye think the Camerons may have come back?"

"I want to make sure they dinna."

The other man gave him a shrewd look. "Ye ken for certain 'twas them?"

"I have nae proof, except here." Rory tapped his head. "And I ken Neal Cameron will nae give up without a fight."

"Does he care so verra much for Juliana then?"

The question made Rory's temper rise. The bastard had no right to Juliana. He should have let her be when she'd declined his attention at the Campbell ball and most definitely when she'd done it again at Ian's wedding. Instead, he'd abducted her. If Rory hadn't caught up to them when he did—or if Cameron had stopped to shelter the first night— who knew what might have happened? He clenched his fists, then unclenched them, since Calum was looking rather pointedly at him.

"Ye care about the lass."

Rory opened his mouth to deny it, then snapped it shut. Calum hadn't stated it as a question. And… Well, damn it, he did care. Or, at least, he was starting to. Who would have thought someone who argued with him constantly and generally drove him barmy would be someone he found attractive? Perhaps not the right word. Certainly, lust lurked in him, had stirred ever since that kiss in MacLean's hall, but since their escape, he'd come to appreciate Juliana's inner strength. She hadn't once complained about conditions, although he knew she'd been miserable on the ship and not felt much better on the horse. The weather had been miserable, too, but, in spite of her tart tongue, she had borne the adversities stoically. And then, when she'd been so ill with the fever…

"I ken Neal Cameron didna like my stealing Juliana from him." Rory ignored Calum's statement and focused on the question he'd asked. "What he cares about is his pride, and he'll nae let it rest that we made a fool of him."

"Ye may be right. Hold a minute and I will ride with ye."

"Ye doona have to—"

"Mayhap not." Calum made quick work of saddling his own horse. "But if he is out there, he will most likely nae be alone. Besides, I ken the territory better than ye do."

Rory could hardly argue the point, since this was MacDonnell land. He mounted. "I'm grateful to ye, then."

"Think nothing of it," Calum said as he settled in the saddle. "My brother will be expecting both of us to go on the hunt this morning, so 'tis better ye have another pair of eyes to look."

"And if we find Cameron?"

"Well, then, the lad will be our guest for Yule." Calum grinned. "Trussed up like a turkey."

Rory laughed and spurred his horse lightly. "A worthy feast indeed!"

• • •

After they'd gone, Morag stepped out of the shadows that she'd slipped into when she'd entered the stable behind Calum. She'd actually planned to surprise Rory—he'd locked his bedchamber door last night, but she'd huddled in a far corner of the hall to make sure that English bitch wasn't going to knock on his door—so she'd seen him leave this morning. Unfortunately, for whatever reason, her uncle had seen fit to rise early as well and had spoiled her chances of a tryst.

They had lied to her. The Sassenach hadn't been accosted on the road at all. Rory had chased after her and stolen her away. Why? Uncle Calum had asked if he cared for the slut. Rory hadn't answered.

Morag narrowed her eyes. No Englishwoman was going to get her hands on Rory MacGregor. He was *hers*. She had the next four days to prove it to him. And…if Neal Cameron wanted the Sassenach, the Morag would be happy to help him get her.

She'd just go back to her nice, warm bed and think of how to do just that.

# Chapter Twenty-One

Rory and Calum returned to the castle, not having found any signs that Neal had circled back. While that was good news, Rory still didn't trust that the man had returned to the MacLean holding for good. His instinct told him Cameron was just lying low...and his instincts were rarely wrong.

Most of the men had already ridden out to hunt, and he would join them, but since he still felt a sense of trepidation, perhaps this would be a good time to give Juliana a lesson on how to defend herself with a knife. A bairn could have taken away the one she'd purloined from the MacLeans.

He glanced down to the *sgian dubh* tucked into his boot. It was a good all-around knife, the double-edged blade not too long, well balanced, and not too heavy. Although it wasn't a lady's weapon, it made an excellent training tool.

Rory went in search of Juliana, finding her as she was leaving the breakfast room. "What are your plans for the next hour or so?"

She shrugged. "I do not really have any. I was going to look for Greer and Aileen."

"Would ye like to have a lesson in handling a knife first?"

Her eyes widened. "Do you think I need to know how?"

"I think ye need to be able to defend yourself, if need be." He grinned. "Your last attempt was nae successful, if ye recall."

She frowned. "You tricked me."

"Mayhap, but 'twas easy for me to do since ye were nae prepared."

The frown deepened, and she raised her chin. "Fine, but I broke my knife."

"A good thing. That blade wouldna do much damage even in skilled hands." He pulled out the *sgian dubh*. "We will use this."

She looked at the finely honed tip and the razor-sharp edges, but she didn't flinch. "I will get my cloak."

"If ye want, but we are only going to the stables. The tack room will provide enough space, and there are bales of straw we can use for a target."

"All right." She pulled the shawl closer. "Then let us be about it."

He hid a grin as she preceded him across the bailey. Apart from his sister, Fiona, he'd never seen a lass so keen on learning to handle a knife.

The stable was nearly empty, since most of the men were gone. A couple of stable lads mucking out stalls gave them curious looks, but before either of them could start smirking about the direction he was headed, he gave them stern looks and they quickly returned to their shoveling.

Still, he left the door to the tack room slightly ajar. There was no use starting rumors about a tryst.

Juliana tossed her shawl across a saddle rack. "So where do I stab a man with that knife?"

"First of all, ye doona want to be close enough to stab a man. 'Tis likely he could overpower ye in a thrice."

She frowned. "Then what is this lesson going to be about?"

"Throwing a knife. Ye can do that while ye are out of arm's reach."

"Does it not take years—or at least, months—to learn to do that?"

"Aye, to be deadly accurate, it does, but if ye have to use it, ye will probably be close enough nae to miss." She looked dubious and he smiled. "Hold out your hand."

As she did, he placed the handle across her palm, then moved her thumb over the top and wrapped her fingers around the handle. "This is a hammer grip and the easiest to learn."

She moved her arm back and forth. "It feels… comfortable."

"'Tis a well-balanced blade, a bit more weight in the handle than the blade. It makes it more accurate to throw." He walked toward the other side of the room and piled three bales on top of each other and patted the top one. "This is about the height of a man's chest, which is where ye want to aim."

"Not…*lower*?"

Rory managed not to wince as he realized where she meant. "That…area…is better served with a knee jab if ye canna avoid your assailant."

Juliana tilted her head to one side. "Will you show me?"

He felt his eyes widen at her request, and, even though she hadn't made contact, he had an urge to shield himself. "Nae. I think 'tis an action that comes naturally to females." She smiled then, and he wondered if she'd been teasing him. In any case, better not to continue the direction of the conversation, since he'd prefer to be able to walk upright when they returned to the castle.

"Let me show ye the proper stance. Ye put your weight

on your right leg and move your left leg forward." He demonstrated, and she followed his example. "Good. Now hold your knife the way I showed ye, then raise your arm even with your shoulder and bend your elbow so the knife is alongside your ear."

She looked at him as though he'd taken leave of his senses, so he held his hand out. "Let me show ye."

After she'd given him back the knife, he assumed the position he'd just shown her, then quickly shifted his weight forward, the knife doing a complete spin before it found its mark in the straw bale. "Like that."

"You moved too fast."

"I will show ye again." Rory retrieved the knife from the straw then held it out to her. "See what ye remember."

She didn't have any trouble placing her feet correctly, but her elbow jutted out and her arm was too low. He stepped closer, mindful to keep to the side where her knee wouldn't make a temporary eunuch of him, and placed his arms around her, guiding her into position. The faint scent of heather soap wafted up from her hair. He briefly thought how interesting it would be to teach her archery, since that would entail being even closer and helping her pull the bow as she drew... He shook his head. *I need to concentrate on what I am doing, not what I want to do.*

"There ye go," he breathed near her ear and thought he heard a quick intake of air from her. *It would be so easy to let my lips brush her lobe and then nibble...* He gave himself another shake. By all that was holy, the woman was enthralling him!

He stepped back. "Now bend your wrist a wee bit, then shift your weight forward, keep your upper arm straight, and throw."

The knife landed halfway to the bales. If he hadn't needed to concentrate on controlling his uncalled-for lustful urges, he would have laughed at her expression. And maybe he did chuckle, because she gave him a baleful look.

"It did not work."

"It just takes practice." He picked up the knife and handed it back to her, careful this time to keep his distance. He was having a hard enough time maintaining his composure as it was. Although *hard* was probably not a word he should be using right now. Still. Better not put temptation back into his arms. "Try again."

She set her mouth and took aim. This time the knife almost made it.

"Again."

Her jaw clenched, and a determined look settled on her face. He'd seen similar expressions on the faces of clansmen preparing to go to battle. Mayhap there was a bit of Viking blood in the lass, even if she was English.

After nearly an hour, he called a stop. Her last few throws had hit the target hard, the knife making a complete spin as it should. She'd become much more proficient than he'd thought possible in such a short time.

"'Tis enough for today," he said after she'd completed another near-perfect throw. "Besides, I canna allow ye to best me." He grinned as she lowered her brows to glare at him. "At least, nae yet." She pursed her lips, making him want to kiss them. He pushed the thought back. Far, far back. *What is wrong with me this morning?*

Juliana sighed. "I suppose you should go join the other men in the hunt."

He'd nearly forgotten about the hunt.

"Here." She held out the knife.

He shook his head. "Ye keep it."

"I cannot accept—"

"Ye can. A good knife is as important as your skill. It seems ye found the right one." He turned to go before he said something foolish about maybe having found the right one, too, only he'd mean *her*.

"Thank you," she called after him. "For everything."

He gave a curt nod, not wanting to think about what *everything* meant.

...

After Rory left, Juliana returned to the castle and wandered the near-empty halls. She was having conflicting feelings over the knife-throwing session. They'd actually gotten along without sparring with each other, but other sensations had surfaced as well. Her first throw had been so abysmal because, with Rory standing so close, her arm had turned to mush. His warm breath had tickled her ear, and it had been all she could do not to rub against his mouth like a purring cat. She grimaced. It wasn't smart to allow herself to be attracted to him. It... *Well, I won't go there. It just is not smart.*

She found herself at the door of the solar. To her surprise, Aileen and Greer were there, although their faces were flushed as though they had been out in the cold. She sniffed the air. It smelled fresh and cool as well.

"What have you been doing?" she asked. "Playing in the snow?"

"We were helping our mother air the sleigh blankets," Aileen said. "To get rid of any vermin that might have nested in the wool since last spring."

Juliana felt a twinge of guilt for not helping, but no one had asked her. "Sleigh blankets? You have a sleigh?"

"Aye." Greer looked at her as though she might be simple-minded. "Ye have never ridden in one?"

She shook her head. "London has snow, but it quickly turns to mud and slush. My sister's husband's estate was in Sussex, where there wasn't much accumulation, either, so a sleigh was not practical."

"Well, it is here, once the storms start," Greer answered. "Ye'll get to ride in one tomorrow."

She frowned slightly. Had Rory changed his mind and said something to the MacDonnells about leaving tomorrow? She had thought the matter settled after the talk yesterday. But surely he wouldn't borrow a sleigh even if he'd decided not to stay. She didn't know much about horses, but she didn't think either Baron or Misty would be used to pulling anything behind them. "I am?" she asked tentatively.

Aileen nodded. "The men will be cutting down the Christmas tree tomorrow, so all of us will go along."

"To make sure they choose the *right* one," Greer added.

She didn't think she much cared to be squeezed into a sleigh with Morag. She'd felt her eyes on her after Rory had left the parlor, and the couple of times she'd turned too quickly for Morag to look away, the girl's eyes had looked like slivers of icy glass before she'd pasted a smile on her face. Morag might be Scottish, but Juliana had seen that false-friendly look too many times among London's *ton* not to recognize the insincerity of it. But she'd also been trained in manners. Not that she didn't mind flaunting them, much to Emily's chagrin at times, but she was a guest here, and the MacDonnells had taken them in. *How could I not be the epitome of well-mannered?*

"Do they go far to find a tree?"

"Sometimes, but doona fash. Ye will nae be cold."

Aileen had obviously taken her question to mean she didn't want to brave the elements. She almost laughed. After sailing on a stormy sea with stinging rain and then facing a howling blizzard with icy pellets lashing her face, being outside in the snow on a sunny day with no wind would seem like springtime.

"'Tis what the blankets are for," Greer said. "They were

woven to be lap size, so each person has her own."

"And we'll have hot bricks on the floor as well," Aileen added, as if to reassure her. "Ye'll be quite warm."

That really wasn't what she was worried about, but she could hardly tell Aileen and Greer that their cousin didn't like her. She'd just have to make sure she managed to sit across from Morag. Or did this sleigh not have two benches? She didn't know, but she supposed she could endure one morning. Then another thought came to her. "Do all of you go out when the men bring in the Yule log, too?" They'd mentioned something about that being a bit of a ceremony.

Aileen shook her head. "Nae. The log was cut weeks ago and put in a shed to dry."

"We canna take a chance on it nae lighting at first try."

Juliana frowned. "Why not? Sometimes it takes several attempts to get a fire going."

That remark got her the look again that doubted her intelligence, although Greer didn't voice the thought. "'Tis tradition that the new log be lighted with a charred stick saved from the year before. If it doesna light right away, 'tis bad luck."

"Ah." Scots did seem to have a healthy respect for superstition, although as she learned about some of the awful things that had happened to them throughout the centuries, perhaps they were justified. "I see."

Greer looked skeptical that Juliana *did* see, but she didn't comment on it. "There will be hot cider waiting when we come home," she said instead.

"Then the tree will be brought in, and the men will get into an argument about who actually found it," Aileen said, "and perhaps have a scuffle or two to prove the point."

"Of course, 'tis we women who made the choice, but we let them think they did." Greer giggled. "Besides, they like having a wee bit of fun by wrestling about."

Juliana hid a smile over the image of grown men—and large, broad-shouldered men like Rory—brawling like boys in a schoolyard over such a matter. She couldn't picture any English aristocrats doing the same. They'd probably tear some of their fancy lace frills if they did. And, while Rory might wear a bruise on his face as a sign of courage, the Englishmen she knew would probably cover it with powder. And then she sobered. *When did I start thinking of Rory as a hero?*

...

The next morning, Rory set out with nearly a score of MacDonnell men for the great tree hunt, as they called it. When Calum had told him it was a clan tradition, he'd wondered why they attached a name to it. The woods between Loch Lochy and Loch Ness were full of pine—different types of fir and spruce—so selecting a decent-size one shouldn't be a problem. But that was before the sleigh had been brought out.

Now he looked over his shoulder as the sleigh, filled with women, slid along the road beside the walking men. As such contraptions went, it wasn't overly large and pulled by just one horse, but it was packed with almost a dozen chattering females. Well, most of them were chattering. Juliana wore the same stoic expression she'd had on their trip up, and Morag was stonily silent.

He sighed as he turned off the road and trooped with the other men to the trees. He hadn't spoken to either of them yesterday, since as soon as he'd returned with Calum from searching for tracks, the MacDonnells had set out to hunt. The Christmas banquet was hugely important for their neighbors, someone had explained. It included a ritual of bringing in the Yule log, and Rory half expected the men to hunt for the traditional boar, even though the animal was near extinct in Britain. Instead, they'd brought in several stags, some rabbits, and a gaggle of geese who'd landed too close not to take advantage of. When they'd gotten back, he'd helped with the cleaning and dressing of the bounty. By the time that had finished, he'd been tired and filthy and had slunk up the servants' stairs to his chamber to wash off the blood and other matter.

But all that was just excuses. He'd been avoiding Morag and Juliana, albeit for different reasons.

Morag's greeting two days ago when she'd returned had unsettled him. He'd hoped for a simple hello when she saw him. He certainly hadn't expected her to throw herself—literally—on him. And then he'd heard the handle on his door being tried that night. He'd bolted it instinctively. When the MacGregors had been proscribed, they'd all too often had to wonder who was friend or enemy. His first inclination had been to open it in case it might be Juliana. Then the head on his shoulders replaced his *other* head's lustful urge with logic. There was no reason for Juliana to come to his door in the dark of night. Definitely not for a tryst. *His* thoughts might be turning—far too often lately—in that direction, but even in his wildest fantasy, he couldn't imagine *her* sneaking through hallways to his door.

But Morag might. The lass was bold—she'd tried rubbing his thigh under the table last year and probably would have fondled him elsewhere—and she was used to getting her way, since her father indulged her. She was also wily, never acting too bold in front of the laird.

Rory would never know for sure if she'd attempted it, since he hadn't opened the door to find out. The last thing he needed was to reject her while he was a guest in her father's house. He supposed he could announce that he was handfasted to Juliana—he *was*, after all—but that would lead to why they weren't sharing the same bedchamber. And *that* would lead to a whole other quagmire of problems. Not the least of which was that Juliana would be furious and blame him for setting things up to get into her bed. Better not venture there. He was already having trouble keeping a tight rein on his feelings.

"Ye look as if ye are carrying the weight of that big tree we're going to cut on your shoulders," Calum said as he came alongside him. "What ails ye?"

Rory snapped out of his reverie. "Just pondering how soon it would be feasible to get on the road." That was partially true. The sooner he could get away from Invergarry, the less of a problem Morag would be.

"Ye are still worried that Cameron will return?"

Calum had mistaken his problem, but he wasn't about to correct him. They hadn't found any tracks yesterday morning, but that didn't mean Neal wasn't still at Spean. "'Tis still a possibility. If he arrives after we are gone, ye MacDonnells will nae be involved."

"'Tis winter, lad. Nae much to do now until the spring thaws come. I imagine many a MacDonnell wouldna mind a bit of a brawl with Camerons." Calum grinned. "Just to stay in practice, ye ken."

Rory shook his head. "Ye doona want to start a clan war because of that eejit."

"Doona fash about that," Calum replied. "The Cameron laird kens the temper his son has, even if he willna admit it out loud. He'll nae bring his men to arms."

"Mayhap, but I doubt Neal is riding alone. His friends might take it upon themselves to stir up trouble."

"Like I said. There's many a MacDonnell who'll be glad to meet them if they do." Calum clapped him on the shoulder. "Now, we had best get looking for that tree, lest my brother claim to find it first."

Ah, the tree. He'd almost forgotten why they were out here, as he and Calum joined the rest of the men at the tree line. The sleigh had stopped, and its occupants were being helped out. As the women headed in their direction, Morag broke away and ran to him.

"I ken where we can find the perfect tree." She put a hand on his arm. "Come with me and I'll show it to ye."

He had a feeling that she wanted to show him a lot more than a tree that was probably conveniently located deep within the forest. He glanced at Juliana, but she had turned away, apparently deep in conversation with Aileen. He managed a small smile as he slowly withdrew his arm on the pretense of flipping his ax handle from hand to hand.

"I think I need to find out what the rules are to this event first."

She pouted. "There are nae rules."

Sima joined them. "Nae rules to what?"

"To selecting a tree," Rory answered. "I am nae sure how ye go about picking one."

"Och, the picking part is easy," Sima said. "'Tis the choosing that is difficult."

Rory felt confused. "'Tis nae one and the same?"

"Nae!" This was from Greer as she and her sister and Juliana approached. "The men each walk about and find a tree, then stand by it. We ladies go around and judge."

"Whoever gets the most votes for his tree is the winner," Aileen added.

"And I think Rory should win, since he is our guest." Morag placed her hand on his arm again. "And I will show him where to find it."

Rory could have sworn that Juliana's hair beneath her cap turned brighter just then. It was a peculiar trait, but her hair did seem to almost set itself on fire when she was agitated. Was she agitated? Usually her fair skin turned pink, but with the cold weather he couldn't assert that. And she'd developed a passive expression worthy of any faro player. She wasn't meeting his eyes, either.

"That would nae be fair, Morag," Sima said. "Ye canna help any man when ye are also a judge."

Her face turned mulish. "Then I'll nae judge."

Sima gave her a firm look. "Your father will nae be pleased to find ye've gone off with a man into the forest."

"And I wouldna want to sully your reputation with your clan, lass." Rory stepped away. "'Tis better I abide by the rules, as Sima said."

Morag narrowed her eyes slightly, but before she could retort, Aileen spoke.

"If we're going to stand here and blether all day, neither Rory or our father will have a chance to win." She gestured. "Some of the men have already picked a tree."

"Aye." Calum gave him a nudge. "We'd best get on with it, then."

He didn't need anyone to make the suggestion twice. For now, he'd been saved from a possible compromising situation, but Christmas was still three days away.

He hoped the weather would hold so Drumochter Pass would be open. The sooner he and Juliana could get on the road to Blair Castle, the better.

. . .

Juliana followed the other women as they moved to inspect the first tree, a chill in her blood that had nothing to do with the cold. She had a plaid wrapped around her cloak, the sun was out, and the wind had died down, but she felt as frosty as the temperature.

It was obvious from Morag's actions and words that she had laid claim to Rory. What was less obvious, and definitely more important, was how Rory felt about it. His remark about finding out what the rules were first was not a rejection of Morag's advances as much as it was being sure he was being fair to the other men. The six months she'd spent in Scotland had taught her that Highlanders placed a great deal of pride in doing the honorable thing. Rory had proved that in spades by rescuing her and *not* claiming his legal handfasting rights. It followed, then, that telling Morag he didn't want to sully her reputation was part of that internal code.

It didn't mean he didn't want the girl.

"'Tis a fine day to be out." Aileen tilted her head. "But ye doona look like ye are enjoying it."

"I..."

"She's upset about Morag," Greer said.

"I am not upset."

Greer ignored that. "Our cousin throws herself at him. I would be mad as a disturbed hornet, if I were ye."

"I have no reason to be angry." When both sisters looked at her skeptically, she continued. "I truly have no claim on Rory."

"Ye are handfasted to him."

"We have already discussed this," Juliana replied. "Even if it is legal in Scotland, he only said it to get us away from Neal Cameron. He did not mean it."

Aileen shook her head. "I am nae sure about that, but whether he meant it or not, he will honor the vow. Mayhap we should tell Morag—"

"*No!*" Juliana lowered her voice when several of the other women turned around to look at her. "Rory is not property any more than I am. I cannot just claim him. Besides," she added, "if he wanted Morag to know, he would tell her himself."

Aileen shrugged. "If he did that, the clan would question why ye are nae sharing a room."

"Sharing..." Juliana stopped herself. Less than a week ago she had nearly panicked at sharing the room at Spean. Now, the prospect didn't seem quite so frightening. Rory had lain half-naked beside her when she was fevered, and he had undressed her, save for her chemise... She managed to stop herself from rolling her eyes. He'd only done that because she was half-frozen, not because he had any intentions. Still, she remembered being more intrigued by his bare chest than frightened at his lack of clothes. She couldn't deny that her body was reacting in strange ways, either. Odd little things like tingling when he touched her. Instead of instinctively drawing away, she actually had urges to touch him, too. But... "Sharing a bed?" She hoped her voice didn't squeak.

"Aye." Greer nodded. "'Tis tradition if ye are handfasted to share a bed."

"Ye ought to think about it before Morag makes more of a fool of herself," Aileen said.

Before she could answer, Sima called to them. "Why are ye lingering behind? We need your vote on this tree so we can move on."

Juliana pasted a smile on her face. "We should not keep the others waiting."

Although both Aileen and Greer gave her inquiring glances, they picked up their pace, leaving her alone with her thoughts. Was Morag making a fool of herself? Or was Rory just acting the gentleman in public? Or—worse thought—was he actually honoring the handfasting because he thought he *had* to when he really wanted Morag?

If that were true then she, Juliana, was holding him back. Perhaps she should have a talk with him and tell him he was a free man...that she would not hold him to a vow he hadn't meant.

The idea didn't sit well. In fact, it felt rather like she'd swallowed a hot coal that was burning a hole in her stomach.

A childish and totally irrational anger swept through her as she remembered Morag clinging to Rory. Why was that bothering her? The answer came so abruptly, she stopped in her tracks. Good Lord. She was *jealous*. It was an unpleasant sensation she'd not experienced before, and she wished she could just wave it away, but she suspected her feelings ran deeper than she wanted to admit.

And maybe that made her the bigger fool.

# Chapter Twenty-Two

Rory rode out of the stable a full two hours before dawn the next morning, alone this time since no one was stirring, although he'd left a note. Even though he and Calum had not found any tracks or evidence that Neal Cameron had returned, Rory wanted to see if the man was staying at the inn at Spean, lying in wait. It would be an all-day round trip, but with the roads clearing, he should be home before dusk.

Of course, this trip was also an excuse to avoid any more Yule adventures. The women had been chattering about gathering holly, ivy, and mistletoe today and he didn't want to have to fend off Morag once again. *Especially* not when it came to plucking the mistletoe.

Now that she had returned and it was evident that she harbored even more amorous feelings than last year, he was in a real debacle while he and Juliana remained at Invergarry. Apart from Calum's family and the laird himself—and Rory had them sworn to secrecy since Juliana didn't consider the vows real—no one knew about the handfasting. Morag, sly as she was, behaved perfectly well when her father was around. Rory had considered having a word with the laird but dismissed the idea. He would be insulting the daughter if he told her father Morag was making overtures as brazen as a wanton. MacDonnell would no doubt take umbrage at the insinuation—and blame Rory for encouraging her somehow—and then throw him out, if not worse.

Besides, there was the matter of Rory's pride. What kind of a man would go sniveling to a woman's father—asking for *help* in keeping his daughter away—because he couldn't handle the situation? If word of that got out, he might well be banned from calling himself a MacGregor, and it wouldn't have anything to do with proscription. His brothers would consider him disgraced.

He'd avoid Morag as much as possible, which wasn't going to be easy with all the Yule festivities about to take place. Tomorrow night was Christmas Eve, and the Yule log would be brought in, followed by the great feast. The bonfire would be held the evening of Christmas Day. He'd already announced they planned to leave the day after if the weather held. Surely he could manage three more days. He hoped.

When he neared the inn several hours later, there was no sign of horses in front, but if Neal were there with his henchmen, they'd have their horses in the stable.

Dismounting, Rory tied Baron's reins to a nearby bush and approached the stable on foot. Peering carefully around the double door, he spotted only one horse. He didn't think Neal would be here by himself, although since it was Christmas, his comrades might have gone back home.

Rory turned and walked toward the inn. If that was Neal's horse, just as well to confront him right now. He adjusted his sword and felt for the two knives he kept on his person. He flexed his hands, fisting them several times. Then he straightened his shoulders and opened the door.

"Can I help ye?" the clerk behind the desk asked.

"Aye. Is Neal Cameron staying here?"

The clerk—a gangly young man—smirked. "We doona give out that information."

Rory put his hand on his sword hilt. "Answer the question."

The clerk gave him a wary look, then widened his eyes as Rory's hand tightened its grasp. "He is nae here."

Rory took a menacing step forward. "Doona speak in riddles. Do ye mean 'he is nae here *now*' or do ye mean he was here and he left?"

The clerk swallowed hard. "He left a few days ago." He pushed the register toward him. "See for yourself."

Rory glanced at the book. According to the dates, Neal and his men had only spent the night of the morning he'd found their makeshift camp. He narrowed his eyes in consternation. It wasn't like Cameron to admit defeat, nor to retreat so quickly. Had he actually returned home? It was possible since the MacLean holding was only about fifteen miles from here and thirty miles from Invergarry. And it probably made sense since it was Yuletide.

Rory pushed the register back and plopped a coin on top of it. "For your troubles," he said.

The clerk grabbed the coin and pocketed it. "No trouble. No trouble at all."

Rory didn't bother to answer as he left. Once he was back on the road home, he considered the facts.

Just because Cameron had gone home didn't mean the man would not be returning once the festivities were done. One more reason to get on the road as quickly as possible. He just wished they could leave tomorrow, but that would be a slap to the MacDonnells, since they'd invited the two of them to stay for Yule. And he didn't need to insult them. He already had Morag to deal with.

It was late afternoon by the time he reined in a tired

Baron to a walk about a mile from the castle. The sun was already low in the west, but he wanted a chance to cool his horse down before they got home. Then, out of his peripheral vision, he sensed movement to his right. Turning in the saddle, he saw what looked like a cloaked figure through the thick pine. Then he caught a glimpse of bright-red hair. He frowned.

What in the world was Juliana doing this far away from the castle?

...

Juliana paused, gazing up at the dense ceiling of conifers that towered over her. It was getting dark among the trees, which meant the sun was setting. She should return to the others. She turned around, searching for the deer trail she'd followed earlier. With the light fading, she couldn't find it. The bracken that covered the forest floor was bare this time of year, and none of it looked broken or even bent. There wasn't even any snow under the thick cover of trees for her to look for tracks.

Tracks. A bubble of hysterical laughter rose in her throat, and she quickly quelled it. Rory would probably have been able to find the invisible trail in seconds. He had managed to follow her to the MacLean holding, and there had been myriad trails through those foothills. But he wasn't here. She looked around. Every tree looked the same. *What direction did I come from?*

A chill slid down her spine that had nothing to do with the weather, although now she realized dampness was seeping through her boots, making her feet cold. And so were her hands, in spite of her mittens. With one hand, she pulled the collar of her cloak closer and forced herself not to panic.

She'd been stupid to wander off from the group, but the thought of spending the whole afternoon with Morag—who alternated between giving her dagger looks and talking about Rory as though the two of *them* were betrothed—made her want to throw something at the girl. While she could probably restrain herself from doing that, she wasn't sure if she could keep foul words from coming out of her mouth, so she'd decided to separate from the rest.

She hadn't realized she'd wandered so far. At first, she could hear the sounds of voices as the women of the castle, servants included, laughed and talked as they collected holly and ivy. The sounds had become muted and had eventually faded as she wandered, although she hadn't been aware, since the forest had a voice of its own.

Now the forest had grown still, its daytime residents settling in for the evening and the night creatures not yet roaming. She had no desire to meet any of those, but she had no idea how to get back to the castle.

Hysteria threatened again, and she took a deep breath. Nothing was going to be accomplished if she gave in to a case of the vapors. Besides, she wasn't a ninnyhammered, delicate debutante, and she wasn't about to spend the night in the cold woods.

Juliana unsheathed the knife Sima had given her to cut the greens. It wasn't as balanced as the one she'd used when Rory had taught her to throw, but she wasn't planning on defending herself. Her intent for now was to make a mark on the side of a tree so she'd see it if she started walking in circles. And also… She bit her lip, not wanting to think on it, but the marks might also serve as clues if someone finally came looking for her. Although it might be too late. She took another deep breath. *I can't think of that right now.*

She made her first mark and took a step, hoping she wasn't going farther into the forest. Then she took another and another. And one more. She looked back. So far, her marks were in a straight line. She moved forward with a little more confidence. And then she heard a shout. It sounded like her name.

*Rory?*

But it couldn't be. He'd left early this morning, and Calum had said he might not be back until tomorrow. Besides, how would he know where she was? *She* didn't know where she was. Then she heard it again. Her name.

"I'm here!" she shouted and began running toward the sound.

"Doona move! Stay where ye are!" The voice sounded louder and was definitely Rory's. "I will come to ye. Just keep shouting, lass!"

Juliana stopped as understanding dawned. With darkness settling in, she might very well pass by him and not know it. She started yelling and heard him crashing through the bracken. In another moment, he burst through the trees.

"What the hell are ye doing out here? 'Tis near dark!"

*Well.* Her relief turned to indignation. *He doesn't have to take that tone, does he?* She knew very well it was near dark. She had two perfectly good eyes.

"And what are ye doing by yourself? Do ye nae ken 'tis dangerous?"

Now he was making it sound like she was stupid. *Which I just called myself minutes ago.* But, still. She lifted her chin.

"I was cutting greens for decorating the hall." She held out the small bunch she had collected to show him. "I was about to return to the castle." *Which isn't a lie.* She desperately wanted to return to the castle.

He crossed his arms and stared at her. "Ye are lost."

"I am not." *Well...that is a lie.*

He raised one brow. "Which direction is the castle, then?"

She frowned. Why was he goading her? *Because that's what we always do.* Had she forgotten how they'd acted at Strae Castle? They'd goaded each other every chance they got. Not this time. She tilted her chin higher and waved her handful of greens in the direction that he'd come from. "That way."

He smirked. "Easy for ye to say, since ye saw me coming from there."

He wasn't going to make this easy for her. Her frown deepened. She would have thanked him—and *maybe* even admitted she'd wandered too far—if he hadn't taken this attitude with her. She waved the greens in what she hoped was a dismissive manner, although she'd never mastered the art of fan waving. "Could we just go home?"

"Aye, we'll go home." He raised his brow once more. "Ye just need to tell me where it is."

"Oh!" She waved the greens again. He was the most infuriating man. "I…I am sure Baron knows the way home."

"I'm sure he does, but I am asking ye." He grabbed the greens that were nearly smacking him in the face. "And I doona think we need these…" His expression changed as he looked down at them, and then he started to grin as he plucked one out. "What have we here?"

Mistletoe. Juliana felt her cheeks heat in spite of the cold. She'd come across the cluster intertwined with the mossy bark of a tree and pulled it loose since Greer had said it was good luck for each girl to bring a sprig back. She reached for it. "I was supposed to bring some back."

He lifted it out of her reach, his eyes darkening as he stepped closer. Her mind registered he was holding it over her head just before he bent and covered her mouth with his.

• • •

All the conflicting emotions that had been roiling inside him since sighting Juliana exploded like gunpowder as his lips touched hers.

That he'd seen her at all was nothing short of divine intervention. The ground near the road had been cleared past arrow-shot decades—if not centuries—ago as a defensive measure, but the woods just beyond were dense. He might have mistaken the movement for a deer, except that her glorious red hair had been a beacon for him.

He'd had an instant of nearly paralyzing fear when he realized she was this far away from the castle by herself, followed by a flash of anger that she *was* out here by herself. Why had someone not watched over her? Or had she deliberately struck out on her own? That was more likely the truth, given that Juliana was Juliana...a conclusion that did little to mitigate his ire. He might have been a bit harsh with his first question, although it was born out of fear and also relief that she appeared to be all right. His temper had risen again with her apparent nonchalance over the situation. *And* the fact that she wouldn't *admit* that she was lost. Stubborn woman.

Then he'd seen the mistletoe. All his tumultuous feelings had swiftly changed to just one—the *need* to kiss her senseless.

Her soft lips heated quickly under his. Although his brain made a feeble attempt to remind him that a mistletoe kiss was not supposed to be a prelude to tearing off one's clothes and tumbling on the ground, he had a hard time recognizing the thought. His mouth plundered hers. Dropping the mistletoe, he cradled her head, angling it for better contact, then he swept his lips across hers, nuzzling, nibbling at the corner of her mouth, then returning to her lips, increasing the pressure until she began to respond. He sucked in her lower lip, causing a mewling sound to come from her, then licked along the crease as she gasped. He took the opportunity to thrust his tongue inside her mouth and began to thoroughly explore its warm wetness as his cock hardened in anticipation of thrusting into another hot, wet area. His hips gyrated against hers instinctively.

Vaguely he became aware that something was pushing at him. Pounding his chest. His mind niggled at him that Juliana was trying to get him to stop. In confusion, he broke the kiss and stepped back.

Juliana stared at him, her ginger eyes dilated so much they looked near black. With desire? He felt a moment of male hubris, then he frowned. If she desired him, why had she pushed...? Rory blinked when he realized she was shaking. She couldn't be cold, not with the heat that had risen between them. Then what...? The answer came to him with the swiftness and clout of a horse's hoof to his stomach.

She was *scared*. He had frightened her. Instinctively he reached out to touch her, but she drew back, reaffirming his conclusion.

He dropped his hands. "I am sorry. I dinna mean to offend ye. Are ye all right?"

She stared at him for a moment longer, her face still pale, then shook her head. "I...am fine."

She didn't look fine. She looked as though she might bolt back into the woods if he even breathed hard. He furrowed his brow, remembering her reaction to his first kiss at MacLean's. There had been nothing demanding about that one, and yet, she'd stiffened as if she'd feared something. He didn't think then—or now—that she was actually afraid of *him*. He didn't even think she disliked him. Not anymore. *And* she had started to respond to him. He'd felt that.

So what was she afraid of? It was a question he wanted to ask, but it would be totally inappropriate. Right now he had more pressing matters to consider. Like how he was going to get her to ride with him on Baron.

"'Tis getting dark. We had best return to the castle." He stepped back, giving her room to walk past him. For a moment he wondered if she would. She was still eyeing him as though he were some wild animal about to pounce. The thought wounded his pride. Surely his finesse wasn't that bad? He couldn't remember any lass ever complaining about his skills... Then he gave himself a shake. Juliana's near panic—and he suspected he'd get a complete dressing-down if he called it that—had something to do with more than stealing a kiss, albeit it a lustful one, under a sprig of mistletoe.

"We need to go before the laird sends out a search party for ye."

That seemed to spur her to action. Color returned to her face, and she walked past him. At least she didn't gather up her skirts to avoid any chance of contact. He supposed he should be grateful for that. Hopefully she wasn't going to argue about getting on the horse with him.

He should have known that she would. They had no more than reached Baron when she began to walk along the road.

"What do ye think ye are doing?"

She stopped. "Am I not going in the right way?"

They weren't going to have that argument again. "Ye are."

"Then I am walking back," she answered.

"Ye are going to ride on Baron."

"I...I prefer to walk."

"But I doona." He grabbed Baron's reins and moved in front of her, causing her to halt once more. "We can be back at the castle in five minutes if we both ride. Ye can get into dry clothes and sit by the fire with a mug of hot cider to warm yourself."

Juliana looked down the road and then up at Baron, but she didn't move.

Rory sighed. "I promise I willna molest ye. Can ye nae bear to ride with me for five minutes?"

She looked at him quickly, her face turning pale, then blood rushing back. "It... is...I mean, I..."

"Ye doona have to say any more." He bent and intertwined his hands to make a stirrup. "Just get on the horse."

She gave him a doubtful look, and he hoped he wasn't going to actually have to lift her onto Baron's back. He'd never been accused of taking advantage of any female, and she might see it that way.

"Please."

Juliana took a deep breath, then grabbed the saddle and put her booted foot in his hands. Once she was on Baron, he vaulted up behind her, careful not to touch or put his arms around her. "Ye can take the reins. Baron kens the way."

Then he spurred the horse forward, and they galloped toward the castle.

. . .

She'd insulted Rory. She'd *hurt* him. Juliana knew she had when he wouldn't even put his arms around her to handle the reins. It was a good thing Baron knew where the stable with his hay and oats was waiting, because her hands were incapable of guiding him.

She felt numb all over. How could she make Rory understand that it wasn't *him* she had shunned? That sheer terror had overcome her when she'd felt his manhood press against her stomach? That the memory of the rape she'd endured had washed over her like storm waves crashing on shore? Vivid, horrible details had pushed her beneath that raging sea and swept everything from her mind except the need to struggle to the surface and breathe. To untangle herself. To survive.

It wasn't something she could *tell* him.

Not wanting to ride with him was an entirely different matter. She didn't trust herself to his touch. For those few moments while he was kissing her, she'd been lost to the sensation of his mouth—and his tongue—doing all sorts of *pleasurable* things, and she'd felt herself falling into a dark abyss of wanting...*something*. Of *surrendering*. Of letting him continue...and then the terror had struck.

When an iota of her mind had returned to sanity, she wasn't sure she wouldn't panic again if she were enclosed within his arms while on Baron. It sometimes took an hour after one of the nightmares to calm down. She couldn't take the chance of going completely mad with him.

*I obviously don't need to worry about that*, she thought as they arrived at the castle. Rory slipped off Baron's rump without so much as a whisper of a touch to her person. When a groomsman came running to take Baron, Rory asked that the man assist her in dismounting and led Baron away himself. He couldn't have made his point more clear that he wasn't he going to *molest* her. He wasn't going to have anything more to do with her at all.

To her added chagrin, she now noticed the group of people assembled near the front door of the castle. Several of the men were dressed for riding, no doubt about to search for her. Sima, Greer, and Aileen had relieved expressions on their faces.

"Come with us, Morag," Aileen said as they started down the steps toward Juliana.

Morag stayed where she was, her gaze following Rory going to the stables, then she gave Juliana a speculative look, her eyes narrowing as she did. Instead of doing as Aileen requested, she turned and went inside, slamming the door behind her.

# Chapter Twenty-Three

Most of the next day was spent decorating the great hall. The male servants helped the maids string ivy and hang holly branches in hard-to-reach spaces, and there was a great deal of giggling from the women—as well as big grins from the men—when they were deciding where to put the mistletoe.

Juliana didn't want to think about mistletoe. She'd tried to put on a cheerful face, but it was hard to join in the general merriment that was affecting Aileen and Greer. Even Morag was being pleasant, although Juliana thought that was probably because she had taken special interest in helping place the mistletoe, no doubt in anticipation of luring Rory to a sprig. And, after what had happened between *them*, he'd probably be more than willing to acquiesce to Morag's invitation.

At least she hadn't had to face Rory since they'd returned yesterday. Sima, concerned that she might have stayed out too long in the cold and could become fevered again, had insisted she take a hot bath and had sent up a tray to her room. Juliana didn't argue the point, and she'd even taken advantage of that assumption by sleeping in late. By the time she went downstairs, Rory had left. He'd ridden out with the laird and Calum, who were delivering personal invitations to surrounding neighbors for the Christmas ball tomorrow night.

"Ye are awfully quiet. Does Christmas nae excite ye?" Greer asked. "Or are ye nae feeling well?"

"Mayhap ye got more of a chill than ye thought?" Morag smiled at her, although it didn't reach her eyes. "It might be better if ye took to your bed for a day or two."

She *almost* sounded concerned. Juliana stifled a smile at the obvious ploy to get her out of the way for the holiday festivities, so Morag would have Rory all to herself. Juliana probably should just tell the girl that she didn't need to worry about her posing a threat. Not after what happened yesterday. But a part of her didn't want to admit that she'd botched things up so badly. Besides, she wasn't feeling very charitable toward Morag at the moment, even though it was Christmas.

"I am quite rested, thank you for your concern," she replied, knowing she didn't sound any more sincere than Morag had. She did need to come up with some excuse why she was so gloomy, though. "I…just will miss not being with my sisters for Christmas."

"Of course you do," Aileen said. "I would hate to be away from home for the holidays, too."

"But ye can pretend we are your family for now," Greer said seriously. "I ken it isna the same, but—"

"But it is nae too late if Juliana wants to go back," Morag broke in. "The roads are clearing, so Father can send an escort with ye to Strae Castle, if ye wish. Ye could be home tomorrow."

Juliana thought that might be how she went back, given the circumstances. It would be Rory's decision to make if he wanted to turn her over to an escort. Would he consider he was still honor-bound to take her to Strae Castle himself? He might want to spend more time here now. She didn't want to dwell on that possibility, and she certainly wasn't about to admit such to Morag.

"*We*"—she put some emphasis on the word, hoping that she and Rory were still a *we*—"decided it would be more prudent not to return the way we came. Rory mentioned going east toward Blair Castle and then over to Strae, so it would be impossible to be home by tomorrow."

She saw anger flash across Morag's face before it was replaced with a calculated look. She was probably thinking taking the longer route would mean several nights on the road with Rory. Juliana allowed herself a small moment of triumph. Let the girl think they might be sharing a room somewhere along the way. Not that it would happen. Rory would probably sooner sleep with his horse than be anywhere near her again.

"'Tis Christmas Eve day." Greer looked at Morag. "Your father wouldna want anyone to miss the festivities by being on the road anyway."

"I suppose waiting until the day after Christmas will not make that much of a difference," Juliana admitted. At least, she hoped it wouldn't.

"Aye. Besides, if ye are going that way, we canna be sure Drumochter Pass will be completely open," Aileen said. "Best to give the snow another day or two to melt."

Morag gave them all a predator smile. "Well, I would nae want Rory to leave before then, either."

Juliana just prayed it wouldn't snow again before they were ready to leave. She really didn't want to spend more time here, and Rory probably didn't want to spend more time with *her*, even though he had kissed her in the woods. There *had* been mistletoe, after all. The sooner Rory got her home, the better it would be for both of them.

...

Rory stopped for a moment after he entered the great hall that evening. Although the voluminous room had always retained a feel of times long past, with its trestle tables and dais, along with the tapestries and weapons lining the walls, tonight it felt as though he had walked into a medieval world.

A harpist, accompanied by a man with a lute, sat near the dais in the front of the hall, strumming a carol. The huge tree they'd brought in was decorated, too. The scent of pine filled the air from the many boughs that served as centerpiece runners on the long tables. Branches of holly adorned the mantelpieces of the two unlit hearths on either of the side walls, and ivy vines ran along the dais, looped and draping down over the edge. Although the large iron chandeliers were not burning, there were candles on all the tables, the smell of beeswax mingling with the pine.

Sima and the household had been busy while he had been gone. Had Juliana enjoyed helping them? He'd spent most of the day vacillating between whether he should apologize for his churlish behavior of walking away from her or giving her a wide berth this evening, since she'd made clear her own feelings. He wasn't even sure which would be harder to do. In the end—really, only minutes ago—he'd decided on the neutral path of being polite but distant.

He looked around the room that was quickly filling up and spotted her with Aileen and Greer taking their places on the dais. As a guest of the MacDonnells, he had a seat there, too. Luckily, at least for tonight, it was on the other side of the laird's place in the middle. He managed a smile and nod as he passed in front of Juliana, who gave him a rather constrained nod back. At least he wouldn't be forced to keep up a conversation.

Unfortunately, he would have to keep up a conversation

with Morag. She had managed to secure the spot next to him.

"Do ye keep the Yule log tradition at Strae Castle?" she asked as he sat down.

"We havena." Did she not remember the MacGregors had not been able to hold *any* traditions for decades, since their clan had been banned? "I am nae sure Ian even thought about it with his recent wedding."

Morag gave him a sideways glance. "Are ye the next brother in line?"

It took a moment for the unspoken part of that question to register, but he wasn't going to discuss *marriage*. "If ye are asking who is the second oldest, that would be Devon."

"Oh." She looked disappointed, then she brightened. "But I forgot. Men doona have to marry in age order like girls, do they?"

He didn't like where her not-so-subtle hints were heading. He could put an end to the conversation by telling Morag he was handfasted to Juliana, but after yesterday, that would be the worst thing he could do. Nor could he take the opposite tact and say he didn't intend to marry for years. Not when, in fact, he was sworn for a year and a day. Before he could think of a suitable answer, a bell tinkled at the far end of the hall, and everyone grew silent.

"What is happening?"

Morag looked annoyed. "They are starting the procession."

It needed no further explanation. Bagpipes sounded at the entrance. In a moment, the piper—dressed in banned Scottish regalia—moved toward the dais, followed by a single candle bearer. Two elderly white-haired men, also dressed in the forbidden tartans, bore a ram's horn, and the other held what looked like a charred stick. They were, in turn, followed by six strapping lads, who carried the big Yule log on their shoulders. Halfway down the hall, the piper turned abruptly to his right, and Rory noticed there was a path between the tables that led to a hearth on that side. The lads put the log down on the kindling that had been laid and stepped away while the piper and the candle bearer took their places on either side.

Laird MacDonnell stepped down from the dais. Rory wouldn't have been surprised, at this point, to see him in full clan colors as well, but the law did not allow recognition of a laird—at least to Englishmen—so he supposed MacDonnell didn't want to tempt fate.

The laird accepted the horn from one of the elders and took a drink, then raised it to their clansmen. "To Scots! We give honor. May we live free."

The crowd roared their approval and then, as if admonished by a soundless voice, grew quiet once more. As the laird handed back the horn and accepted the stick, people leaned forward to extinguish the candles on the tables, leaving the hall in near darkness save for the single candle that the candle bearer held. The laird lit the stick he held and raised it up.

"With the remnant of last year's Yule log, I light this one. We welcome a new year full of prosperity and peace."

He laid the piece on top of the dry kindling, where it caught immediately. Rory heard a collective sigh as though people had been holding their breaths. MacDonnell smiled.

"The log is lit. Our future will be bright."

That explained the holding of breath, then. Although Rory was pretty sure everything had been done to ensure the log would light, from drying it out for weeks to making sure the kindling was laid properly and the edge of the stick probably swabbed with lamp oil, it was still a nice symbolic gesture for good luck in the new year.

As the candles were lit on the tables again and conversation returned to normal, the servants carried the food in. Rory wondered if maybe the MacGregors should have been observing this custom as well. They could have used good luck through the years of banishment. Then again, the MacGregors had been known as Children of the Mist for so long that the faeries may have decided it would be grand fun to make sure the log did not light if they tried it.

Although he kept telling himself he was not superstitious, he was growing more sure the fae had had a hand in yesterday's events, after all.

...

Normally, Juliana was an early riser, and, when she was younger, she would be awake and dressed well before dawn on Christmas morning, but this time she would much rather have stayed in bed with the covers pulled over her head. Unfortunately, she didn't have that choice. Greer and Aileen had both knocked on her door to make sure she was awake to join them. She wasn't really sure why they'd be so eager to include her in what would probably include a family exchange of presents, but that wasn't the sole reason she preferred to stay secluded.

Rory had been coolly distant to her as he passed the dais last night, even though he'd kept up a conversation with Morag, who just happened to have the seat beside him. They'd even walked around together—Morag with a possessive hand tucked into his elbow—after the feast, talking to various MacDonnell clansmen. Juliana hadn't seen him venturing near any of the hanging mistletoe, but she'd occupied herself by helping Sima supervise the packing of food boxes that neighbors would be taking home. In England, they boxed food the day after Christmas, but here they did it so the folks who'd attended could share the food on Christmas itself with the crofters and others who couldn't come to the castle.

When she'd returned to the great hall, there had been no sign of Rory, although Morag was still there, talking to Greer and Aileen. Juliana wondered if they'd deliberately separated the two, especially when Greer had given her a wink.

This morning was another story. Would Rory even speak to her? She took a deep breath before she entered the front parlor, where she'd been told to meet.

For a minute, she didn't think she'd be noticed, since there was a flurry of movement, which included gifts being opened amid a tearing of paper and ribbon tossing. Aileen and Greer were sharing one sofa, each unwrapping gifts. Morag sat alone on the second sofa, looking decidedly put out. Rory was standing near the hearth, speaking to Calum. Just to tweak the girl's nose, Juliana was tempted to fill the obviously empty space beside Morag—before Rory did—but that would look childish and petulant. Besides, it would *also* involve talking to her. She was looking for a spot to sit when Sima called to her.

"Come over here." She indicated an armchair near the hearth. "'Tis a nice, warm spot by the fire."

It was also close to Rory. She hesitated a moment, wondering if he would move away. That would be worse than getting a cut direct from the snobbish *ton*. She didn't really care what Society matrons thought, but Rory was a different matter. In spite of how she'd reacted—and it had been an instinctive reaction—she did care about him. Still. She couldn't just stand there. She pasted a smile on her face and walked over.

"Thank you," she said to Sima.

Although Rory didn't turn his head, she caught a side glance and thought a muscle in his jaw twitched. Was he angry with her? Or had she imagined the twitch? Maybe she was making too much ado about nothing? At least he hadn't moved away. Yet.

"These are for you."

Sima thrust two large presents onto her lap. Smiling, Greer and Aileen turned in her direction, and even Rory and Calum stopped talking. Juliana felt her face warm. "You did not need to do this. I have nothing to give any of you."

"That doesna matter," Sima replied. "Ye are far from home—"

"She could have gone home if she'd wanted to," Morag mumbled.

The laird gave her a stern look. "'Tis uncharitable of ye to say so, daughter."

Morag lapsed into silence, although she certainly didn't look as though she considered charity to be a virtue. Juliana concentrated on the packages to avoid any more embarrassment.

The first held a finely woven, dark-blue wool half cloak with a hood and the other a pair of matching woolen breeches.

"'Tis a riding habit of sorts," Sima explained. "I ken English ladies doona wear breeches, but 'twill be practical on your ride home."

"Yes, it will," Juliana answered, "and I have found breeches to be much better suited for riding than a split skirt. Thank you."

"And the cloak will settle on the horse's rump," Greer said, "so ye won't have to keep pulling at it."

"And it can be worn over your other one," Aileen added, "to keep ye warm."

Juliana remembered how warm she'd been wrapped in Rory's cloak when they'd ridden to Fort William. She ventured a glance in his direction, wondering if he remembered, too, but his expression was neutral. She felt her face heat again. What had she expected? Even though she hadn't meant to, she'd rejected him.

"Well, now that everyone has opened gifts, can we go in

to breakfast?" Morag asked. "I am starved."

The others apparently were, too, as everyone muttered assent. Morag looked at Rory expectantly, but he gestured for her to go on. "I need a word with Juliana."

The girl's eyes narrowed slightly, but she must have remembered her father was there, for she turned on her heel, lifted her chin, and marched out.

He waited until everyone had cleared the room, which gave Juliana a moment of trepidation. He certainly didn't look as though what he had to say would be pleasant. Her breath caught. Was he going to tell her he'd decided to send her off with an escort while he remained here?

"I spoke with one of the MacDonnells last night—Keneth. His brother Tate has a house in Dalwhinnie near Drumochter Pass…" He paused.

Juliana stared at him. Was he going to say that was as far as he was taking her? She steeled herself for his next words. Whatever they were, she was not going to show her feelings. "Yes?"

"He offered us his brother's hospitality."

Rory had said *us*. That meant he was going to take her himself, didn't it? She didn't quite dare to breathe a sigh of relief. "And?"

He took a deep breath himself. "I wanted to ken what arrangements ye want made."

She furrowed her brows. "Arrangements?"

"I ken ye will want your own room." A muscle ticked in his jaw. "I can say we are avoiding another attempt by Cameron to abduct ye because one of my brothers is paying ye court."

"One of your *brothers*?"

"Aye. That way there will be nae question why I am escorting ye and nae questions about having your own room."

"I…" She swallowed. "I see."

And she did. Rory could not have made it more clear that he was through with any silly notions about actually being handfasted to her. Not that she'd ever intended to hold him to such, but... She sighed. But nothing. There had been *nothing* between them. She lifted her chin.

"Perhaps that would be best."

The rest of Christmas Day passed in a blur for Juliana. It hadn't taken her much time to pack the few pieces of clothing she'd purchased in Fort William, and the new woolen cloak and breeches she'd wear tomorrow morning were on the chair for when they left. She'd spent most of the afternoon in the solar with Greer and Aileen, partly because they'd become friends over the days she'd been at Invergarry, but it was also a good way to avoid Rory. They'd soon be forced to keep company on the road. She wasn't looking forward to being properly formal for the entire time it took to get home, but Rory had already demonstrated that he was going to do just that. Who knew she'd miss *arguing* with him?

He hadn't been at dinner, nor had Calum. Sima said they'd ridden out to check for any possibility that Camerons were lurking in the woods. Juliana supposed she should be grateful that Rory was taking such precautions.

Now, as the sun set and what they called the gloaming was quickly turning into darkness, there was just one more Yule festivity for them to get through. People were already gathering in the bailey for the big bonfire that would soon be lit. She saw Rory coming across the bailey from the stables and wondered if he'd just returned. Then she saw Morag run to him. Juliana turned away.

"I think I remember reading something once about pagan religions using bonfires in their ceremonies," she said to Aileen as they watched the laird lead eleven other men to the stack of wood, "but I thought it was done in the spring to ensure good crops and healthy livestock."

Aileen nodded. "'Twas the practice of Beltane, I think, but this custom dates back to our Viking roots. Our Norse ancestors were used to the sun completely disappearing where they came from, and it would not appear again until the twelfth night." She gestured to the twelve men who were now lighting the fire at intervals. "So, even though we all ken why the sun disappears on the winter solstice, 'tis symbolic of bringing back the light."

"And of the next year being better than the past," Greer added.

Juliana wondered if her new year would be better. Her sister Emily was happily married and more than glad to remain at Strae Castle. Her other sister, Lorelei, was planning to return to London for the Season under the chaperonage of the Countess of Bute, whose husband, the former prime minister, had been instrumental in ending the proscription of the MacGregors.

Should she go back to London with her sister? Juliana had no interest in going through the Season, since its primary goal was for young ladies to acquire husbands. Besides, she'd always scoffed at what Society referred to as the "marriage mart" when it really was more like a horse sale at Tattersalls—the best bloodlines sold to the highest bidder. The last thing she wanted was to become chattel to a stranger. She wasn't sure she could tolerate what marriage demanded... She tried not to flinch, thinking of how she'd reacted to Rory—and she *liked* him and, to be truthful, she was attracted to him. She also trusted him. But someone else? No. Better—*safer*—to become a spinster.

"Do ye want to join in the dancing?" Greer asked.

Juliana snapped out of her reverie and noticed that people were gathering around the fire, linking arms. "I have never been much of a dancer."

"'Tis easy," Greer said. "All we do is skip in a circle to the right, then skip in a circle to the left."

Would Rory be joining in? She scanned the crowd that was now beginning to move. Then she caught sight of him walking toward the castle. She glanced around for Morag but didn't see her. Perhaps this would be a good time to catch him and try to explain that she hadn't meant to wound his pride. She didn't think she'd get much sleep tonight if she didn't at least attempt to make amends.

"I think I will just go in. We have an early start planned for tomorrow."

Aileen gave her a sharp glance, then nodded. "Ye have a good night, then."

"I will." At least, she hoped she would. It would depend on if she could find Rory and how amenable he would be.

She walked up the front steps through the open door. The great hall was empty now, although she gave a cursory look around. Maybe Rory had gone to the library. She knew that's where the MacDonnells kept a decanter of their good whisky. If he were there, maybe they could share a dram. It would make the conversation easier.

She'd just started past the parlor when she heard a muffled sound. Something that sounded like a groan. Pausing, she looked at the half-open door. A chair—or something—scraped the floor. Was some drunkard lurching about? She took a step closer and looked through the small space between the frame and the door. Then she recoiled.

Rory and Morag were kissing under mistletoe suspended from the chandelier. His hands were on Morag's arms, hers were entwined around his neck, and she was pressed full length against him.

Juliana pressed a hand to her mouth to stifle her gasp and then turned and rushed out into the cold night air.

There would be no making amends this night. At least, not for her.

# Chapter Twenty-Four

When dawn broke, Rory felt like he'd just—finally—drifted off to sleep. He sat up and yawned, looking at the mantel clock atop the small hearth in his bedchamber. When he'd looked at it last, it had been an hour ago. He *had* only drifted off to sleep.

This was not the best way to start off a trip that would likely be at least ten hours in the saddle over rough terrain.

But the terrain wouldn't be as rough as making the trip with Juliana.

Rory rose, rubbing the sleep from his eyes, and made quick work of his ablutions, not bothering to call for hot water to shave. He probably didn't even need to shave, since he doubted Juliana would deign to look at him unless she absolutely had to. Of all the ill-fated timing…having her walk by the parlor last night just as he was trying to untangle himself from Morag.

Somewhere a very mean-spirited faerie was probably laughing herself silly, but it certainly wasn't a laughing matter for him. He'd been a real eejit for allowing himself to be duped. When he'd received the note asking him to meet in the parlor, he'd assumed—*eejit* that he was—it was from Juliana. The initial at the bottom of it seemed to be a *J*. He'd looked around the bonfire before he left and had seen Juliana—*eejit, eejit!*—but he thought maybe she'd been waiting for him to leave first.

It had been Morag waiting for him. The hair at his nape had risen when he saw her, but she said she'd only wanted to talk. To clear the air about how things stood between them so there would be no misunderstandings before he left the next morning. He didn't realize until he was well inside the parlor that she meant she was going to wait for him to return to her, and he'd definitely not seen the mistletoe hanging from the chandelier, either. Who would hang mistletoe from something fifteen feet in the air? It would have taken a ladder to get up that high.

He should have checked, though, once he realized Morag's ruse for what it was. He was a tracker, and he knew not all traces of tracks were on the ground. He also knew most people never looked up, which made it easy to spy on a foe. Both he and Devon had spent time in trees doing just that when they'd followed English dragoons several years ago, but had he bothered to survey his surroundings last night?

*Eejit. Eejit. Eejit.*

And then—this was where he was pretty sure the fae had a hand in it—Juliana appeared in the hall just as Morag had leaped at him. He'd stumbled back, banging into a chair and grabbed her arms to push her away when he'd caught a glimpse of red hair. Before he could disengage, Juliana had disappeared.

This did not bode well for the beginning of a trip that would take several days.

Rory finished dressing and took a final look in the mirror, touching the slight discoloring below his left eye. Morag hadn't taken the news that he was handfasted to Juliana very well.

He was somewhat surprised to see Juliana sitting at the table when he came down for breakfast. He gave her a wary look before helping himself to food from the sideboard, but she only smiled at him.

The hair at his nape prickled.

Everything else seemed normal, though. Juliana was engaged in conversation with Greer and Aileen, Calum and Sima were eating, and the laird had just sat down.

"I want to thank ye for your hospitality."

"Yes." Juliana said, "you have been most gracious."

She didn't look at Morag, but she glanced at him. She didn't mention his bruise, so maybe it didn't show as much as he thought it did. Right now, he just wanted to get on the road before any more trouble—faerie-instigated or otherwise—came their way.

The laird shrugged. "Think nothing of it."

"If circumstances were reversed, the MacGregors would have done the same," Sima said.

"And I did make a final check this morning to make sure no Camerons were lurking about," Calum added.

"I'm thankful to ye for that as well." Rory looked at Juliana's plate and saw she'd finished. "Are ye ready then?"

She nodded and rose as did the others. "My valise is by the door."

"I saw your horses brought around earlier," Morag said, as she smiled sweetly and broke open a scone. "Have a good ride."

The rest of the family followed them out to say farewell. Because he didn't trust Morag's smile, Rory double-checked the girths on each horse to make sure it was tight, and he inspected their hooves to make sure a stone hadn't been put inside a shoe that would make a horse lame down the road.

Everything seemed to be in order. He took the sack of food Sima had packed and tied it to his saddle, then turned to help Juliana mount, only to see one of the stable lads do the honors. *Is she determined to shun me completely?* Well, he could keep his distance, too. They would be home in a few days.

But as they rode away, the hair at his nape still prickled.

...

Juliana nudged Misty to come alongside Baron. In spite of Rory's aloofness—there was frost in the air around him that had nothing to do with the weather—she was not going to follow docilely behind him. Besides, she was curious about the bruise beneath his eye. Had he and Morag crashed to the floor and he'd hit his head on something? They'd certainly bumped into the furniture before Juliana had run up to her room. The thought of him rolling around on the floor with Morag was unsettling. Not that it was her business. It was not. *Not*. No doubt *Morag* hadn't been afraid to welcome Rory's kisses…and more. Juliana had liked his kisses, too—*I had*—before the panic had struck. But the dice had been rolled. Something that felt like a hot poker seared her stomach. Rory had made his choice, and it wasn't her. She swallowed. She might not want to hear the answer, but she had to ask.

"How did you get that bruise?"

He glanced over. "I doona want to say."

Of course not. Another knife-sharp pain pierced her. He was protecting Morag by not discussing their *in flagrante delicto*, as English Society called it. That meant he cared and it hadn't been just a quick tryst. She pursed her lips. She really was a glutton for punishment, but she wanted him to admit it. That way she could push it out of her mind, too.

"You can tell me. We are away from Invergarry now, so

no one will know what you did."

He raised a brow. "What I *did*?"

She waved her free hand vaguely. "You know."

"I ken a lot of things."

Was he being deliberately obtuse? If she were prudent, she'd let the matter drop. It wasn't even a proper subject, regardless. But. She'd never been overly concerned with being either prudent or totally proper, so this was not a time she wanted to start.

"I was referring to the parlor." When he looked stoically ahead, she added, "Last night." She was rewarded with a slight muscle twitch in his jaw and took a deep breath. "You were with Morag."

He reined in. Misty stopped of her own accord when Baron did. "What, precisely, do *ye* think I did?"

So he was turning the tables on her. He wasn't going to admit what he did. He wanted her to *tell* him what she saw. She heard Emily's voice in her head admonishing her—no, *telling* her in no uncertain terms—to let the matter lie. That it was not her business. Ladies didn't inquire about such things. But there seemed to be a devilish imp on her shoulder, prodding her to go ahead. Maybe it was one of those faeries that the Scots talked about, but she could almost feel it poking her.

"I saw you kissing Morag under the mistletoe." Juliana threw caution to the winds. "You were quite...*involved*."

A corner of his mouth quirked up. "Are ye jealous, lass?"

She drew her brows down. "No. Of course not."

"Ah." He tilted his head to the side, the half smile still on his lips. "Then why do ye bring it up?"

Her face heated in spite of the cold. "I..." Suddenly, she felt foolish. No. *I am a fool.* "My apologies. I should not have brought the subject up. You are free to engage in whatever carnal pleasures you like." She fought to keep her voice from rising. "With whomever you please."

His eyes darkened. "With whomever?"

She was sliding on already slippery ground here. She certainly didn't want Rory bringing up that debacle in the woods. She waved her hand again. "It was obvious to everyone that Morag liked you—"

"I am known to be likable, believe it or not."

"That is not what I meant! She *wanted* you. She made it plain..." Juliana stopped to collect her thoughts. She was sounding like a harpy. A *jealous* harpy. Taking a deep breath, she finished, "I am not blaming you for taking what she offered."

"*Hmm.*" He shrugged. "*She* kissed *me*, nae the other way around."

"That is not what it looked like." The words were no sooner out of her mouth, but she could have bitten off her tongue. "Never mind. Forget I said that."

Rory studied her for a moment. "For what 'tis worth, I didna take anything that Morag offered." He lifted the reins and nudged Baron forward. "We've a long ride ahead, so 'tis best we doona delay."

Juliana nodded, letting him lead the way this time. He obviously didn't want to discuss the subject further, which was quite all right. She could remain quiet now, since she'd gotten his answer. An odd feeling of elation filled her as she recalled his words. *I didna take anything that Morag offered.*

...

The terrain grew steeper and more rugged as they rode east toward the Monadhliath mountain range, necessitating riding single file most of the time. That arrangement suited Rory just fine and, he suspected, Juliana as well, since she was lagging farther behind as time went on. He looked over his shoulder regularly to keep her in sight, but he was pretty sure she wanted to put some space between them after their exchange. And he had his own thoughts to muddle through.

She'd sounded quite peeved about seeing Morag kissing him, which didn't make sense, since Juliana had literally pushed him away when he'd kissed her in the woods. That gesture didn't need an explanation. She'd rejected him. Why would she care if he were kissing someone else? He could have said that, but instead he couldn't resist asking whether she was jealous. Then he couldn't seem to let it go, especially when she made her remark about "whomever." It had *almost* sounded like… He pushed the thought aside. Juliana had *not* meant she wouldn't mind if he kissed *her* again. She'd pretty much said he could do what he liked. Then again, she *had* sounded rather petulant when she'd contradicted his explanation *and* she had blushed furiously right after. Why would she do that?

Rory snorted, causing Baron to do the same. The horse turned his ears back inquiringly, as if asking if they were going to continue a horse conversation. Rory leaned over and petted the gelding's neck. "Ye wouldna understand. I doona understand myself."

What he did understand was that he was going to be completely and totally barmy by the time they reached Strae Castle if he kept this kind of thinking up. He wasn't some green lad dazzled with the first girl who let him put his hand under her skirts, nor was he some besotted mooncalf. Juliana Caldwell was one of the most exasperating, quarrelsome, and maddening females he knew, and yet, he was drawn to her. He enjoyed matching wits with her, and she had grudgingly earned his respect and even admiration because she had not complained once about anything since the night he'd gotten her away from Cameron. And then there'd been the kiss in the woods. Her lips had been lush and ripe and she'd fitted against him perfectly…until she'd pushed him away. He shook his head silently this time. He would be completely and totally barmy halfway through the trip if he kept this up.

The sound of a horse galloping behind him brought him out of his convoluted thinking. Why in the world was Juliana approaching at such a speed over this kind of ground? The horse could lose her footing...

The thought died when he turned and saw the mare was riderless.

He wheeled Baron around, searching the trail. He hadn't noticed how much it twisted, and he cursed at his own dereliction. Grabbing Misty's reins, he headed back. He didn't have to go far before he saw Juliana lying on the ground.

He slipped from the saddle before Baron had come to a complete stop, praying she wasn't dead. There was no spattered blood, and he saw no rock near her head as he knelt beside her. Her eyes were closed, but she was breathing steadily. Perhaps it was better that she was not conscious. It would give him time to check for broken bones, since she probably wouldn't appreciate him running his hands over her body.

He tried not to dwell on that as he felt her shoulders, arms, ribs, and worked down her legs, although his obstinate mind couldn't completely deny the image of doing this when she would be naked beneath him. To trail his fingers—slowly—over every inch of bare skin. To feel her warm, silky... He cursed again and reached for her ankle.

"Ouch! *Ow! Ow! Ow!*"

He released her ankle and sat back on his haunches. Juliana had risen up on her elbows and was glaring at him. He nearly laughed with relief. If she were already angry with him, she couldn't be too severely hurt.

"What did you think you were doing touching me all over?"

He struggled to hide his grin. So she had been awake for his examination. At least she hadn't clobbered him.

"I was checking for broken bones. Ye fell off Misty."

"I did not *fall*."

He raised both brows. "Then why are ye on the ground?"

"Misty started acting strange."

"Strange?"

Juliana raised herself to a sitting position. "She started sidestepping, then tossing her head and rearing. When she kicked out her back legs, I couldn't stay on."

Rory looked over at the docile mare, now pulling on some dry grass. "Did something spook her? A rabbit, mayhap?"

Juliana shook her head. "We had fallen behind, and I tapped her to trot. We were rounding that bend"—she pointed behind her—"and I started to slip a little in the saddle. When I pulled myself straight, she started acting funny."

The hair at his nape began to prickle as he rose and walked toward the mare. Quickly, he unsaddled her and took off the blanket. As he turned it over, he saw the thorns. Pulling them from the wool, he held them up.

"What's that?" Juliana asked from where she still sat on the ground.

He brought it over along with the blanket. "'Tis a thistle. 'Twas what was hurting Misty and made her act like that."

"How did it get there?"

Rory clenched his jaw. *Morag.* He examined the blanket again and saw the small indentation where the thistle had been placed. "It was originally between the saddle and the blanket." He grimaced. The conniving harridan had placed it there so it would not go all the way through until they were well away from Invergarry. Well away from *help.* "As we rode, the pressure of ye sitting in the saddle pushed it through the cloth. It probably happened when ye lost your balance and pulled yourself up."

Juliana frowned. "Would the grooms not have checked the blanket before they saddled the horses?"

"They should have." He hesitated, hating himself for not thinking of it sooner. "I am nae sure who saddled the horses this morning."

"But even if someone else did...Morag told us the horses had been brought around." Juliana's voice trailed off, and her eyes widened. "Do you think she would have put it there?"

He was silent for a moment, then nodded. "I am almost certain of it."

"But...why? Why would she want to hurt me? I was leaving."

Rory took a deep breath. "I told her we were handfasted."

"You...*what*?"

"I ken ye didna want anyone else to find out, but it was the one thing I kenned would stop her." He touched his face. "I didna want to tell ye, but 'tis how I got the bruise."

"She slapped you?"

"Nae. She punched me quite proper."

"I...I am so sorry."

"I should have expected it." He held out his hand. "Let's see if ye can walk."

Juliana started to get up, then winced and fell back. "I do not think I can."

Rory leaned down, scooped her up, and carried her to the horses. "I doona think 'tis broken, but ye might have a sprain. We may have to stay at Dalwhinnie a day or two."

"I seem to be an ongoing burden to you," Juliana said even as her arms wound around his neck.

"Ye are nae a burden, lass." He grinned to make her feel better. "Ye hardly weigh anything at all."

Juliana rolled her eyes. "You know that is not what I meant."

"Do I?" Then he sobered as he clenched her closer. "At

least Morag can do no more damage."

• • •

Neal Cameron looked around the MacLean bailey, trying to find his second-in-command in the firelight and smoke from the Yule bonfire. The hour was not yet late, but couples were already beginning to drift away. He had to find his men before they took to their beds for a night of wenching.

He fingered the letter in the pocket of the coat he wore. It had arrived two days ago and bore no outside address. He'd almost not seen it, since it had been in a stack of mail tossed on a small table in the foyer. He hadn't recognized the handwriting, either, and, for a moment, he had contemplated whether it was from someone to whom he owed a debt. Trepidation had turned to elation when he saw the contents, though.

Morag MacDonnell had given him the date MacGregor would be leaving with Juliana and the path he would take.

Seeing his men on the far side of the bailey, he walked over to them. "Mind ye keep clear heads tonight. We ride for Drumochter Pass in the morning."

# Chapter Twenty-Five

Rory stood with Juliana in his arms, looking at her unsaddled horse and gauging what to do. They needed to get back on the road toward Dalwhinnie, but the thistle had rubbed a spot on Misty's back, and the mare might well get buckish again if pressure were put on the spot.

Juliana began to wiggle. "You can put me down."

"I doona want ye putting any weight on your foot," he said as he bent and eased her into a sitting position. "I doona think ye broke your ankle, but it would be better nae to risk further injury."

"Just this once, I will agree that you are right," she said, wincing a bit when as she settled.

"Well, that's a first for ye." Rory grinned to take any sting out of the words. "Ye actually think I may be right about something."

"I did say 'just this once.'" Her lips twitched as if she were trying not to smile. "You should not let it go to your head."

Was she actually jesting with him? He hoped her congenial mood would remain after he said his next piece. "I doona think ye can ride Misty."

"Of course I can. You might have to help me into the saddle, but once I am on her back, I will be fine."

He shook his head. "Her back has a sore. Ye will make it worse if ye ride her."

"I do not want to hurt her, but how will we…" Her voice trailed off as she looked from Misty to Baron. "We cannot ride pillion for miles."

He wasn't sure if she thought it would be a burden for the horse or because she didn't want to be that close to him for that long. The thought rankled. Why would she mind? She'd just acted like she was upset over what he might have done with Morag. She almost *had* sounded jealous, although that could be his wounded pride niggling at him. Still, she hadn't objected to being carried just now. He sighed. She truly was driving him mad. She'd had no choice but to let him carry her. She couldn't walk. Well, she had no choice now, either.

"We are going to have to." When she looked contemplative, he waved his hand around. "There is nae a village anywhere near here. We are several hours away from Dalwhinnie and more than three hours from Invergarry. Either way, we will have to ride." He looked at her. "Do ye want to go back?"

He hoped she didn't. Although a part of him wanted to let MacDonnell know what his daughter had done, taking Juliana back might put her in more danger. Morag had proven herself to be conniving. Besides, going back meant the possibility that Cameron might be lurking near the castle as well.

Juliana shook her head. "I do not want to go back."

He breathed a sigh of relief. "Then I'll put the saddle on Misty and leave it loose while ye ride with me."

Several emotions swept across her face, each moving so quickly that he wasn't able to decipher any of them, but she finally nodded.

Taking care to cinch the saddle only tightly enough that it would not slide around, he led Misty toward Baron and hitched her reins to the gelding's saddle. Then he returned for Juliana. She tried to stand, then fell quickly back.

He crouched down. "Let me lift ye."

She frowned as he stood up with her. "I hate feeling helpless."

"I ken, but if ye do more damage to your ankle, we may be stuck at Dalwhinnie for days. I thought ye wanted to get home."

"I do." She glanced at him. "I am sure you do, too. I am most definitely a burden to you now."

"Are we going to have that conversation again?" He placed her in the saddle, careful not to bump her ankle.

"I do not wish to be trouble for you."

"I dinna say ye were nae trouble." That got him an eye roll, and he grinned. "But I think I am getting used to it."

She frowned. "Am I supposed to be flattered?"

He shrugged. "Ye do seem to like vexing me."

One of her brows rose. "You seem to delight in vexing me as well."

"I'll admit I do like seeing your hair turn on fire."

"My hair?" She instinctively touched a curl as if to make sure it was unlit. "I have no idea what you mean."

He grinned again as he vaulted up behind her. "It turns redder when your temper rises. 'Tis intriguing."

She glanced over her shoulder. "You try to make me angry so you can be *intrigued*?"

"Aye." He reached around her for the reins. "And right now, your hair seems to be getting brighter."

"*Humph!*" She turned around. "I am glad I amuse you."

"Well, 'tis a long ride." He nudged Baron forward. "I'll have to see what else I can do to irritate ye along the way."

"*Humph!*" she said again and settled back against him.

And he realized he'd spoken much too soon. Having her arse settled so firmly over his groin was going to be damn irritating.

...

She hadn't meant to settle against *that* part of him, but now that she had, she wasn't going to admit her error by adjusting her position. It would probably just *amuse* him further to think she was embarrassed.

*My hair does* not *get brighter when I am angry.*

Her ire was not up, either. Now that he'd confessed to deliberately trying to pique her temper, she was not going to succumb. For the rest of the ride, no matter what he said or did, she was going to remain calm and composed. She was.

Her face did feel a little flushed, though, and she was quite warm in spite of the winter weather, but that had nothing to do with her being annoyed. She was wearing wool breeches and the heavy woolen cloak the MacDonnells had given her, after all, and she was practically cocooned by Rory. Her back was pressed against his chest, and his arms were around her, using the reins to guide the horse. Anyone, even a placid and perfectly in-control lady, would be warm under the circumstances. It did not mean she was doing a slow boil. Or that maybe...*maybe*...she was enjoying his attention a bit.

She spent the next several miles mulling proper replies that she could give to any question—no matter how irritating—that Rory might ask. It was harder to do than she thought it would be. She huffed in frustration. As much as she resented it, until they reached Dalwhinnie, she was going to have to bite her tongue and act like a docile and demure idiot.

*My hair does* not *grow brighter. What a ridiculous idea.*

Lost in her resolve that she would not be fodder for further entertainment, she didn't realize until nearly an hour had passed that Rory wasn't talking. Now that she was focusing on it, she'd only heard a few grunts and groans as he did a lot of shifting behind her. She grimaced. The saddle was really not meant to hold two people, but if she brought her leg over so she was sitting sideways across it, she'd not only see his face, she'd have to hold on to him as well. Better she stay astride like she was.

As they continued to ride, his shifting grew worse. She was about to ask him what was wrong when realization crept up on her. He *felt* different than when she had first settled against him. There was no denying that his manhood had grown hard. Very hard.

Juliana waited for the sense of panic to take over, like it had in the woods. Her rational mind knew they were both fully dressed, but they were in the forest as well. Logic had nothing to do with the near hysteria anytime she had close contact with a male.

And yet...it didn't come. She didn't experience the urge to swat or kick Rory, to fight and claw at him. No scream rose in her throat, and the grey haze that normally blurred her vision didn't happen. Her heart was beating faster, but it wasn't pounding. Her breathing might be a bit more shallow, but she wasn't gasping for air. Instead, she was actually able to *think*. To assess the situation.

She recognized now that all of Rory's squirming was because he didn't want her to realize his predicament. A sense of guilt niggled at her. She'd created the situation. Inadvertently, to be sure, but she still had been the cause. Instead of adjusting her own position, she'd stubbornly refused to move. The trotting, even though Baron's gait was smooth, still had them bouncing a bit. She couldn't have been making this easy for Rory.

And then she became aware of another sensation. This one was completely foreign. Her lower belly clenched, and an odd little throbbing that she'd never felt began to pulse between her thighs. A moment later when Baron stumbled on a jutting rock and caused both her and Rory to sway, her bottom came down directly on his hard shaft. The contact made her inner core soften, and she felt a wetness between her legs. *What is happening?* Behind her, Rory made a sound that came close to a growl.

"Are you all right?" she asked.

He didn't answer immediately, and when he did, his voice was raspy, as though he'd inhaled too much peat smoke. "I… will…be…fine."

...

Except, of course, he wasn't. Rory didn't think he'd ever been so grateful to see a house come into sight as he was a few minutes later when they rode around a curve and the village of Dalwhinnie appeared. It wouldn't be much farther to Keneth MacDonnell's brother's house now. He hoped.

He'd not been in such miserable pain in his life. Hours spent with Juliana's soft arse rubbing against his hard cock had been pure agony, much worse than any physical wound he'd ever received. No matter which way he moved, he couldn't get away from the constant friction arousing him. He'd seriously considered stopping, making his way behind some bushes, and taking himself in hand for relief, but he suspected such relief would not have lasted long once he was back in the saddle. Besides, he didn't want to leave Juliana alone with two horses to manage. The last thing he needed was for them to bolt.

"Do you know which house is Keneth's brother Tate's?" Juliana asked.

"He said it was a square sandstone at the edge of town." Rory had hoped it was *this* edge of town so he could dismount soon, but no such luck. "It looks like we will have to ride through the village."

He was all too aware of the curious looks they were getting from people as they rode past an assortment of market stalls, a dry-goods store with a cooper's sign hanging above it, the stables with the village blacksmith shop, a coaching inn in need of paint, and a small stone church.

Perhaps they should have waited until dusk fell before they rode through, but Juliana's ankle needed tending to. Hanging down as it did, her foot had swelled, and God knew—and the devil as well—that he *needed* to get off the horse soon. Still, he would have preferred that they'd managed to get to the MacDonnell house without being noticed. The fewer people who saw them, the fewer lies he'd have to tell regarding why they were there. He couldn't just say he'd simply been escorting Juliana through the central Highlands for nigh unto two weeks after her abduction without ruining her reputation. Since she didn't want to claim to be handfasted to him, that left him with the plausible excuse that his brother Alasdair—who was presently in Ireland—was courting her. Rory grimaced. If word of that got back to Strae Castle, it would ruin Alasdair's chances with Lorelei, the sister his brother really wanted to court.

"I do not see a sandstone house."

Rory frowned and looked around. Cottages were scattered behind the buildings, but he saw no sandstone structure, either. Keneth had been quite clear in his description, and houses didn't just disappear.

Juliana glanced over her shoulder at him. "Maybe we should stop and ask someone?"

"I doona think that necessary."

She shook her head. "Why is it men never want to seek help? It will not make you a lesser man if you do."

"A lesser man?" Good Lord. Did she think his manhood

was too fragile to ask for directions? Well, his male pride anyway. His *manhood* was certainly intact, as he could certainly attest. Not that he *actually* would. Attest to it, that is. He growled. He was dangerously close to total madness.

"You do not have to get angry about it." She shook her head again. "If you just stop the horse, I will ask for directions."

By all that was holy! Did she think him too *cowardly* to ask? He cursed silently and reined in Baron next to a man carrying a pail of coal. "Do ye ken where Tate MacDonnell lives?"

The man looked at him and then at Juliana before he turned his gaze to their riderless horse. It seemed he might be weighing whether they were reputable people or not. Just as Rory was about to ask again, the man finally pointed.

"If ye ride about a half mile more, ye'll find him."

He nodded to the man as he nudged Baron on. "Thank ye."

"Now, was that so hard?" Juliana asked as they left the village behind them.

Rory gritted his teeth. "I didna think 'twas difficult."

"Well"—she patted his knee as if reassuring a bairn—"we will soon be there."

It couldn't be soon enough for him. *Women.*

...

Tate MacDonnell's house stood near the frozen shore of Loch Ericht. Juliana looked out at the winter woodlands of Glen Truim from the window of the bedchamber she'd been given. It was a quiet, secluded area, and she could imagine how beautiful and serene the place would be in the midst of summer, with the trees in full leaf and the loch shimmering blue in the sunshine.

Highlander hospitality still amazed her. She sat back in

the stuffed chair near the window with her swollen ankle resting on the ottoman in front of her. They'd arrived less than two hours ago, and she'd already had a heavenly hot bath and a tray of bread, cheese, salted venison, and tea—tea!—had been sent up. The village healer—who reminded her of old Gwendolyn at Strae Castle—had been sent for and had declared nothing broken. She'd prepared a poultice to bring the swelling down, wrapped the foot, and ordered Juliana to stay off it until morning. She wasn't going to argue the point, since her backside was nearly as sore as her ankle.

It also gave her some time to reflect. Juliana poured the rest of the tea into her cup and took a sip. That the old panic hadn't risen this afternoon when she'd felt Rory's obvious condition was somewhat of a miracle. What was even more of a wonderment, though, was how *her* body had reacted. For the first time in her life she'd felt...*desire*. As if she wanted something...*more*.

The thought was confusing. She couldn't fathom how a man shoving his engorged member into a woman, impaling her, could be pleasant. When it had happened to her, it had felt like her insides were being ripped apart, and she'd bled for two days afterward. And yet...today that odd little spot between her thighs had throbbed and pulsed, and she'd felt herself turning to mush. The sensation *had* been...*pleasant*. She'd wanted to press herself against the hardness of Rory's shaft and *rub*.

She hadn't understood what she was experiencing, so she'd done the only thing she could think of. Act like nothing was happening. Change the subject. Be bossy. At least that had taken her mind off what her body had been feeling. But she had no idea why she had decided to touch his leg afterward. As though her hand had a mind of its own. His leg, of all places. Women did not touch men's legs.

Someone rapped on her door, and a moment later it

opened and Rory poked his head around. "Ah, ye are decent," he said and then stepped through.

"You should not be in here."

"I left the door open." He pointed to it as he took the other chair in the room. "Besides, the MacDonnells think I am escorting ye back to my brother, remember?"

She frowned, suddenly not relishing that lie, although it was probably preferable to declaring them handfasted, which had all sorts of complications that she didn't want to add to her already confused state. She had considered confronting him after Sima had explained to her that the handfasting was lawful, but since Rory had never brought it up, much less tried to take his rightful place in her bed, it was too embarrassing to ask. And, by now, it was far too late. She pushed the thought aside. "The brother is not Devon, is it?"

Rory laughed. "No one who has ever met Devon would ever believe he would court a Sassenach."

"It would be interesting if he ever met my cousin Anne." Juliana smiled at him. "She distrusts the Scots as much as he does the English."

Rory raised a brow. "Isn't she the one who sent gowns with ye because she thought we all ran around in pieces of plaid?"

"Well, yes, but she thought there were no seamstresses north of the border."

"She thinks us barbarians, then."

"I am afraid so." Juliana grinned suddenly. "It would be enjoyable to be a mouse in the corner if they ever did meet."

"'Tis unlikely, but mayhap the world is a safer place for it." Rory grinned, too. "But going back to my story, I told Tate 'tis Alasdair, since he's in Ireland."

Juliana grimaced. "Let's hope he never hears of it, since he's sweet on Lorelei."

"Aye." Rory shrugged. "I doubt the rumor will follow us

and, if it does, ye can always cry off, like ye'll do with the handfasting."

Juliana gave him a sideways glance. Of course, he would want her to do that if anyone at Strae Castle found out. He would want his life back once they got home. For the first time, the thought was somewhat unsettling. She realized that in the past two weeks she had grown rather used to having him near. She gave herself a mental shake.

"So why have you decided to visit me?"

"Ah. That." He grimaced. "There is another storm coming."

She frowned. "How do you know? Will it be as bad as the last?"

Rory shrugged. "Although General Wade built a good road through Drumochter Pass forty-five years ago, it doesna keep the snow from blocking the way. I doona ken when it will reopen."

"So you want us to leave now?"

Juliana straightened and started to put her foot down, but Rory placed his hand on her knee. "The wind has nae clocked around yet. Tomorrow at dawn should be early enough. Ye need to rest your foot."

"What about Misty?"

"She should be fine. The thistle dinna break her skin." Rory rose to leave. "I just wanted to give ye fair warning that we will be on our way early."

She looked at the closed door after he left. He'd only placed his hand on her for an instant, but she could have sworn she still felt lingering heat on her leg. And she hadn't minded his touch. At all. *What in the world is happening to me?*

Maybe she had changed? Emily had commiserated with her after what had happened, since her own marriage wasn't a good one, but there wasn't much she could say. Now, however, things were very different for her sister since she'd married Ian. Emily practically glowed, and they were always touching each other. Her sister couldn't seem to get close enough to her new husband.

However, Juliana hadn't expected that kind of thing with any man, never mind Rory. He certainly was not in love with her, and she wasn't in love with him. But he had been there for her and he had not taken advantage, even when he'd had the chance. She trusted him.

Could it possibly be that some of the ice packed around her heart was melting?

...

"Are ye sure ye want to leave today?" Tate asked as Rory was saddling the horses the next morning. "Ye ken ye are welcome to stay."

"Aye, but they'll be worried at Strae Castle if we doona get home soon." Although that was true, he wanted to get Juliana back for another reason. He wasn't sure how much longer his willpower would hold out over these increasingly strong, lustful urges. Yesterday's ride had just about done him in. "Besides, we will nae be sure how long the pass could be blocked, so 'tis better we try and beat the storm."

"I suppose ye are right about that," Tate answered. "But I doona think ye will be able to make it all the way to Blair Castle before it hits."

Rory had been thinking about that, too. In good conditions, it would be a solid ten to twelve hours in the saddle. "Hopefully, the mountains will slow the storm down and we can beat it. 'Tis one reason I want to leave by sunup."

Tate followed him as he led the horses out. To his surprise, Juliana was not only up and dressed for riding, she was waiting on the front steps with her valise and a satchel.

"Mrs. MacDonnell was kind enough to pack us some food," she said as she handed the bag to him.

He tied it to his saddle along with his whisky and water flasks, then slung her valise over Misty's saddle before helping her mount. He tried not to think about how his hands fit around her waist under the woolen cloak. He definitely didn't need his wayward cock to start torturing him this early in the day.

He vaulted onto Baron and dipped his head to Tate. "Many thanks."

"For naught." Tate looked up at the sky where low-hanging clouds obliterated the rising sun. "There is a royal hunting lodge about halfway to Blair Atholl on the other side of the pass. 'Tis called Dalnacardoch. Ye could take refuge there if ye need it."

Rory raised an eyebrow. "Is it open this time of year?"

"Nae. 'Tis most likely empty." Tate's mouth twitched. "But 'tis the king's responsibility to abide by Highlander hospitality if he has a lodge here, is it nae?"

Rory nodded. The idea of King George offering hospitality—to anyone anywhere who wasn't an aristocrat—was about as likely as a mermaid popping out of the loch. But then, the king wouldn't know, would he? "I will keep it in mind."

"God's speed, then."

With a wave, Rory turned Baron down the carriageway to the road, Misty following of her own accord. He glanced at Juliana, huddled in her cloak against the morning cold.

"How is your ankle?"

"Much better. I put the rest of the poultice on it, and Mrs. MacDonnell had a clean bandage to wrap it tight."

"It didna hurt to walk on it?"

"Only a little. The boot helps support it." Juliana reached down to pet Misty's neck. "And how is she doing?"

"She'll be fine. I made an extra pad of my dirty shirt so the saddle blanket wouldn't rub her if she was still sore."

"That was clever of you."

He grinned at her. "Aye, I can be clever."

Her mouth quirked. "First you tell me you are likable and now clever. What will be next?"

"I'll have to think on it." His grin widened as he urged the horses to a fast trot. "I wouldna want to overwhelm ye with all my talents." That earned him an eye roll, and he nearly laughed out loud. He was beginning to think the gesture was Juliana's way of not admitting that he was right.

But he sobered a few minutes later as he felt the first snowflake hit his face. He looked up at the now leaden sky. "We are going to have to hurry if we want to clear the pass before this storm unleashes its fury."

Juliana took a deep breath and tightened her grip on the saddle with her free hand. "I'll hang on."

Luckily, Misty had a smooth rocking-chair gait, and Rory held the horses to a slow canter because the road was somewhat rutted. By the time they reached the pass, though, the snow was falling heavily, already building up along the sides of the road and narrowing the passage. He breathed a sigh of relief that they'd made it in time.

"'Tis better we go single file. Wait until I'm through so we don't risk bringing more snow down," he said. "Once on the other side, we should be fine."

Juliana nodded and pulled Misty back to let him go first. As he entered, he looked up the mountainous sides, hoping the new snow wouldn't loosen heavy clumps already hanging from jutting ledges and start a small avalanche. He hated having to walk Baron through, but trotting or cantering could shake the earth enough to get him buried, leaving Juliana stranded.

He'd just made it through and reined in Baron to wait for Juliana when he felt a sharp pain in his thigh. Looking down, he saw an arrow protruding from his leg. Then something hard hit his head, and his world turned black.

# Chapter Twenty-Six

Juliana waited until Baron had rounded the slight curve in the pass and disappeared from view. She eased up on the reins, and Misty eagerly moved forward. It seemed her horse had taken a liking to Baron. Or maybe the mare felt protected close to him, same as—oddly—Juliana was beginning to feel toward Rory. He was...

Her thought broke off abruptly as she saw him lying on the ground. She slid off Misty and ran to him, ignoring her sore ankle. Just as she was kneeling down, she felt herself being grabbed roughly by her arms and yanked upright.

"I've finally caught up to ye."

She recognized Neal Cameron's voice even before she twisted halfway around trying to free herself. "Let go of me, you vile brute!"

He held fast. "I am going to teach ye some manners."

"You will teach me nothing." She tried to claw at him, but she couldn't get her hands up. "You could have killed Rory! I need to make sure he is all right."

"Doona fash about him. MacGregors have hard heads."

He pulled her away, half dragging her several yards around some boulders. "I want to be well away from here before he wakes up."

She saw his two henchmen then. One of them had caught Misty. The other stood holding the reins of their three horses.

"Let me go!" Juliana flailed at Neal, struggling against his hold as fury began to simmer inside her. "I am not leaving with you!"

"Aye, ye are."

"*No!*" She tried to dig in her heels to no avail. "I need to make sure Rory is alive."

He gave her a shake that rattled her teeth. "I told ye nae to fash about him."

"We are handfasted! He… I am going to marry him!"

"'Tis a lie. Margaret told us the truth."

She tried to pull away once more. "I've changed my mind. I…love him!" Where that came from, she didn't know, but hopefully the words would sink in.

Neal narrowed his eyes. "Has he taken your virtue? I'll kill him right now if he has."

Juliana opened her mouth. Closed it. Started to open it again. Tried to tamp down her rising fear and think calmly. This was worse than the dilemma she'd been in when she'd been raped. If she hadn't acquiesced to the lord's demands, he'd have ruined Lorelei. This time, the choice meant Rory's life. Right now, he was lying helpless in the snow and couldn't defend himself. Well, then. It was up to her. She lifted her chin.

"I am untouched. Rory has been a gentleman."

"MacGregor has been stupid. I'd have swived ye until ye couldna walk."

She had no doubt that he would—vile, despicable creature that he was. She refused to look away as he leered at her.

"Mayhap I should teach ye that lesson now before we

move on." He grabbed a breast and squeezed hard before letting go. "Would nae take long to show ye who's the one in charge here."

Cold sweat ran down her spine. Never was she going to allow herself to be raped again. Somehow, she managed to get some traction, and she kicked Neal's shin with her good foot, only to strike a boot. "Get away from me, you *eejit*!"

Neal grinned. "Ye are learning the Gaelic? Good lass—umph!"

The last came out as her knee connected with his groin. He bent over while the man by Misty stifled a laugh. She jerked one arm free and balled her hand into a fist. Before she could strike, however, Neal grabbed it with a snarl and twisted her arm behind her back. She clenched her jaw from crying out in pain.

"If ye try anything like that again, I'll—"

"We best be going if we're going to outride the storm," the man holding the three horses said.

"Aye, ye can handle the hellion later," the other one added.

Neal yanked her arm a bit higher, and, in spite of herself, she screamed.

"I can easily break it," he said as calmly as if he were deciding what to wear. "Ye'd best remember that."

He gave her a shove that had her stumbling forward. She managed to catch herself before falling. Red-hot rage spread through her, nearly obscuring her vision with its haze.

"Get her on her horse," he said, "and make sure one of you stays on either side."

The first man led Misty to a rock. "Ye can climb on from here."

At least now there was some distance between her and Neal. She tried to keep from shaking. She needed to *think*. Maybe once she got on Misty, she could get away? But Rory was lying on the ground. She couldn't leave him. Then she remembered that this morning, she'd strapped on the *sgian dubh* Rory had given her. Her fiery anger disappeared, to be replaced with icy-cold resolve.

She'd done it almost as a lark, as part of her new traveling outfit, but perhaps divine intervention—or one of the Scottish faeries—had prodded her to do it. Neal wasn't that far away... She took another step, pretending to stumble again, and pulled the blade from its sheath beneath her breeches. Holding the knife close to her side, she straightened. She no longer shook. Instead, she felt calm. Almost detached.

"Neal."

He turned at the sound of her voice. "What?"

"I have something for you." Even as she said the words, she quickly took her stance—thank God Rory had made her practice until she could move with lightning speed—and the blade hurled through the air, striking Neal just below the ribs.

His eyes widened as he grasped the handle, yanked the blade out, and threw it to the ground. Then he clenched his hands over his belly as he fell to his knees.

For a moment nobody moved.

Then all hell broke loose.

• • •

Rory stirred, coming back to consciousness abruptly as sharp pain tore through his leg. He sat up and waited for the world to stop swirling around him. As his head cleared, he saw the damn arrow stuck in his thigh. He couldn't pull it out without causing the wound to gush blood, and he didn't know how deep it was, either. Better to leave it in for now. Clenching his teeth, he grabbed the shaft near his leg to hold it steady while he broke off the rest of it. Even so, the world went black momentarily as the pain seared through him again.

*How long have I been out?* He looked around, but there was no sign of Juliana or Misty. He didn't see any signs of a struggle, either, but the ground was rocky and the horses had trampled the snow. Had she been able to escape to safety? He hoped she'd turned around when she saw him and ridden back to Dalwhinnie.

Who had attacked them, anyway? He studied the broken shaft and fletching. He didn't recognize the cock feather as unique, but the clans had ceased making their own arrows decades ago, since they were generally used for hunting and not identification in battle anymore. He tossed it aside and picked up the good-size rock that had apparently hit him in the head. Whoever aimed it must have been close to be so accurate.

Which meant someone had been waiting. Highly unlikely for highwaymen to stake out the pass, hoping to catch an unwary traveler at the onset of a blizzard. Much more likely that it had been Neal Cameron… But how would he have known they'd be taking this long route home? Rory cursed suddenly.

*Morag.* It was no secret at Invergarry which way he and Juliana had planned to go. Nor was it any secret why they were taking that route. He and Calum had discussed outwitting Cameron on more than one occasion. If Morag had been malicious enough to put a thistle under Misty's saddle, the wretched woman could very well have sent word to Neal.

The question was: Did they have Juliana, and which way did they go?

The question was answered by a piercing scream.

Rory leaped to his feet, steeling himself against the hot-iron agony burning his leg, and limped to Baron. With near superhuman effort, he managed to get a foot in the stirrup and haul himself up while at the same time turning the gelding toward the sound. He'd just rounded the boulders when he saw Neal Cameron fall to his knees.

Then things happened simultaneously. The man who'd been tending the horses ran toward Neal. In a vague, peripheral way, Rory was aware that blood was gushing from Neal's belly and a knife lay on the ground, but it was the blur of movement to his right that caught his attention. Another man who'd been near Misty had drawn his dagger and was approaching Juliana, who stood in the middle of the small clearing with no place to go.

"*Àrd Choille!*" Rory yelled the MacGregor battle cry as he drew his sword and bore down on the man.

The man turned, dropped the knife, and attempted to draw his own sword, but it was too late. Rory swung, wanting to lop the man's head off, but he managed to hold back his rage and slice through the man's weapon arm instead. The cur howled as he clenched it and hobbled toward Neal and his partner.

"Shoot the damn bastard!" Neal managed to say.

Rory whirled Baron, intending to pull Juliana up behind him and get the hell out of there before the unwounded man could pull his musket. Instead, his fierce little warrior had picked up the knife the wounded one had dropped and assumed a throwing stance.

"Do not move," she said—assumedly to the three Camerons, but Rory wasn't sure if she meant him, too. "I am not going anywhere with you. Do I have to make myself clearer?"

In spite of the dire circumstances, Rory bit back a grin. Juliana's hair looked as if it were about to ignite. She reminded him of Boudicca just then, but even that war queen had needed help. He gestured with his sword.

"Throw all your muskets over here. Slowly."

The unharmed man tossed his, then pulled the other two from his companions. Neal glared at Rory from the ground, but he ignored it.

"There is a healer in Dalwhinnie. I suggest ye all ride there before ye bleed to death." Then he turned to Juliana and held out his hand, hoping for once she'd listen to him because his strength was fast fading. "I suggest we leave."

But of course, she didn't. Instead, she walked over to the men—much too close—and retrieved her *sgian dubh*.

"I've grown rather fond of this," she said, and then she walked to where Misty still waited by the rock. In another moment, she had mounted by herself. "Now we can leave," she said as she spurred Misty to a canter.

Baron followed, and one of the last coherent thoughts Rory had as he leaned low in the saddle to wrap his arms around his horse's neck was that Juliana had just ridden to his rescue.

• • •

Juliana refused to think. Or maybe she *couldn't* think. She was aware that Misty was galloping along a road, but she felt a strange, numb detachment, as though she were someone observing from afar the events that had just taken place. Watching as some coolly calculating woman had calmly threatened to kill three men. The woman had *wanted* to do that. Had only been waiting for someone to make a wrong move so she could avenge every woman who had ever been molested by a man. The weapon in her hand had felt good. Powerful. She was the one wielding power, not some damn man.

But Rory had come to her rescue. Maybe not all men were monsters. She recalled that moment of terror when she'd been defenseless. Rory had charged like some gallant knight of old. Not that she believed in gallant knights.

The pounding of the horse's hooves was jarring her back

to reality. She heard Baron thundering behind her, trying to catch up, and glanced over her shoulder. Then she nearly unseated herself at the sight of Rory sagging over Baron's neck. She reined in Misty.

"Are you—"

"Just ride," he managed to grit out. "We have to get to Dalnacardoch."

"You are hurt. Should we not go back to Dalwhinnie?"

"Doona argue." His voice was barely audible. "Just. This. Once."

Juliana frowned. "But…" She stopped when he completely slumped over Baron's neck, eyes closed. Good Lord! He'd passed out. What was she going to do if he fell off? There wasn't any way she could lift him. She fought the panic that was rising in her. She needed to secure him to his saddle. How? She thought a moment, then opened her valise and pulled out a shawl.

Slipping off Misty, she rolled the wool tightly until she had a rope of sorts. Tying one side around his wrist, she dipped under Baron's neck and secured his other wrist as closely to the first as she could. It was a makeshift manacle at best, but hopefully it would keep him from sliding off. She tugged Baron's reins loose so she could lead him and remounted Misty.

She looked in both directions. Should she return to Dalwhinnie in spite of what Rory had said? The healer was there…but the Camerons would be there as well. There was a real possibility she would run into them on the road before they got to Dalwhinnie. Neal Cameron would be as angry as a poked bear. Worse than a poked bear. He would be more like a rabid wolf. She couldn't fight three of them, even if two were wounded. And they could easily kill Rory.

Sighing, Juliana turned Misty's head to the south. She would have to keep both horses at a walk, since Rory's position was precarious. It was probably just as well, since the snow was falling more thickly now and she couldn't see that far ahead. The last thing she needed to do was wander off the road.

Rory's eyes remained closed as they made their slow way, but his lips weren't blue, so at least he was breathing. His mouth was slightly open and looked rather soft against the coarse hair of Baron's mane. She remembered how his lips had felt that day in the woods... How skillfully he'd used them to nibble and nuzzle, tempt and tease...

Juliana felt a hysterical bubble rising in her throat. She was thinking of Rory's kisses *now*? She was out in the middle of snow-covered mountains—in a near blizzard—trying to manage two horses when she was no horsewoman. *And* she had an unconscious man tied to his saddle. And where were her thoughts straying? She giggled at the absurdity of it, then hiccuped and wiped her eyes, realizing the laughter had turned to tears. She rarely cried. She *never* giggled. And yet she had a strange desire to start laughing out loud or even shriek and scream. She never did those things, either. *What is the matter with me?*

Taking a deep breath, she forced herself to focus. She had no idea how badly Rory was hurt. He'd been hit in the head, and she remembered old Gwendolyn telling everyone to keep Emily awake after her sister had had an accident at Strae Castle, but she could hardly stop the horses and try to do that now. They'd freeze to death if they didn't find that hunting lodge.

As they proceeded slowly along, wrapped in a swirling haze of white, she began to talk to Rory, even though she knew he could not hear her. She told him how sorry she was that she'd been rude to him. She told him that most of the time she thought he was right, even though she wouldn't admit it. She even told him—finally, when she'd run out of things to confess—*why* she'd run away from him in the woods that day. Other than Emily and Lorelei, she'd never told anyone about that awful day. But at least her secret was still safe. Rory hadn't made a sound or even so much as shifted once since he'd passed out.

Finally, after her voice grew raspy from talking and the horses had slowed their walk to a plod, she saw the hunting lodge. She almost missed it, since the buildings were painted white and set off the road.

There was no sign of life as she turned the tired horses into the carriageway in front of the main building. No door opened to them, but perhaps their arrival hadn't been noticed. Surely the king must keep a small staff here, even when he wasn't in attendance? But it was just after Yule and the mid of winter.

Juliana had a growing sense of trepidation as she walked to the entrance and banged the heavy brass knocker several times. Hearing no sound from within, she tried again. Nothing. She tried turning the knob, but the door was locked. Had she really expected it to be open?

She looked around. She knew they had arrived at Dalnacardoch, because they had passed a sign by the road. It seemed the entire place was deserted. *What are we to do?*

• • •

Rory stirred as warm air swept his face. At least, it felt warm, and he'd been so cold. His nose twitched. Something coarse was rubbing his face, and it smelled...like horse. He opened his eyes. One of them, anyway. The other seemed pressed closed.

He sniffed again, and this time the sweet aroma of hay filled his nostrils. With his open eye, he assessed what he could see. Exposed beams, not too high. A wooden wall...

no, a stall. He was definitely in a stable. And using his horse for a pillow.

He started to sit up, only to be pulled back down on Baron's neck. He tugged at his hands and realized they were bound. By the devil's own horns! Had he been taken captive by the damn Camerons? But he remembered riding away. Following Juliana. *Have we been captured? Where is she?* He attuned his hearing for sounds, but could discern only a soft nicker. The mare? No other horse responded, so maybe the Camerons weren't there. Raising his head as much as he could with his arms shackled around Baron's neck, he looked around, breathing a sigh of relief as Juliana stepped out of a stall.

"Are we safe?"

She started, then hurried toward him. "You are awake."

"I wasna sleeping."

"You lost consciousness hours ago."

Hours ago? He grimaced. *I passed out when I was supposed to be protecting Juliana? Good God almighty. What must she think of me?* "I am sorry."

Her brow furrowed. "For what? You were hit on the head, and you have a leg wound. It was probably better you did not have to endure the ride."

*Better that I went blank and left her to manage?* He studied her with his open eye. She didn't seem angry when, for once, she had every right to be. Perhaps best not to push that issue. "Why am I tied?"

"I should think it obvious." The look she gave him was one she might have used on a halfwit, which, at the moment, might be accurate. "I had to secure you to Baron so you wouldn't fall off."

"I havena fallen off a horse since I was a wee bairn."

Her eyebrows rose. "Well, you weigh more than a wee bairn now. I would not have been able to lift you back into the saddle, unconscious that you were."

She did have a point. "Can ye untie me now? I think I can get off Baron by myself."

Nodding, she leaned down and undid the binding on one wrist. As soon as it was free, he straightened and swung his leg over the saddle to dismount.

And promptly collapsed in a heap.

Juliana knelt beside him. "You cannot walk? Is your leg broken?"

He shook his head, not trusting his voice to come out an octave higher, as needle-sharp pain seared through his thigh. Clenching his teeth, he finally managed to get words out. "There is an arrowhead in my leg."

Her eyes grew round. "It...it's still in your leg?"

He nodded wordlessly and scooted back, in case Baron should accidently place a hoof on his leg as well. "You need to—"

"Of course!" Juliana stood and took Baron's bridle. "I'll put him in a stall."

That wasn't what he was going to say, but he might as well wait until she returned to tell her he needed to get the arrow out. Perhaps he could get control of his voice by then.

In a few minutes she was back. "I unsaddled him and gave him hay. There may be oats in one of the bins, but I have not looked yet." She paused. "If you will be all right for a few minutes, I will bring in some buckets of snow to melt for water."

He nodded again, still not trusting his voice. It didn't take long before she returned, carrying two buckets. "I should be helping with those."

"You have an arrow in your leg."

As if he didn't know. The pain, now that he was awake, was steadily increasing. He hoped infection hadn't already set in, but it wasn't something he wanted to voice. He looked around again. "Are we at Dalnacardoch?"

"Yes. That is what the sign said."

"Then why are we out here? A servant dinna refuse to let us in, did he?" He frowned as a disquieting thought hit him. "And where is the stable master? Ye shouldna be taking care of the horses."

"There is no one about. Maybe the servants have all gone home for Yule." She shrugged. "The door to the lodge was locked."

*"Mhic an Diabhail!"*

One brow rose. "I assume you are cursing?"

"Aye." He grimaced. "I am sorry."

She waved away his apology. "I would say we are in a *bloody* sorry state ourselves."

In spite of the pain shooting through his leg, he managed a smile. Juliana wasn't one to mince words. "I think I'm beginning to like that English word."

"We will have to make do. Would ye mind getting the whisky flask from my saddle?"

She frowned at him. "You want to get drunk? Now?"

"Aye, I would love to." He thought he saw her hair get brighter and decided not to tease her further. "But I need it for another purpose."

She gave him a skeptical look. "What would that be?"

"I'll need to pour it on my wound."

Her gaze went to his leg. "Will it soak through the wool?"

"Nae." He watched her face. "My breeches will have to come off."

"Ah…of course." Her face turned an interesting shade of pink as she rose. "I will get one of the saddle blankets so you can cover yourself."

"It probably willna help."

"Of course it will. You cannot…cannot just lie about… with no breeches—"

"'Tis just the two of us, lass." He raised a hand before she could protest. "And I think ye can see I am in nae shape to take advantage of ye."

She drew her brows together and pursed her lips as she appeared to contemplate that. "I suppose you are right. Still, I would rather you have a cover."

"'Twill just get in your way."

That drew a startled look. "Get in the way? You just said you would not—"

"Take advantage of ye," he finished. "But in a way I need to."

She looked wary. "You said—"

"I need ye to do something else."

"What?" Her voice still sounded unsure.

He drew a deep breath. "Ye will need to remove the arrow for me."

# Chapter Twenty-Seven

Juliana stared down at him, still seated on the stable floor, not quite sure what she'd heard. "You want me to remove the arrow?"

"Aye." He winced. "The sooner, the better, to avoid infection."

"But I do not know anything about treating wounds."

A muscle in his jaw clenched. "There is nobody else here."

Juliana opened her mouth, then closed it with a snap. He was right. He needed tending. This was not the time to act like a cabbage head. She turned away.

"Where are you going?"

She paused. The question had come out almost as a plaintive wail, something she was *sure* Rory hadn't intended. He must be in more pain than he'd acknowledged. "I'm going to see if there is any kind of accommodation so you do not have to lie on the floor. I will be right back."

He looked a little mollified at her assurance, and, for some reason, she suddenly thought of him as a boy who didn't want to admit that a scraped knee hurt. Except Rory was a man with an arrow in his thigh.

It didn't take her long to check out the stables. The snow in the buckets she'd brought in had just started to melt. "We are in luck. There is a small room that seems like the stable master's. It's got a cot and some living essentials."

"Good."

While she had been gone, Rory had scooted toward a rail and used it to pull himself up. He gingerly put weight on his wounded leg and took a step. His face went from grey to white, and she moved instinctively to drape his arm over her shoulder, trying to support part of his weight. "Lean on me."

"I doona need—"

"Just. Do. It." *What is it about men? They can't ever be anything but strong?* "It is all right—"

"I can walk."

"*Gabh air do shocair,*" Juliana snapped.

Rory blinked. "Are ye are telling me to shut my mouth?"

"I am. You need to conserve your energy."

They hobbled a few more steps before he frowned. "When did ye learn Gaelic?"

She didn't answer until she had, rather unceremoniously, plopped him on the cot in the stable master's room. She didn't have enough strength to talk and assist at the same time. "There are a few words and phrases I like. That's one of them."

"I can teach ye more."

"Right now, you need to tell me what to do." She straightened. "In English."

He tried to smile, but it turned into a grimace as he slid back against the wall and started to tug off a boot.

"Let me." Juliana bent to put one hand under the heel to wiggle it loose, but it wouldn't budge. "How do you get these things off?"

One of his brows rose. "Ye have never taken a man's boots off?"

She frowned. "Of course not. Why would I?"

He gave her a long look. "Never mind. If ye will turn your back to me and straddle my leg—"

*"What?"*

He sighed. "'Tis the easiest way to get a boot off."

"But it...does not seem—"

"I need to get the boots off, lass."

She snapped her mouth shut. It might be an awkward position—at least for her—but she doubted he had anything lecherous in mind, given that his pallor was near ghostly. Doing as he asked, the boot did come off fairly easily. However, she almost changed her mind about lechery when, as she pulled on the second boot, his stocking-encased foot came in contact with her derriere and nudged her. Startled, she jumped, the boot coming loose in her hand suddenly, and she lurched forward to fall on her hands and knees.

From behind her, Rory made a strange choking sound.

Trying to muster some dignity, she turned on him as she stood. "Was that called for?"

"Aye. 'Tis the easiest way to get the boots off. I dinna mean to send ye flying across the room."

"I did not fly..." She clamped her mouth closed once more and set the boots aside. "I will go and get our supplies."

"Light the fire first in the brazier. We will need it for the knife."

She swallowed hard. "You expect me to cut your leg open?"

"Nae. I hope ye can just grip the end of the shaft and pull the arrowhead out."

"Then why do I need a knife?"

"Because the wound will bleed freely once ye remove the arrow." Rory shrugged. "Ye will need to cauterize it."

"Caut… You mean put hot iron to your skin?"

"Aye."

"But…" She didn't finish the inane question. Of course it was going to hurt. She didn't need to point that out. He must be well aware of it. "Um…if you will…remove…your breeches, I will gather the things I need."

"Doona forget the whisky."

"I won't." She was beginning to think she needed a drink herself.

Kindling and a small log had already been laid in the brazier, which, she noticed as she lit it, was well placed in the midst of a cobblestone circle and not near any wall, for the safety of the animals. A pitcher and basin sat on top of a chest of drawers across from the cot. She found a few eating utensils in one drawer and a wash cloth and towel in another, along with an extra shirt. She made quick work of hacking the sleeves off it to use for bandages and laid everything by the cot, then she went back to the main room to fetch the whisky and melted snow. She nearly dropped one of the buckets when she returned.

While she'd been gone, Rory had divested himself of his breeches. She probably should be grateful he hadn't asked for help with *that*. At least he'd draped the towel over his nether parts as well as the wound, but the sight of the rest of his hard, muscular legs did funny things to her insides.

She approached him slowly, laying the things she'd brought from the other room on the floor. "I think I have everything I need."

"Whisky first."

"Am I not supposed to pour that on your wound after I remove the arrow?"

"Aye, but I think I need a fortifying swallow." He managed a wan smile. "Ye might take one for yourself."

"I will wait." She handed him the flask. The last thing she

needed was a shaky hand. She was already shaking like the last autumn leaf in a gale.

He took three swallows. Healthy ones. Then handed back the flask.

"Tell me what to do."

As he explained what she would need to do once the arrow was out, she wasn't sure she was capable. But there was no one else, so she nodded.

"Now," he said once he'd finished, "take your *sgian dubh* and lay the blade across the coals." When she'd done that, he picked up one of the makeshift bandages she'd torn from the shirt. "Take this—it will work like a tourniquet and keep the bleeding down—and wrap it tight around my leg above the wound."

Above the wound? That meant she'd have to lift the towel and…see…his…his… She took a deep breath, chiding herself. She was going to have to move the towel anyway to see the *wound*. She simply wouldn't look at…his…*thing*. Gingerly, as though she were reaching for a coiled snake, she picked up a corner of the towel, inching it upward.

"I'll die of old age if ye keep that pace." Rory yanked the towel away. "Let's get this done."

He was wearing small clothes. Relief flooded her, blood returning to her face in such a rush that her ears rang and she scarcely made out his words. Of course he was wearing an undergarment. Her face felt on fire. "I thought… I mean, I did not…ah—"

"I would nae mind stripping naked for ye, lass, but I doona think much would come of it if I did right now, so ye doona have to fash."

She frowned. "I am not…*fashing*."

"If ye say so." He bent his knee. "The tourniquet?"

It was then that she actually saw the arrow. It had lodged near the back of his thigh, the skin around it ruby red. "It does not look good."

"I dinna think it would. Just get the bandage on."

Juliana gave herself a shake in order to focus. The arrow was midthigh, and she placed the cloth a good two inches away from the swelling around it, which was dangerously close to his manhood. Although she took care to avoid touching him there, when she started to secure the bandage by pulling it tight, his leg jerked and her hand brushed against the bulge, which instantly enlarged. She pulled her hands back. "I did not mean—"

"Just. Get. On. With. It."

For a fleeting second, she thought he meant he wanted her to fondle him. She waited for the familiar sense of panic to set in, but it didn't. In another moment, her mind cleared and she realized he meant to get the arrow out. Why was she thinking such foolish thoughts? He had not acknowledged the reaction. He probably hadn't even felt it.

She took a deep breath to steady her hands. "Do I just grasp and pull?"

For an instant, something sparked in his eyes, and she realized her words may have come out wrong, since that part of him twitched again. She certainly didn't mean to grab *him*. Was he trying not to smile? She drew her brows together. "Where do I grasp the *arrow*?"

"Press your left hand around the puncture and hold it down while ye grab what's left of the shaft with your right. Count to three so I can ready myself, then yank hard. It has to come out all at once."

She took another fortifying breath. She could do this. She *must* do this. There was no other choice. Doing as he asked, she counted aloud. "One. Two. *Three*." She pulled, trying not to squirm as she felt flesh tear, but she held up the arrow. "It is out."

His face had gone white as the snow outside. "Pour the

whisky on it."

She did, watching as his jaw clenched and his lips formed a tight, pale line. "I do not want to hurt you."

He shook his head, then gestured to the brazier. "The...knife...next."

*Dear Lord. How am I going to do this?* How was she going to place red-hot steel against his skin when just the alcohol had such a horrible effect? "I do not think—"

"Ye...*must*."

She looked down and saw, to her horror, blood was flowing down his leg. Quickly she went to the brazier and wrapped the wash cloth around the handle of the knife before picking it up and bringing it back to the bed. She stopped just inches away.

"You are sure?"

"Aye. Do it."

Juliana bit her lip, then closed her eyes as she pressed the hot metal down. The sound that came from Rory was neither human nor beast, but it was a sound she would never forget for the rest of her life... Nor the smell of searing flesh.

She lifted the knife away quickly, opening her eyes at the same time. Rory lay slumped over, unconscious, for which she gave thanks. The pain would be excruciating if he woke any time soon.

Laying the knife on the cobblestones to cool, she slowly loosened the tourniquet, keeping it tied until she was sure the cauterization had stopped the blood flow, then she wrapped a clean bandage around the leg. It was all she could do for now.

Suddenly, exhaustion overtook her. The events of the day—the ambush by the Camerons, Rory lying wounded on the ground, the attempted abduction, her own attack on Neal, the escape, and then the long, bone-chilling ride here.

She desperately needed sleep, but there was only the one cot. A hysterical bubble rose in her throat as she thought of the argument they'd had over the one bed at Spean and how she'd offered to sleep on the floor, only to have Rory leave instead.

It was obvious he would not be going anywhere tonight. Nor did she want to sleep on the floor. She eyed the cot. It might be big enough for two if she didn't mind nestling against him. The thought should have been unsettling, but it wasn't. Taking care not to bump his injured leg, she rolled him to his side, then she quickly removed her boots and outer clothing to crawl in beside him.

Her last thought before she fell asleep was how ironic that she felt safe now.

...

When Rory woke the next morning, his nose was practically against a wooden wall and he wasn't sure where he was. The room smelled vaguely of hay and horses. A stable? Why would he be in a stable? His thigh hurt like hell, and he was stiff and sore. *What...?* Memories began to drift back. He remembered being shot with an arrow, and then something had hit his head. There'd been some kind of skirmish, too. Juliana had galloped away like the devil was behind her, and he'd followed. Except he wasn't the devil. That would have been Cameron. Cameron had ambushed them, and he and Juliana had managed to escape to Dalnacardoch. He hoped that's where they were.

At least his leg didn't feel like it was on fire any longer. He'd somehow rolled on his good side—which was why he was looking at a blank wall—but that had probably helped as well. He needed to thank Juliana for the job she'd done. Not just in patching him up, but for having managed by herself to get them to safety after he'd passed out on Baron yesterday. She had been quite clever to tie him to his horse.

Slowly, so he wouldn't disturb the bandage or cause further injury to his leg, he began to turn over and then realized he was blocked. Had Juliana rolled something behind him to keep him on his side? He raised his head to glance over his shoulder and blinked.

*Juliana* was blocking him. She lay with her back to him, but she was definitely up against him. Quite solidly. For a moment, his disoriented mind wondered if they'd done anything the night before, since she was in his bed. He didn't think he was capable of doing much, but his cock hadn't been injured. Then, as his thinking cleared, he chided himself. There was only one bed. That was the reason she was in it.

Carefully, he turned on his back and eased an arm behind her head to make her more comfortable. As he moved his hand down her arm to tuck her closer, she turned again, her breast, beneath the tunic she'd left on, filling his hand. Instinctively, his fingers squeezed gently, feeling the soft plumpness.

The next minute his ear was boxed and the she-devil flew out of the bed.

"What do you think you are doing?" she shrieked.

"I'm sorry." He rubbed his ear. "'Twas an accident."

"An accident?" Juliana pulled on her breeches and wrapped her cloak around her. She looked around as though she might want to put more of a barrier between them. "You touched my breast."

"I ken." Rory looked at his offending hand. "I was only trying to make ye more comfortable."

She glared at him. "I was not uncomfortable. You... took...advantage."

"I dinna!" Rory sat up, ignoring the pain shooting through his thigh as he swung his legs over the edge of the cot. "Ye just happened to turn as I was moving your arm..." He let his voice trail off. His fingers *had* squeezed her breast, even if he had not intentionally meant to do so. "I am sorry. 'Twill nae happen again."

She looked wary, as though she didn't completely believe him. Then he noticed something else. Juliana was shaking. With all the clothing she'd just donned, she couldn't be cold. Besides, the brazier was still emitting some heat. He looked back to her face and realized she had that same unfocused expression she'd had in the woods that day. *Fear.*

"Ye doona have to be afraid of me, lass."

She blinked and looked at him, her eyes clearing. "I'm not. Afraid of you, that is."

He pulled on his own breeches and stood. She looked as though she'd skitter away like a scared rabbit any minute. "What are ye scared of then?"

"Nothing."

"'Tis *something*," he responded. "Ye are acting like ye did the day in the woods. Ye acted strange when I kissed ye in front of the Camerons, too—"

"I did not expect it. You surprised me."

"At the time," he went on as though she hadn't interrupted, "I thought mayhap ye didna like me, but—"

"Do not be ridiculous. I like you well enough." Juliana shrugged. "I would not have agreed to ride pillion with you otherwise."

Each of those times there had been no other option, although he didn't point that out. But she *had* returned his kiss in the woods before he'd pressed himself against her, so she had to have some feelings for him. While he had been in his comatose state, he'd dreamed she'd talked to him, apologizing for being rude and admitting he was right most of the time. When he'd awoken in the stable, he'd decided it had been a fever dream, a wishful fantasy of his unconsciousness. But there had been something else, too. Something that hadn't really made sense. She'd cried and told him she wished he would understand why she'd reacted like she had. Suddenly, a nasty suspicion began to grow. He tilted his head to study her.

"Some man has misused ye." When she began to study the floor as though the words to the Acts of Union were written on it, an even uglier suspicion raised its head. "Were ye raped?"

Her quick intake of breath told him he was right. A red haze formed in front of his eyes. He wanted to kill whoever the bastard was. *Would* kill him if he found out who it was. What kind of cur would do that? He'd wanted to beat Cameron to a bloody pulp for forcing the MacFarlane lass, but this was worse. *This* bastard he wanted to tear limb from limb. Slowly. With his bare hands.

Another emotion warred with the first. He wanted to go to Juliana, gather her in his arms and hold her close, but that was probably the last thing she wanted.

"Who..." he began, "when...?"

She shook her head. "It is over."

He moved then, taking her hands so she could not run away, but careful not to stand close enough to frighten her. "It is *nae* over, lass. Nae when ye canna endure a man's touch or kiss." Thankful that she didn't attempt to pull her hands away, he gave them a little squeeze, then dropped his. "Tell me again."

Her eyes went wide as she looked up. "Again?"

"Aye. I think ye tried to explain while I was lying over my horse—"

"You heard me?" She turned pale, then blood rushed back to her face. "You were awake?"

"I thought I was dreaming. Ye might as well tell me again since I've already heard part of it. I want to ken all of it." When she looked hesitant, he took her hand again. "I will avenge ye. I swear it."

Juliana's mouth quivered as she tried to smile in spite of

a tear rolling down her cheek. "You will have to dig him up for that."

"The swine is dead?"

She nodded. "Killed in a duel last year."

Rory sat down on the cot and tugged her gently down beside him, careful to leave space. "Tell me everything."

When she'd finished, he was sorry the bastard was dead. Dueling was too easy a death for a maggot like him, even if he had been an aristocrat. Rory looked down at Juliana, who had somehow come to be in his arms and was currently drenching his shirt with her tears, not that he cared one whit about the shirt. What he cared about was *her*. He kissed the top of her head and stroked her back. "It will be better now."

She looked up with red-rimmed eyes and a swollen nose, and he thought she was beautiful. He kissed her forehead. "Ye will heal."

"I…I do not know if I can." She sat up and brushed at her wet cheeks. "Besides the…humiliation, it hurt so much. I do not want to ever go through that again."

"Ye may nae believe me and 'tis nae the time to say it, but when ye give yourself willingly to a man, the act will nae hurt." He gave her a smile. "Bairns would nae come into the world if it did."

She wiped at her tears again. "I do not think I am brave enough to find out."

There were a thousand things he wanted to say to that. To tell her how good it could be. How much pleasure there was to be had. How much he wanted to be the one to show her, but that would have to wait.

"Time will tell," he said instead.

# Chapter Twenty-Eight

"We should have left yesterday," Rory grumbled as they saddled the horses the next morning to leave for Blair Castle.

"And have your wound open and start bleeding again?"

"I'd have been fine."

"Why are you men so obstinate?" She shook her head. "I told you I never wanted to have to put a searing iron to anyone's flesh again."

"But we've wasted time. Neal may be following us."

She frowned. "Highly unlikely. He had a gut wound that needed stitching. One that I put there, I might add."

He growled at that, even as he helped her mount. "I should have been the one to slash him. Ye shouldna have to defend yourself."

She was rather proud of the fact that she had, although she managed not to retort *and* refrained from rolling her eyes as Misty followed Baron along the rutted road. Arguing between them was never going to change.

But one thing definitely had. She had told him her terrible secret. Once unburdened, she felt like a bird must when let out of its cage. She thought she might fly herself, if only she lifted her arms and tried. She certainly felt light as a feather.

Juliana glanced at Rory. Riding slightly behind him had its advantages, since she could study him without being obvious. His reaction to what had happened to her had surprised her. He didn't think her ruined, as an English nobleman would. He didn't even seem to take into account that she had lost her virtue. Instead, he'd promised to avenge her, had been willing to *kill* for her. Although Juliana had always scoffed at the tales of gallant knights, she couldn't deny that his vowing to protect and defend her felt good. Something one of those medieval heroes would do. But then, Rory had been acting the hero since he'd first rescued her from Neal Cameron.

Rory glanced back. "Ye have been awfully quiet."

"Just thinking."

He reined Baron in so Misty could come alongside. "About what?"

She certainly couldn't tell him she'd been comparing him to one of King Arthur's knights. He'd probably laugh and then tuck the information away to gloat about in future arguments. And she definitely did not want him thinking she'd gone soft in the head like some silly ninnyhammer. "Nothing, really."

He gave her a long look. "Ye are nae thinking about what ye told me?"

She shook her head. "That is in the past. I will not waste more time on it."

That, she realized, was surprisingly true. The pain—the *guilt* that she hadn't fought back, the *anger* that she hadn't dared—was fading. Though not gone, once all the horrid details had come tumbling out, it was almost like an ebbing tide had taken most of the debris with it.

"Ye are sure? We can stop and rest if ye have more to say."

"No. Everything I needed to say has been said." Maybe Rory had worked some magic with the faeries, because she really did feel things could get better. "Well, except maybe—"

"What?"

She smiled at him. "Maybe to thank you. I do not remember thanking you for being so kind."

"*Humph.*" His cheeks turned ruddy. "We'd best move on, then."

She allowed herself a wider grin once Misty lagged behind him again. So he had difficulty accepting compliments. That might be a useful tool to have in *her* arsenal—for future arguments. It might end one quite quickly in her favor.

But she'd meant it. He had been kind. He'd comforted her, let her drench his shirt, and had held her for a long, long time. Nothing more. Just that. Even when they'd gone to bed last night, sharing the cot again, he'd cradled her head on his shoulder, but he'd been careful to keep his hands away from her breasts. Kind. Gallant. Protective. Her hero.

...

They approached Blair Castle well after sunset. Rory considered continuing past the castle itself and going to the inn in Blair Atholl but rejected the idea. With the blizzard just a couple of days ago, any coaches planning to go through the pass would no doubt wait until an outrider could ascertain if the pass was open. They'd be lucky if the inn had a room available, let alone two.

"Are you sure we will be made welcome?" Juliana asked. "I remember Ian saying the new duke was not able to attend your un-proscription celebration because his father had recently drowned himself. Will they not be in mourning?"

"Aye, but they've also just had a wedding," Rory replied. "There is a new duchess in the keep, so I suspect she will be glad to have guests for a day or two."

He was right. The duke himself greeted them, apologizing for having missed the MacGregor celebration, and his young wife, Jane—just twenty and daughter of a knight—was anxious to prove her new station. She welcomed them with all the fervor Rory would expect for a close family member.

He bowed and gestured. "This is Miss Juliana Caldwell. She is—"

"I am handfasted to him."

Rory felt his mouth gape and quickly closed it. Had he heard her right? Had she just announced—admitted, for the first time—that they were handfasted?

Jane clapped her hands. "That is wonderful! We just got married ourselves"—she turned pink and looked at her husband—"so I can imagine how excited ye are! We will give ye our best guest chamber!"

"That is nae necessary—"

"Of course it is!" Jane glanced at him as though he might lack wits and then turned to Juliana. "Men just doona understand these things. Ye have been on the road in this horrible weather, and a bride wants to feel special."

Juliana gave him a furtive look at that and, since he was completely flummoxed, he raised an eyebrow. Her brow creased ever so slightly—a harbinger of a *discussion* they were sure to have later—then she put a bright smile on her face.

"It does feel wonderful to be off my horse and somewhere warm and dry."

"We have already eaten, but I will have Cook send ye a tray and some wine to celebrate your handfasting. And I'll have a hot bath sent up as well. Do ye require the assistance of a maid? Or..." Jane gave her a wink. "Will your husband assist ye?"

Rory managed to stifle a grin as Juliana turned the color

of a summer sunset. He really should let her untangle herself from this web she was weaving. His wayward cock was already trying to stand at attention at the thought of *helping* her with her bath, but then he remembered all that she had confessed. Whatever her reason had been for telling the Murrays they were handfasted, he was not about to force himself—in any manner—on her.

"My *bride* is still getting used to the idea of being handfasted, since it hasna been long," he said, thinking all of five minutes. "She is still a wee bit shy"—he didn't dare look Juliana's way—"so I think she might enjoy privacy."

This time it was the duke who looked at him as though he were addle-brained, but he held his peace.

"That is very chivalrous of ye to consider her feelings," Jane said. "How gallant."

Juliana made a choking sound. "He has been...very kind."

Kind. *She thinks I'm kind.* It wasn't exactly an exciting word. Certainly not one hinting at any kind of passion. And it definitely put a damper on the way his thoughts were leading. *Had* been leading. Whatever her reason, it was clear she was not extending an invitation of any sort. More than likely, she didn't want to be alone in a strange castle and wanted him to hold her like he had last night.

When Rory finally got to the guest chamber more than two hours later, Juliana was already in bed asleep. He shut the door quietly behind him. The duke had invited him to the library for brandy while Juliana was bathing and had ordered some venison and cheese to be brought. Murray no doubt wondered, though, why Rory lingered over the brandy and then asked for a second. He'd made some sort of lame-sounding excuse that his "bride" was *sore*—a poor play on words since she'd been in the saddle all day and not naked under him in bed—and he was giving her a bit of respite. The duke—only nine and ten himself—had looked puzzled at that, and Rory had hastily changed the subject. He just hoped word never got back to Strae Castle about his seeming lack of prowess. His brothers would never let him live it down.

He kicked off his boots and quickly divested himself of his outer garments. He considered leaving his small clothes on, but Juliana was sound asleep, so she wouldn't know if he slept nude or not. He'd be up before she was, since it would be another long day to get home. Taking that last piece off, he slipped into the bed beside her and sighed. It was going to be another painful night for him, which would have nothing to do with his wounded leg.

• • •

Juliana kept her eyes closed as she heard Rory enter the bedchamber and begin removing his clothes. Was she going to be able to go through with this? Her thoughts had changed so much. She knew she could trust Rory. He had proved himself to be a good man, kind and considerate. Even when they argued, he didn't demean her. And...she was *feeling* things. Things that made her body tingle in odd places. She wanted to have Rory touch her. Wanted to feel his lips on hers. Wanted to *respond* like a woman should when she desired a man. And, yes, she did *desire* him. Yet... *Dear Lord. What if...*

She felt the mattress cave slightly as he lay down, and for a moment, the old panic threatened to rise. She swallowed hard, then turned and opened her eyes.

"Did I wake ye?" Rory's voice sounded a bit strange.

"No." She hesitated. Did she have the courage? *If I don't act now, will I ever?* Another swallow, then a deep breath. "I want you."

"I am here. Ye are safe."

"I know." She paused again, then tentatively put her hand on his bare shoulder. "I want you to"—she took a second deep breath and closed her eyes—"to consummate our handfasting."

There was complete silence on his part. Was he not going to say anything? Worse, was he going to *refuse*? Slowly she opened her eyes to find him searching her face.

"Are ye sure?"

Juliana looked into his eyes and saw desire burning there. *Yes.* She wanted this. This was Rory. He would not hurt her. Taking yet another deep breath, she nodded. "I am sure."

He smiled. "Then let me show you pleasure."

As Rory rose up on one elbow to lean over her, she closed her eyes again. He'd part her thighs now and soon his weight would be on her, holding her down, and then he would... She tensed, in spite of herself.

"Relax, lass." He brushed strands of hair away from her face and caressed her cheek with a hand so gentle it might have been a butterfly skimming across her skin. "I willna do anything ye doona want me to do. Ye can tell me to stop at any time. Do ye understand?"

Slowly, she opened her eyes to gaze at him. His eyes were dark as sapphires in the low light of the candle on the bedside table. He touched her nose with a fingertip. "Understand?"

She nodded and spread her legs. "Go about it then."

He chuckled. "We might—or mayhap nae—get to that area later."

She felt her eyes widen at the *mayhap nae...might not*. Did he actually mean he might not complete the act if she didn't want him to? Bringing her legs back together, she whispered, "What do you want me to do?"

"Nothing. I want ye to enjoy what I do."

*Enjoy.* She wasn't sure that was possible for her. But... she had enjoyed his kisses. Her body had turned to mush...

was that just physical? Did everyone who was kissed expertly react like that? Or...was she capable of truly *feeling*? Because this was Rory. That was what she wanted to find out, didn't she? "I...I will try."

"Trust me."

*And I do.* The sudden realization struck her like the huge wave that had once knocked her over when she had waded into the sea. The force of the truth sucked the air out of her lungs. She had trusted Rory from the very start, when he'd gotten her away from Neal at the MacLean's. She just hadn't let herself...*wouldn't* let herself feel...

The rest of the thought was cut off by the brush of his lips across hers.

It was the softest of kisses, gone before she could respond. She felt his breath fan her cheek as he kissed her forehead, then he feathered small kisses across her eyelids before moving to her ear. He nuzzled the tender spot behind it, then licked the lobe, causing little shivers to run down her spine. When he nipped it lightly, a moan escaped her.

His mouth found hers again, but he teased it with brushing swipes, allowing her to savor the touch before he pressed his lips against hers with a gentle, firm pressure. He taunted by running the tip of his tongue along the crease, coaxing but not demanding she open to him. Her lips parted of their own accord, but he did not take advantage by plundering. Instead, he nibbled at one corner, then slowly sucked her lower lip, causing her to gasp, before he returned to kissing her. She was openmouthed now, but still his tongue did not intrude. Instead, he feasted on her lips, angling his head for different effects as he kept kissing her. He played with her mouth as though he had nothing else in mind. A feeling of frustration rose in her. Tentatively, she let her tongue touch him. For a moment, she felt him pause, and then his tongue joined hers.

She made a soft mewling sound as his tongue, with its

warmth and velvety texture, explored slowly, entwining with hers. There was no demanding pressure, only a feeling that he could go on forever, like he had with his kisses. An odd sensation shot through her, pooling in her lower belly.

She started to protest when he finally withdrew, but he only placed a finger across her lips. He nuzzled her neck once more, then trailed kisses down her throat, causing her to instinctively turn her head to give him better access. Who knew that would feel so good? Or the nibbling that he was doing now?

Cool air across her chest was her first indication that Rory had somehow loosed the ribbons on her night rail without her noticing. Or that his busy hands had slipped it off her shoulders? She reached to tug it back up, but he stayed her.

"I want to see your breasts."

"Why?"

He grinned. "Ye will find out in a moment if ye let me pull this down."

No man had ever seen her breasts, not even when… She cut off the thought before it could fester. Curiosity rose in its place. "All right."

He inched the night rail down slowly, letting his fingertips slide along her collarbone, then down her arms as the garment slid lower. She felt a moment of embarrassment as it gathered at her waist, fully exposing her breasts to him.

"So beautiful," Rory murmured as he cupped them gently into his palms. "They fit perfectly."

She hadn't ever considered her breasts fitting anywhere, but before she could ponder that, he began to knead them, his thumbs flicking across her nipples and causing any rational thoughts to flee.

"Ye react as I knew ye would."

Rory rolled one suddenly hard peak between two fingers, eliciting a short gasp from her, but when he bent his head and took the other one in his mouth—laving the areola—she nearly shrieked. The sensation was like nothing she'd *ever* experienced. Juliana felt her breasts grow heavy, and she needed…*more*. His hand alternately pinched and tugged at the first nipple, causing a tingling sensation to rack her body in strange places. When he stopped his ministrations, she almost cried, but then he cupped her breasts again, pressing them together so he could alternate flicking his tongue over both tips. She arched her back for him and thought she heard him growl. And then his mouth covered the breast that his hand had manipulated, and he began to suckle. The heat that had been pooling in her belly intensified, and that special spot between her thighs began to pulse. "My God! Do not stop!"

"There is more," he said as he pulled his mouth from her nipple with a final lick.

"Better than this?" Her voice sounded shaky to her.

He grinned again. "Ye be the judge."

Before she realized what he was up to, he shifted, taking the night rail with him as he positioned himself on his knees between her legs. She hadn't even realized he'd separated them, but now he placed a thigh on either of his shoulders, leaving her totally and completely open to him. It seemed a strange position if he was going to… "What are you—"

"Shh. Ye will find out."

He placed a soft kiss on her inner thigh, causing her to quiver. Then he placed another, higher on her thigh. He splayed her folds with his hands, one finger stroking along the slickness.

"So wet."

She felt like she was practically gushing—another foreign sensation—and everything had gone mushy down there, except for that rapidly pulsating spot that felt engorged. When his finger encircled the little bud, she nearly levitated off the bed.

"Ye like that?"

It was a rhetorical question. Or, at least, she hoped it was, because she was incapable of speech. When he began to flick his thumb over it, she forgot to breathe. Something was beginning to build inside her body that she didn't recognize.

Rory pressed another kiss to her thigh, this one closer to her core and then another. She could hardly concentrate, given what his clever hand was doing, but was he going to... Surely, he wasn't... *Oh. My. God.* He *was*.

His tongue thrust into her opening, mimicking what his penis would do, and then he began to lick her folds, lapping at her juices with long, slow strokes, as if he had all the world at his leisure. The simmering heat in her belly began to boil, then all thought left her completely as he covered that throbbing nub with his mouth and sucked hard. A red haze blurred her sight, and she erupted like a volcano spewing lava.

She drew a shaky breath as her world came back into focus and then became aware of another sensation. Rory had entered her. His manhood filled and stretched her, but it didn't hurt. She wiggled a little. There was no pain at all. In fact, it felt...rather good.

Rory started to move, withdrawing partially and then thrusting gently, watching her as he did. "Are ye all right?"

She had never been more all right than just a minute ago. "What you did was wonderful." She gave him a wobbly smile. She'd no idea she was capable of disintegrating into boneless nothingness and yet feeling *everything* at the same time. Rory had sent her to those heights... She felt desire stirring once more. And she wanted to please him. "Now it is your turn to take what you want."

One eyebrow lifted as he continued his slow thrusting. "Ye will be wanting it, too."

"But I—"

"Trust me, love."

She opened her mouth to reply, but only a little squeak came out as he filled her again. The feel of him rocking against her core as he moved made all those parts start to tingle again. "Oh…my."

And that was her last coherent thought as all the sensations she'd just felt magnified tenfold with Rory's increasingly faster and deeper thrusts. Her body began to writhe beneath him. Her toes curled and muscles tightened into near spasms, shuddered to a peak and exploded once more.

•••

Juliana wasn't going to drive him barmy. She was going to kill him instead. He'd unwittingly lit a powder keg and almost gone up in flames. Rory allowed a self-satisfied smirk as he gazed at the woman lying beneath him, totally satiated to the point that her eyes were fluttering in a swoon. Carefully, he eased himself to the side and propped his head on his hand, waiting for her to return to her senses.

Even though he'd withdrawn before he could get her with child, it was probably the most difficult thing he'd ever done. He didn't think he'd ever seen—or felt—something as wonderful as watching Juliana come for him. Not once, but twice. Shattering completely. He'd wanted nothing more than to bury his seed in her.

That thought alone should have caused him sheer panic. He had not wanted marriage, let alone creating bairns. And yet, a new emotion niggled at him, and he realized this was exactly what he wanted. He wanted Juliana as his wife. Life with her would never be boring. And, as feisty as she was, she would not hold him back from helping his brothers restore their clan. He could almost see her leading the charge, somewhat like Boudicca. But would she want to marry him? As he was mulling those thoughts, her eyes opened groggily, as though she'd imbibed too much spirits. And maybe she had, but it wasn't alcohol-related. She'd just been introduced to an entirely different kind of headiness, one intensely more pleasurable, in his opinion.

He tapped the tip of her nose. "Ye are back."

She gave him a half-focused look. "Where... What happened to me?"

He pretended to frown, although he was having a hard time not laughing. "If ye doona recall, we will have to do it all over again." Although he hoped she'd give him a few minutes to recover...

Her face turned pink as her eyes cleared. "Oh! Ah... I... You—"

"Us." He grinned. "It was *us* who came together."

Her blush deepened. "Yes. I...did not expect it to be so... pleasant."

"Pleasant?" His male pride took exception to the word. Pleasant was a sunny day without rain. Pleasant was taking Baron for a gallop. Pleasant was a hot bath and a soft bed after a hard day's work. Not...not what had just occurred. "Just...*pleasant*?"

"Um. Very nice."

That was probably even worse. He'd just had the best experience he'd ever had—which was saying a lot, no brag intended—and he thought he'd given her equal measure. Before he could summon up a dignified retort, she added a few words that nearly broke him.

"It did not hurt." Tears welled in her eyes, and her smile wobbled. "Thank you."

Shame immediately washed over him. What a sot he was for nursing his wounded pride when he'd forgotten what she had been through. How much courage it must have taken for her to come to him at all. She'd meant those words as compliments, not disparagement. He frowned slightly. Would she want to repeat the act? Or was it something she'd just wanted to prove to herself she could do? He wanted to ask, but he wasn't going to push her. Instead, he leaned over and kissed her forehead. "Ye are quite welcome, lass."

She yawned, her eyes half closing. "I am so tired."

That was a good sign, at least, although he didn't voice that thought, either. "We should get some sleep."

"Um," she murmured and turned over, giving him her back.

He stared at it for a moment. They'd slept this way last night. Maybe now that she was through with her experiment, she wanted to go back to the way things were? He didn't like the idea at all. Now that he'd felt her passion, he didn't want it to be just a onetime thing. His cock was already growing hard, remembering what if had felt like to be inside her.

He sighed and punched his pillow into shape. He'd given her everything he could. If that was all she wanted, he'd have to leave it at that. Not that he liked the idea, but given what had happened to her, she didn't need another man forcing himself on her. He grunted and punched the pillow again.

Just as he was about to close his eyes, he felt her nudging backward until her back was against his chest and her lovely arse nestled against his groin. They fit together like two spoons. His cock, unfortunately, decided that was a very good thing. Rory took a deep breath, willing himself not to react. She was probably already half-asleep and nestling against him like a bairn seeking warmth and comfort. He would not take advantage of her. He wouldn't.

And then she reached back and brought his arm around her waist. With a contented mewling sound, she took his hand and cupped it around her breast. She sighed contentedly, and her breathing deepened as she drifted into sleep.

But Rory lay awake a long while, not moving his hand at all. Maybe she had answered his unspoken question after all.

# Chapter Twenty-Nine

When Juliana descended the stairs the next morning, she suddenly felt...shy. What would her hosts—the young duke and his duchess—think of her? They would surely know what had taken place. She gave herself a little shake. Of course they would know what had taken place. She had told them they were handfasted. They had referred to her as Rory's bride. They'd expect *something* to have taken place.

And then there was Rory. He'd awakened her before dawn with slow kisses and gentle strokes and then had made love to her again, showing her even more areas of her body that she didn't know were so sensitive. She was sore this morning, but it was a nice soreness. A tenderness between her thighs that reminded her of what pleasure could be had. Who would have known? A flood of emotions washed over her. Conflicting and confusing and unsettling.

When she entered the breakfast room, a number of people were already there, helping themselves to the dishes on the sideboard. Rory was standing by the window, speaking to the duke. From the remnants of food left on their plates, they must have already eaten.

He glanced her way and gave her a quick nod before turning his attention back to the duke, and she had a moment of foreboding. Was that all he was going to do? No mischievous grin? No desirous look that would remind her of what they'd just done half an hour ago? Of course, there were other people around, and she certainly didn't expect him to hurry over and sweep her off her feet. That was nonsense. But… She chewed her lip. Maybe their lovemaking hadn't been as spectacular for him as it had been for her. He was experienced, after all, and had used those skills because she had asked him to. *Then let me show you pleasure.* Those had been his words. And he'd done that. Perhaps that was all it had been to him. A pleasurable interlude. Men had them all the time with willing women. And she had been willing. She'd actually *asked*.

But this morning, he'd given her pleasure again. Was it because she was there? Not that he'd taken her without permission. She'd readily responded.

It was all so confusing.

"Be sure ye eat well this morning," Jane said as she came over to her. "I've had Cook pack food for ye, but ye have a long, hard ride today."

Rory had already eaten. "I am not sure I have time. We should perhaps be on the road since we…overslept." She caught herself on the last word, but Jane grinned.

"We *oversleep* a lot ourselves."

Juliana felt her face warm, and it heated even more as Rory gave her an amused glance.

"Break your fast, lass. I'll go see to the horses." With that, he was gone.

She wasn't sure she could eat a bite, as uneasy as she was, but the delicious scent of cinnamon in the porridge and the succulent smell of ham soon had her wolfing down a full plate. Perhaps lovemaking stimulated the appetite as well.

Fifteen minutes later, she said her good-byes to the Murrays and she and Rory started out for the last day of the journey home. Not wanting to bring up the subject of whether or not he had enjoyed what they had done as much as she had—maybe he pleasured all his bed partners like that and she was just another—she chattered away about every mundane thing she could think of. Then, when she ran out of bland topics, she started asking questions. How long did the snows last in Scotland? When would they begin planting barley? Were there spring festivities the MacGregors would participate in now that they were un-proscribed? Finally, when they were within a few miles of Strae Castle, Rory reined Baron in. Misty sidled so close their thighs nearly touched.

"We need to talk, lass."

"We have been talking." She pretended not to understand what he meant. "You have been telling me about—"

"—about everything that is nae important." He fixed her with a steady look. "Are ye regretting last night and this morning?"

She stared at him. "*What?*"

"Ye heard me quite well."

Of course she'd heard him. But it was the last question she'd expected him to ask. "I…I…"

His face fell. "I am sorry, then. I wanted to make it very special for ye."

"You did?" Juliana gave herself a shake. "I mean, you *did*. You made it very, very special for me."

Rory gave her a wary look. "Then why have ye avoided talking about it all day?"

"Me?" She felt indignation rising. "*You* were the one avoiding the topic."

An eyebrow rose. "I was?"

"Yes." She lifted her chin. "You acted like nothing had

happened this morning when I came in to the breakfast room."

The brow went higher. "Ye wanted to me to announce what we did to everyone?"

Her face heated. "Of course not. I just thought... Oh, never mind."

"What I wanted to do this morning was kiss ye senseless."

She blinked. "You did?"

"Aye." He smiled. "And I would have liked to carry ye back upstairs and have my way with ye all over again, but there was nae time."

"Oh." A perfectly inane, stupid word, but all she could manage.

"Would ye have liked that?"

She nodded, her brain still not quite functioning fully. Finally, she managed to find words. "I would like to do it again."

"I would as well, but I doona want to make ye my leman."

"Leman?"

He thought. "Ye English would call it mistress, I think."

"Ah. I do not wish that, either. But according to Sima, we are already married. In Scotland, anyway." She felt herself blush. "Besides, we have already consummated..."

"The deed, aye, but I took care nae to get ye with child, so ye doona have to agree to the handfasting. No one at Strae Castle needs to find out."

Juliana studied him, swallowed hard. She wasn't sure if she wanted to hear the answer, but she had to ask. "I will not hold you to any promises you did not want to make. Do *you* want to be free?"

He took a moment before he answered. "When I spoke the words at MacLean's, it was a means to get ye away from Neal Cameron. But even then, I kenned I would honor the vow."

"But did you *want* to?"

"Mayhap nae then." He shrugged. "I had nae thought to get married for years. I certainly dinna think it would be to a Sassenach. And I wanted a biddable lass when I did decide—"

"You need not finish. None of that describes me." Juliana lifted her reins. "Let's just ride, shall we? The sooner we can get home—"

"Wait, lass." He grabbed the reins. "Ye dinna let me finish."

She lifted a brow. "I am sure that is not necessary. You made your point. I do not need any more—"

"Will ye *hush*? Just this once?"

She pursed her mouth and glared at him.

He gave her a wary look. "What I was going to add, was—ye have changed my mind. Somehow, ye managed to get under my skin."

Her brow lifted again. "That hardly sounds like a compliment."

He smiled. "It may nae sound like one, but 'tis, lass. I have never had such feelings as I have for ye." The smile broadened into a grin. "Ye are the only woman who has managed to irritate me enough to ken I doona want to let ye go."

"Such flattery," Juliana said. "My heart is fluttering so, I may swoon."

"Ye doona swoon." He tilted his head. "I cause your heart to flutter?"

She opened her mouth to retort, then closed it. Her heart *was* fluttering. His words were hardly romantic, but she didn't believe in such flowery sentiments anyway. She enjoyed sparring with this man. No one could roil her temper as quickly as he did, but anticipating which of them would win the argument made her tingle in several places that he'd explored last night and this morning. She lifted a shoulder. "It might be fluttering a little."

"Just a little?"

"I do not want to give you cause for conceit."

He placed his hand over his own heart. "Ye wound me, lass."

She rolled her eyes, then she straightened in her saddle. "But I will admit this. I would like to stay handfasted to you."

Rory's eyes darkened, and he sobered. "Ye ken what that means?"

"I *ken*. It means that after a year, if neither of us objects, we will be considered truly married for life."

"'Tis what ye want?"

Juliana nodded. She'd never felt more sure of something. "It is."

"'Tis what I want, too, lass." Rory leaned over, half lifting her out of the saddle, and gave her a soul-deep kiss, not releasing her until both horses began to shift below them. "My brothers are never going to believe this."

"Nor are my sisters."

"'Twill be interesting to see which is more shocked, aye?"

"I am sure Emily and Lorelei will be."

Rory shook his head. "I think Ian, Devon, and Carr will be more."

"Are we going to argue about this?"

"Mayhap. I will win, though."

"I do not think so, sir. I know my sisters."

"And I ken my brothers."

They grinned at each other then and spurred their horses toward home. It would soon be a new year and a new beginning. Juliana was sure there would be new challenges nearly every day, but those were to be looked forward to.

For who knew who would win them?

# Epilogue

THREE MONTHS LATER

Rory returned the smile Juliana gave him as she settled next to him on the sofa in the library. They'd just spent nearly half the morning lying abed before Devon had pounded on their door and reminded them that there was *other* business to attend to.

"I suppose ye are a bit surprised over what ye've missed?" Rory asked his brother Alasdair, who'd just returned home from Ireland.

"Ye might say that." He poured a second dram of whisky from the decanter on the desk. "I've heard rumors of building unrest and possible revolution in the Colonies, but I hadn't expected to come home to find Strae Castle turned upside down."

"'Tis nae completely turned upside down."

"Nae?" He turned back to look at his assembled brothers and the Caldwell sisters. "I missed the un-proscription celebration in December because I was in Ireland. I didn't realize it would also be a joint celebration that included Ian marrying Emily, although in hindsight, that wasn't a total surprise. But *ye*, Rory…handfasted?" He shook his head. "Maybe I should be surprised that ye are nae married, too."

Juliana shot him a look. "I wanted to wait for a proper wedding when my sister comes back from her Season."

"To say nothing of the fact that we have to get the distillery up and running again," Rory added and smiled at Juliana. "It seems my intended is rather good with keeping the books."

"And I'm learning to drink whisky," she said with a grin. "I wouldn't want to pass out at my own wedding."

"I canna argue with that." Alasdair finished his own dram and changed the subject. "So ye are telling me we almost got into a clan war within days of getting our clan name back?"

"Ye can blame Neal Cameron for that," Rory said. "He stole Juliana from under our noses." He took her hand and held it.

Alasdair stifled a smirk as he looked at their hands. "Before I left, Juliana would have clawed ye like a feral cat for doing that. Now she is all but purring like a kitten, and ye have stopped growling like a rabid dog."

"I doona *growl*."

"And I do not *claw*."

Alasdair grinned at them. "Apparently, whatever transpired on your journey back has changed your perceptions of each other. Ye've tamed each other."

"Nae woman will ever *tame* me, brother."

Juliana shot him a look. "I will hardly be subdued by a man, either."

"I ken." Rory gave her a heavy-lidded look. "I wouldna want ye tame, lass."

She blushed, and her sister Emily cleared her throat.

"Perhaps we should finish explaining to Alasdair what happened?" she asked.

"Aye. I can torment Rory later," Alasdair said. "I take it ye rescued your damsel from Cameron's clutches?"

"Regardless—" Ian held up a hand for peace before Rory could retort. "I suppose we are lucky the bastard didn't die."

"He might wish he had," Rory said.

Juliana laughed. "I think living in hell will be more fitting."

Rory laughed, too. She was referring to the fact that a wounded Neal and his companions had stopped at Invergarry Castle on their way home and Morag had taken a liking to him. A *strong* liking.

"The two deserve each other," he said after he'd explained, "but the important thing is he willna be bothering us again."

"Besides, with Lorelei and Fiona both gone, there is not anyone else available at Strae Castle to abduct," Emily added.

Alasdair frowned. "Ye are sure it was wise to send Fiona along with Lorelei to London?"

Ian raised a brow. "Have ye ever succeeded in talking our sister out of anything?"

"Nae, but Lorelei will be more than a willing accomplice in whatever scrapes and adventures our sister might think of. Ye do ken that Lorelei doesna think before acting."

Emily gave a short nod in agreement. "That is true, but they should be fine since they are staying with the Countess of Bute. She will act as their chaperone for the Season."

"That is not especially encouraging," Alasdair answered. "The Earl of Bute doesna often stay in London since he left the prime ministership. His wife is near sixty years of age and probably likes to retire early. Who kens what kind of adventures Fiona and Lorelei are plotting? 'Tis a recipe for disaster."

"Well, ye'll be going to London to sort out the land titles for the MacGregors who are returning from Ireland," Ian said. "Ye can keep an eye on both of them."

"They'll nae appreciate it, ye ken," Rory said. "Ye'll have your work cut out for ye."

Alasdair paused. "I do enjoy a challenge."

He smiled as though he were harboring a secret, which made Rory wonder if he weren't more than a wee bit *personally* interested in Lorelei.

His brother's grin widened as if he knew what Rory was thinking. "I think I will leave for London in the morning."

# About the Author

Cynthia Breeding is an award-winning author of twenty-three novels and twenty-nine novellas. She currently lives on the bay in Corpus Christi, Texas, and enjoys sailing and horseback riding on the beach. She also loves traveling, with Scotland a favorite destination…hopefully *soon*.

***Don't miss the Children of the Mist series...***

HIGHLAND RENEGADE

***Also by Cynthia Breeding...***

A RAKE'S REDEMPTION

A RAKE'S REVENGE

A RAKE'S REBELLION

ROGUE OF THE HIGHLANDS

ROGUE OF THE ISLES

ROGUE OF THE BORDERS

SISTER OF ROGUES

ROGUE OF THE HIGH SEAS

ROGUE OF THE MOORS

***Discover more historical romance...***

## HIGHLAND WARRIOR
### a Sons of Sinclair novel by Heather McCollum

Joshua Sinclair was once the fiercest and most notorious warrior of the mighty Sinclair clan of Northern Scotland. But now there's nothing and no one that can make him take up arms again. Except a beautiful woman, it seems. When Kára Flett, daughter of a fallen Norse chief, finds herself unexpectedly sheltering the strongest, most brutal warrior in the land, she throws together a risky and outrageous plan to bring him to her side...

## HER RELUCTANT HIGHLANDER HUSBAND
### a *Clan MacKinlay* novel by Allison B. Hanson

After years as her father's prisoner, Dorie McCurdy is forced to marry the new war chief of clan MacKinlay. While Bryce can provide for her needs, he can't give her his heart—not after his wife and child were taken by illness. In her new husband's strong arms, Dorie slowly emerges from her silence...and gradually the ice around Bryce's heart begins to melt. But when she is unexpectedly offered an annulment, she must choose—stay with the man she's fallen in love with but who never wanted her, or choose the unknown possibilities of a different future.

## Twelfth Knight's Bride
a novel by E. Elizabeth Watson

To help her starving clan at Christmastide, Lady Aileana pilfers vegetables. Except the bastard Laird James MacDonald shows up and demands marriage as recompense. She's able to negotiate a severance on Twelfth Night, but that's still two weeks in enemy territory. James needs to marry in order to inherit his fortune. He might as well handfast with the spitfire Aileana. He'd get his money, and a bonny lass he can't help but admire. If only she'd give him a chance.


## A Scot to Wed
a Scottish Hearts novel by Callie Hutton

Katie has nowhere else to go but MacDuff Castle and she refuses to bow down to the arrogant and handsome Evan MacNeil. She's through with men controlling her. Now that Evan must spar with a beautiful lass for the rights to the lands, he will fight to the end. This battle is nothing like the ones his Highlander ancestors fought with crossbows and boiling oil. They never wanted to bed the enemy.

Manufactured by Amazon.ca
Acheson, AB